I0613107

Charles Wells Russell

Roebuck :

A Novel

Charles Wells Russell

Roebuck :
A Novel

ISBN/EAN: 9783337001049

Printed in Europe, USA, Canada, Australia, Japan

Cover: Foto ©Andreas Hilbeck / pixelio.de

More available books at **www.hansebooks.com**

ROEBUCK:

A Novel.

~~~~~~~~~~~~~~~~~~~~

NEW YORK:

M. DOOLADY, PUBLISHER,

448 BROOME STREET.

1866.

Entered according to Act of Congress, in the year 1866,

BY M. DOOLADY,

In the Clerk's Office of the District Court of the United States,
for the Southern District of New York.

W. GANNON, STEREOTYPER,
No. 105 Nassau St., N. Y.

JOHN J. REED, PRINTER,
Rear 43 Centre St., N. Y.

CONTENTS.

4 CONTENTS.

ROEBUCK.

CHAPTER I.

THE FAIRFAXES OF ROEBUCK.

ROEBUCK was one of the finest estates in the country. Its acres were reckoned by thousands, and the slaves upon it were numbered by hundreds. It has been equally admired for beauty and fertility. Before it was laid waste by the ravages of invasion, taste, skill and industry in improving, cultivating and adorning it had brought the effects of art to rival the luxuriant beauty of nature. In front of the plantation Deer River sweeps with gentle curves—a pretty stream, scarcely entitled to the appellation of a river. From the margin of the stream spreads out a wide and fertile bottom to a bluff about fifty feet high, and from the bluff a table of undulating land extends to the foot of a hill called Elk Ridge. Several brooks, flowing from the ridge to the river, cut the plateau with ravines and dells, and supply the fields with water. The native forest, covering many hundred acres together, and scattered here and there in small groves, contributes to the various beauties of the landscape and to the more substantial uses of the plantation. Upon the table land, a furlong from the bluff, and surmounting a gentle eminence, stands (stood.

alas!) a large and elegant mansion, which, a few years
ago, replaced a more ancient edifice, then destroyed
by accidental fire. Before the house a grassy lawn
extended below the bluff, which there declined into
the bottom with gradual slope. About the mansion
trim walks, edged with box, led among evergreen or
flowering shrubs and trees of rare foliage or stately
altitude, both of native and foreign origin, and
through a flower-garden blooming with all the floral
glories of Virginia. At a greater distance orchards,
vineyards, meadows and fields of corn, tobacco, wheat
and other crops, in the orderly circle of their seasons,
rewarded the busy hand of skilful culture with the
ripe gifts of a genial climate and prolific soil. In
various directions might be seen the negro quarters,
hamlets of white cabins, with their "patches," or
kitchen-gardens attached. On every side the buildings, fences, implements and modes of cultivation,
showed the intelligent spirit of modern improvement,
though here and there might be detected, also, traits
of the pride of inheritance and marks of veneration
for old usages and traditions.

The new mansion and the modern improvements
were the work of Colonel Frederick Fairfax, the
last who has borne that name. Both the name of
Frederick and the title of Colonel devolved upon him
by a kind of inheritance, as if they were annexed to
the estate. During three generations they designated
the proprietor. The first Colonel Frederick had won
the rank in actual service. The title was transmitted
by country courtesy to the son, who inherited his
name and estate, and, after two generations, it became
an easy trick of inheritance, by custom, to invest Frederick, the succeeding son and heir, with the same title

when he came into possession of the same estate. This was a natural expression of courtesy on the part of a community that always respected pedigrees, nourished traditions, admired martial virtues and affected military honors. But the title, thus derived, was seldom conferred with his name in full upon the third Frederick Fairfax. He was usually but "Colonel Fred." to his neighbors. The humblest of them often saluted him with that familiar brevity, and he was thus commonly styled throughout the country. It may be thence inferred that he had affable manners, and a frank, cheerful, sunny disposition. This happy temper relieved, without disguising, his pride of birth. His fortune excited no envy, yet familiarity never degraded the dignity of his demeanor. He was a man of tall, commanding stature, of vigorous frame and graceful action, with bold, but regular features. His complexion was fair and fresh, but imbrowned by the sun. His eyes were blue, and his hair, of light brown, was soft, wavy and inclined to curl. It began to note the years with a few silver threads—white marks of happy years. He was nearly sixty. His mind was large, penetrating and remarkable for sound judgment in the affairs of life. In conduct he was gentle, honorable, brave and energetic. When he was young he carried away the honors of the University. Then he spent in the healthy pleasures of the country and in visiting cities, the period assigned by custom to young gentlemen of wealth for recreation between the discipline of youth and the responsibilities of manhood. Whilst he was thus enjoying leisure, his popular manners, the reputation of his scholastic triumphs and the general respect for his family, induced the people of the county to elect him as their represen-

tative in the legislature of that State. He had served
several sessions in that body with rising credit, when
the death of his father called him, at the age of thirty,
to the care of his estate. Thenceforth he devoted
himself to agriculture and to the duties of a private
citizen. In the management of a large estate, and in
the performance of his proper part as a gentleman of
prominent position and leading influence in his
county, he found employment for his ability and
energy. He was among the most successful planters
of Virginia. Free from the canker of avarice, he felt
an honorable ambition to excel in whatever he attempted and a liberal pleasure in the profitable employment of all the means intrusted to his care. He
was proud of the public benefits which resulted from
the improvements he introduced; he had pride in a
princely revenue; but his benevolence was not less
princely.

As a slaveholder a numerous population depended
upon him, and, with his accustomed energy, he exercised over them the functions both of guardian and
governor. No slaves had their wants supplied with
more judicious or provident liberality than his; none
were more contented, or with better reason; but none
yielded larger profits from their labor. By regulating
their industry according to a well-devised system, by
attention to their health, comfort and cheerfulness—
by the employment of proper overseers, and by the
constant supervision of his own intelligence, he derived from the moderate exertions of all ample prosperity, of which they all partook. Believing the servitude of negroes under a superior race to be a needful supplement to their improvident nature, he did
not, with sentimental inconsistency, shrink from the

exercise of the authority and discipline which servitude implies. He was a humane master, but he was master. The community under his control was burdened with no drones, unless two or three able-bodied but idle pensioners deserved that opprobrious epithet. It was a community which produced within itself nearly everything that its essential wants required. Among the servants were carpenters, shoemakers, smiths, weavers and other artisans, skilful in their trades. Besides the staple crops, the plantation produced flax, wool and other materials, to be fabricated for the use of the negroes. Every married slave was allowed a "patch," or kitchen-garden, proportioned in size to the number of his family, and the most thrifty among them made more profit from these patches and from sales of fowls and eggs, than the ordinary wages of laborers. They were, of course, supplied with food and clothing by the master.

He was not the least industrious member of the community. It was his habit to give the day to business, until near the hour of dinner, which was about four o'clock. He spent the morning in correspondence, or examining accounts or other in-door work, or, more commonly, in riding over his plantation, and giving his personal attention to all its operations. This had been his habit for many years, and now, as he approached the age of three score, his industry was not relaxed. So benignly crept the shadow of age over his active and useful life that "his eye was not dim nor his natural force abased."

His wife, some five years younger than himself, was a lady of comely person, and, in character and manners, an agreeable type of mature womanhood. She was the daughter of a distinguished public man, and

1*

before her marriage had been a toast and a belle in
the most elevated circle of society. But when she
was led to the altar, she left upon it all the gay gar-
lands of maidenly vanity, and, with the ring, she wore
thenceforth the graceful dignities of wedded love.
As a matron, she was proud of matronhood as the
proper consummation of a woman's ambition—the
natural sphere of her highest duties, honors and delights. In Virginia, by the grace of God, women are
feminine. They aim to excel in the lovely qualities
of their own sex, without competing for the prizes of
the other. The form of Mrs. Fairfax had once been
delicate, but years, which threatened wrinkles,
brought a smooth and pleasant roundness to her
cheeks and a more ample dignity to her form. As
the wife of a planter and mistress of an extensive establishment, she had many responsibilities and not a
few anxieties. But a sense of responsibility, suited
to such a station in life, had been cultivated as part
of her education, and had been exercised ever since
her marriage. Sustained by her husband, she fulfilled
the duties of her position with constant and cheerful
fidelity. Her life was one of daily usefulness, and
her servants were scarcely less indebted to her
womanly kindness than to the provident care of their
master. Yet, the nature of this gentlewoman was of
such delicate texture that she leaned continually upon
the strength of her husband, and was dependent upon
his society and affection for every hour of her happiness. She, to whom so many feeble creatures looked
up for protection, looked up to him with a trust
almost religious.

There was no living son to inherit the name and
title of "Colonel Fred." Several children had died.
There remained only one daughter. The loss of chil-

dren had been almost the sole affliction of Colonel
Fairfax and his wife during their married lives.
Their parental affection was now concentrated upon
their daughter, Julia. She was about the age of
twenty. She had the fair skin and brown hair of her
father, with the hazel eyes of her mother. In person
she rather surpassed the middle height of woman,
but was not quite tall. Her form might have been
deemed too slender for perfect beauty, but its outlines
were round enough for grace. Her face cannot be
described feature by feature, without producing a
false idea of its character. All who saw it pronounced it beautiful; but those who saw it only once
might dispute with each other what was its chief attribute. Such was the transparent sincerity of her
countenance, that the special charm of her beauty
changed with her emotions. Her customary manner
was one of modest and winning gentleness. But she
often displayed the gaiety of girlhood and innocence.
Every tender sentiment, every pure passion impressed
itself upon her heart, and flashed its expression in her
eyes as pictures are made by a glance of sunlight.
Under this versatile delicacy, however, her essential
character had the firmness of high principle and
almost masculine courage. Being an only child, and
loving her parents with reverential devotion, she endeavored to fill for them the vacant places of sons
and daughters. She interested herself in all her
father's pursuits, promoting his plans and sharing his
counsels. She often rode with him over the plantation, chatting of crops with a tongue as lively as
maidens use to discuss the latest fashion of artificial
flowers. By frequent association with her father in
manly avocations and pleasures, she may have con-

tracted some modes of thought and feeling somewhat more masculine than the native traits of her character.

In introducing to the reader the Fairfaxes of Roebuck, we should not pass over the Colonel's bachelor brother, Richard; but his loquacious habit will make him known to all who come within the sound of his voice. He had an estate of his own, and kept up a domestic establishment upon it; but the greater part of his time was spent at Roebuck, or, in winter, at Richmond. He was two years younger than his brother, the Colonel, and was a man of small stature. But by some forgotten trick of nursery nomenclature he had been called in childhood "big brother," and so he was still sometimes playfully styled by the larger and elder Frederick. He had been educated as a physician, and entered upon the practice of his profession under the influence of young ambition. But, after a few years, the easy independence of hereditary acres tempted him away from a vocation so laborious. He was once disappointed in an affair of love, and that ordinary event, touching one of the keys of a whimsical nature, made him forswear matrimony altogether. He retained the title of Doctor, and as he grew to be an old bacheör, he was generally named, with curt familiarity, Doctor Dick. His style of conversation did not repress the liberty which men were inclined to take with his name, for it was frequently a style of satirical banter and half-comic extravagance. He sometimes affected a bitterness of invective that might have convicted him of extreme ill-nature, if his conduct had not proved that the roughness of his tongue was to his heart as a crabbed preface to a generous volume.

CHAPTER II.

SLAVES AT ROEBUCK.

ONE morning in the spring of the year eighteen hundred and sixty-one, Colonel Fairfax, according to his custom, rode out from his house to make the grand round of his plantation. We are not to accompany him with a view of observing the scenery of the farm, or of noting the information he obtained or the orders he gave or the progress of cultivation. Those who would learn in detail how the agriculture of Virginia was so greatly improved, as it has been during the last quarter of a century, with immense advantage to both races who inhabit there, will find more authentic sources of information. We are to chronicle only a few incidents of the colonel's morning ride that have an interest more personal and less grave than the topics of an agricultural report.

. Not far from the mansion stood several negro cabins in a cluster, and around them swarmed a number of young Africans, looking like bees about their hives, but idling like butterflies in the early sunshine. Riding to the door of one of those cabins, the colonel dismounted and entered it to make a visit, which he repeated almost daily. Within was an old negro man lying upon a bed, from which he rose when he saw his master coming to the door. His age was evidently very great, and he reckoned it roundly at a hundred. He wore a long white beard, which he preserved at the request of his master. IIis hair was nearly as white as wool. Rising from the bed he walked feebly with the help of a long cane to a stool, on which he seated himself in obedience to a gesture of the colonel, after they had shaken hands with each other. The master stood while they held the brief conversation which was so often repeated, and for which old Valentine looked forward as the leading event of his daily life. Before age had impaired his faculties he had been a fair though rather favorable type of his race in Virginia. It was his pride to have served three generations of the Fairfaxes of Roebuck. All the respectability of the family was appropriated to himself, but only in comparing his station with that of other negroes. IIe yielded the place of superiority to the white race without doubt or reluctance, and as he assigned the highest rank in that race to the Fairfax family, he and the other servants of that family were at the top of the black ladder. Fidelity and obedience were the two prime virtues of his class, according to his moral code. For the rest of morality the masters were responsible. Reason, principle and free will would not have kept him in a right path long if left to himself, but he was capable of understanding and practicing such simple and direct duties as fidelity and obedience to a master. Through them he was made useful and happy, and was civilized beyond the highest conception of his grandfather, who was a native African, and above the independent attainments of his race during forty centuries. The brutality and treachery of savage blood were nearly extinguished in him, and, as a docile and contented slave, he spent his life in cheerful labor with many merry holidays. In servitude he had the pleasures which his better nature craved, but not those higher enjoyments which could not be his in any condition. Among temples which all the tribes in Africa could never have built, he learned the practical precepts of a religion whose sublime dogmas his ancesters could not have preserved in memory from the rising to the setting of the sun. And now it was his boast that he had been always a faithful servant, and his master, recognizing the claim which such servitude established, treated the old man with the kindest care and with sincere respect.

"How are you to-day, Uncle Valentine?" he asked, when the antique African was seated.

"Pretty mis'able, thanks be to de Lord, Master Fred."

"What's your misery, Uncle?"

"On'y waitin' for de Lord to take his servant to hesef."

"Do you want to die then?"

"Never, Master Fred., Lord bless your dear soul, never."

"How old are you, now?"

"Well, you can count it up. I seed Gin'al Washinton a crossin' de Delaware when I was seven or fifteen or along thar, and I seed de black filly dey called Flora beat Colonel Dixon's hoss Thunder, but you know ef black Dick he had rid Thunder"——

"Oh, I remember, Uncle. Do you get everything you want? Do the chaps wait on you properly? Is your bed attended to, and your fire and everything?"

"Yes, everything, Master Fred., thank you. Dis mis'able old nigger gits everything he wants till de Lord he do come."

"Very well, make them attend to you. Don't forget, Uncle Valentine, when that white beard grows a little longer I am going to have your picture taken to be hung up beside my grandfather's."

"Your grandfather, he was de first Colonel Frederick. When he tuk me to de army for his body sarvant, he rode de English hoss Rover, and when we come to de camp"——

"Tell me about that to-morrow. Now come out here into the sunshine. Let me carry your stool for you. There—good-bye."

"Lord bless dat boy," said the old man, as his master rode away, "and bless old master, too; but he's gone afore me long ago to Abram's bosom, thank de Lord for all His marcies."

At a later hour, and in another part of the plantation, the Colonel saw a negro fellow jump up from the ground where he had been lying on his back with his face turned to the sun as duly as a sunflower. He ran towards a gate through which his master was about to pass and held it open. He was very black. His head and heels both stood out rearward almost as far as his hips, and his nose lay in ambush behind his lips. An elaborate bow and a sheepish twinkle of his eyes denoted to the Colonel that Ben was waiting there to ask some favor.

"Well, Ben," he said when he came to the gate, "what do you want?"

"Nuflin, Master."

"You do want something; why can't you tell the truth?"

"Dat's it, Master," replied Ben with a grin, showing more red than white, "no nigger don't tell truth; on'y you's found Ben out, and you knows he lies." Ben giggled as if he relished his own satire, or would laugh his master into favorable humor.

" What do you want, Ben ?"

" I bin a thinkin', Master, maybe you'd like to sell this 'ere lazy, lyin' nigger."

" Sell you! Do you want to be sold ?"

" Yes, Master. I can't keep from lyin', an' I ain't good enough for you."

" That's not your reason ; but what master have you chosen ?"

" Dar's Squire Anderson, maybe he mout buy me, 'case he don't know much about me ?"

" Tell me, Ben, why you wish to be sold ? Are you worked too hard ? Are you not well treated ? Has the overseer done anything to you ?"

" No, Master, de God's truth is, it's jis my wife."

" You want to get rid of Nancy ?"

" Dat's a fac'."

" Why ?"

" 'Case she's done got religion, and I can't bide her no how."

" When did she get religion, Ben ?"

" She done come through last Sunday night."

" Religion should make her a better wife."

" No, Master, beg your pardon, religion ain't good for nigger women. She goes prayin' and singin' and beggin' among them religious fellers, and when she comes home from de prayer-meetin's she goes a rollin' on de floor and kickin' up her heels, and won't come to bed all night. She never gives me a good word no more, on'y poor sinner, poor sinner."

" And what have you done ?"

" I done switch her two, three times, but de religion ain't switched out of her yit. I can't stand it, Master, indeed I can't. I's afeard I'll drown myse'f, and you'll lose dis nigger ef you don't sell me."

"You have your eye on another woman at Squire Anderson's."

"Lord, Master, I have never spoke to his Jinny, but once."

"I understand you, Ben. You are tired of one wife and want another. You are married to Nancy, and have two children. You must stay with her. You make religion an excuse to quarrel with her. You must treat her as a good husband ought, and she shall behave herself as a good wife. If you switch her again I'll direct the overseer to switch you. Go to your work. Begone!"

Another police case came before the Colonel the same day, that may be worth reporting, as the subject of it will appear again in this narrative. On this occasion he came running up from a ravine to intercept his master as he rode along. He was a tall fellow with a powerful frame and a bullet-head. On his head he wore nothing but a circular fringe of ravelled straw which had been the rim of a hat. Even this he doffed as he approached his master.

"What's the matter, Juba?"

"I's jis gwine to find you, Master."

"Where do you come from now?"

"From de bush, Master, dat's de truth."

"How long have you been in the bush?"

"Mighty nigh on to three days."

"Why did you run away, Juba?"

"'Case de overseer was gwine to whip me."

"Didn't you deserve a whipping?"

"I reckon I did, Master, but I don't like to be whipped by dat overseer no how. He's come of a mighty mean family of poor white folks and he don't know how to treat niggers."

"You are impudent, Juba. Don't you think you ought to be whipped now?"

"Sartin I ought. But now, Master, would you jis please to switch me yourse'f—jis dis once, Master."

"No, Juba; go, ask the overseer to come here."

He obeyed and soon returned with the overseer, a man not so tall as Juba, but of stout, athletic frame.

"Mr. Higgs," said the colonel, "Juba confesses that he deserves to be punished and I wish him to know that you have my special authority and request to punish him now. Please attend to his case when you have time."

"Now, Master, please whip me yourse'f, do; I'll fetch de switches."

Juba ran away toward a wood and the colonel supposed he was taking to the bush again. But he was soon seen returning with an honest bundle of switches in his hand. While he was absent, the overseer said:

"Colonel Fairfax, it seems useless to whip Juba. He is a strange fellow. I have had a great deal of trouble with him, and have tried every way I could think of to manage him. He is a capital hand to work when he is in the humor, but he pays no respect to my authority. He is very proud of his strength, and sometimes looks at me as if he was thinking that he is a better man than I am. One more plan to bring him to subjection has occurred to me, and, if you have no objection, I will try it on him."

"What is it?"

"For me to fight him on equal terms and whip him. That will take the conceit out of him and make him respect me."

"That will never do, Mr. Higgs."

"I believe nothing else will do with Juba."

"If there were no other objection, he might beat you."

"Then you will have to get another overseer. I am willing to take the risk, if you consent. I was once active and had some skill at boxing. I am older now and out of practice. But I'll risk it."

The colonel shook his head doubtfully at this novel proposition, but Juba came up and he merely said, "go with the overseer" as he rode away.

"Now, Juba," said Higgs, "lay down the switches. You will need your fists. You must fight me. I give you a white man's chance. It's a fair fight."

"Fa'r fight? White man's chance? Sure enough?"

"Yes, that's what I say."

"Whoop!" shouted Juba so loud that he was heard by some of his fellow-servants in a neighboring field, and, leaning on their hoes, they became spectators of the scene.

"Get ready, Juba."

"I's always ready for a fa'r fight."

"Come on, then."

Juba was not slow to act upon this hint. He made a lunge with his great maul of a fist at the overseer's face, and would have flattened his features if the blow had not been dexterously parried. Juba opened his eyes with wonder to see that so much force had done no mischief. He repeated the effort several times with little variation and with no better success. Then the overseer in turn began to plant his blows. He struck Juba on the head—his least vulnerable part—and Juba fell flat on the grass. He rose and came to the scratch again, but almost instantly he measured

his length upon the ground. He took a third fall, but
then, when he rose, he turned his back upon his
adversary and took to his heels. He did not stop
until he joined the laborers in the adjoining field.
He there seized a hoe and went to work without
saying a word. After a long time he looked round
and said with a rueful grin:

"Dat ain't such a mean overseer after all; I reckon
his folks is pretty decent for poor white folks."

In the meantime Colonel Fairfax passed into a field
where a dozen slaves were at work under the lead of
one of their own class, who acted as headman of the
gang. He was a cotemporary of the colonel, and
they had played together, and sometimes fought too,
when they were boys. As he remained a boy all his
life, and would have protracted also the boyhood of
his master, he continued to call him "Master Fred."
His nose was like a pack-saddle. He was short, and
though not corpulent, his head, face, body and limbs
were all round, and his plump little figure might have
been rolled about like a ball. He was called Joe.
With the bland serenity of ancient and undisputed
authority, he led a bevy of sleek, well-fed negroes,
who whistled or sung at their labor, quite satisfied
with their prospective share of the products of the
plantation. When the colonel approached Joe, took
off his hat and saluted him with a grave bow, saying,
"your sarvant, Master Fred."

"How goes it, Joe, and how do you get on with
the work to-day?"

"Mighty well, sir; de boys is workin' up lively to-
day, lively, Master Fred. But I bin thinkin', sir,
maybe you'd allow old Joe to 'spress his 'pinion on
dis 'ere corn-plantin' subjec'."

"Certainly, Joe, I would like to hear your opinion."

"Den, Master Fred, my 'pinion is dat dis 'e~e way of plantin' corn, what the overseer is gwine to make us plant corn, is a new way, and it ain't the way the Fairfaxes always planted corn, and my 'pinion is, sir, we won't git no crap."

"Then, Joe," replied his master, laughing, "you think we ought to plant corn still just as the Fairfaxes did when you were a chap?"

"Well, my 'pinion is, Master Fred, dat a family as old as ourn oughtn't to take up with these new ways of the upstarts—no offence to the overseer, sir."

"The Fairfaxes," said the colonel, laughing again, "were always a very good family, Joe, since you and I knew them, and in the ways of honor and duty we cannot do better than follow their examples. But as to planting, perhaps we may learn something by experience which they did not know. The fact is, this new way is one of my own, Joe."

"Oh, dat's another thing, Master Fred. You's one of the same old Fairfaxes yourse'f, and you has a right to think for yourse'f and for your folks too. I's got no 'pinion on dat subjec' ef it's your subjec', sir."

The colonel was about to ride away, when Joe signified by a respectful gesture that he had something more to say.

"What else, Joe?" he asked.

"One of my gang—it's roundhead Bill—says he's got two children over his patch, Master Fred, and he wants, ef you please, to git his patch made up to his family."

"Is that so, Bill?"

"Yes, Master, I done got two 'sponsibilities since you give dat patch, and I most 'spectin' another."

"Very well, Bill; your patch shall be enlarged to fit your responsibilities."

"Thank you, Master," said roundhead Bill.

"Bill is a mighty good boy, Master Fred," added Headman Joe; "he's worth twelve hundred dollars dis blessed day; dat is, ef you was a gentleman would sell a sarvant while he behaves hese'f."

When he had moved away, the colonel saw a young lady riding at a canter across the fields towards him on a white horse of high spirit and beautiful form. She was followed by a gentleman who, in turn, was followed by a servant. "There," said the colonel to himself, "comes Julia, worrying her Uncle Dick with a gallop over plowed ground." He gazed at her with affectionate pride, and his cheerful face beamed with a smile. "What are you after, brother Dick?" he exclaimed, as they drew near.

"After Colonel Julia, of course. She would make a cavalry raid on the village this morning, and I had to follow my colonel."

It was one of his whims to call her colonel, as the destined heir of an estate which should always have a Colonel Frederick for its proprietor, according to the customary law of descent in the family. In default of a Colonel Frederick, he dubbed the niece whom he admired and loved, "Colonel Julia."

"Papa," she said, "your big brother and I have come to take you home. We think you have done work enough while we were at play. Uncle Dick says he intends to preach up a new abolition society for the emancipation of masters."

"Certainly," the doctor added, "the masters are the real objects of compassion in this peculiar institution of ours. My heart bleeds for them. Behold me, an apostle of emancipation, and be the first of the wretches I am to rescue."

"What, brother Dick," said the colonel, "have you done with your old theory that the negroes have the natural right to be slaves and therefore to have masters, servitude being necessary, as you have often affirmed, for their preservation and happiness according to the constitution of nature?"

"I have thrown up the constitution of nature and taken to abolitionist tracts. But I improve on the plan of the abolitionists. I am convinced that the emancipation of masters is the shortest way to the grand result."

"Pray, what is to be this grand result?"

"The extinction of the negro race on this continent."

"That is desirable, is it?" said the colonel, laughing.

"Root out the blacks and you know we shall have a more intelligent and profitable set of laborers."

"But humanity, my big brother!"

"Nonsense, my little brother! Humanity was in last year's almanac. It is out of date. Abolition takes its place this year. Free the negroes! Perish mankind! Come, Julia, you shall turn lecturer. What will a humanitarian society—humanitarian, mark you, not humane—be worth unless it turns the world topsy-turvy and makes women perform the functions of men?"

"Will you emancipate me without my wife?" asked the Colonel. "She is a greater slave to our dependents than I am. See, there she goes now to that cabin, probably to look after a sick child or to render some other service to her numerous family."

"No; it is useless to offer freedom to women. They all rush into matrimony, the most galling kind of bondage. Let them alone."

"Begone, you heathen," said Julia, flourishing her riding-switch.

"Yes, I am a heathen and a republican—I confess all my sins at once. Ostentatious confession is a trick of the Pharisees whom I am going to imitate. It is a proclamation of humility—a proud virtue."

"Ah, brother Dick, you jest, but these negroes are the poor whom we have always with us."

"Unless they run away."

"Well, if they run away from their homes we must pity their folly. And here comes Dainty Dave. What place will there be for him in your new scheme?"

"A fellow you have ruined and made a fool of by discharging him from all labor because once upon a time"——

"He saved my dear daughter's life by an act of devoted courage when our old house was burnt."

"Be it so. Here he comes riding his fat mule and dressed fantastically, as usual. Where are you going, Dave?"

Before answering Dave lifted his high-crowned hat from his head and three times bowed profoundly over the mule's neck, saying, "sarvant, Master; sarvant, Miss Julia; sarvant, Master Dick." Straightening himself up, he gravely added: "I'm gwine to be waxinated, sir."

"Vaccinated? Are you afraid of taking small-pox?"

2

"No, Master Dick, but dere is a dirty nigger on dis plantation wat's got de itch. I reckon, ef de small-pox is de killingest 'stemper of dem two, w'at will keep off de small-pox will keep off de itch."

"You draw conclusions, Dave, with the force of a a mule. You ought to be a doctor."

"Same as you, Master Dick?" said Dave with an impudent leer in his eyes, sheltered by the projecting gravity of his lips. The doctor rode at him with a threatening gesture and Dave rapidly receded from the scene.

"Yes, Julia," said the doctor, "there's your own maid, Grace, you make a fool of her too with your indulgence and your presents and finery and all that."

"But, Uncle Dick, she loves me so truly and then we were play-mates in childhood, you know. She is really a good girl and altogether devoted to me."

"Fudge! She will run away the first time she has a chance—for that I'll wager my horse against your switch."

"Never, Uncle Dick."

"You will find there is a great deal of human nature in these negroes when they are free to show it."

"What do you think of that, Caleb?" said Julia, turning towards the servant who followed Doctor Fairfax, and who now sat in stately fashion on his horse near them. He was dressed quite foppishly, though his master was rather slovenly. Caleb pronounced his opinion.

"Miss Julia, when extremes meet, the ebullition of human nature explodes in a cataclasm of the elements."

"There, now," exclaimed the doctor, "Caleb gives opinions that cannot be refuted, because they cannot be understood. There is matter in his words, no doubt, if we had the wit to find it. There is a fellow, Colonel Julia, who has served me, man and boy, more than forty years, and in all that time he has not uttered an intelligible sentence or failed of a single duty. He is the best servant I ever saw."

Caleb, accepting the praise as customary and due, replied to the doctor.

"Master, if you would investigate the collateral inheritance of my signification, you would see that virtue is the better half of wisdom."

"Why, where did you filch that apothegm? I did not know that I ever entertained a sententious philosopher, though gentlemen do sit at my table sometimes who supply you with sesquipedalian phrases. Now, Julia, there is a long word that he will lug in the next time he discourses to the servants."

"Pardon, Master, I never talk the high English to the niggers. Their craniums is so transfigured by the burnished livery of the burning sun that they cannot prefigure the sentiments."

"Come away, Julia; we shall need an ark to save us from a deluge of words if we remain here."

"Will you go with us, papa?"

"Not yet; I will follow you in a short time."

"Remember, brother Fred! No more talk of humanity in relation to your betters. The negro is not only a man and a brother, but the elder brother of the human family. I am sure," he muttered as he rode off, "nature learned on the negro, before she made the white man, and a black botch she made of her first experiment—a mere mud-pie."

"Come, Arab," said Julia, touching her horse, and he galloped away, Doctor Dick following at his heels.

CHAPTER III.

VISITORS AT ROEBUCK.

FROM the country road or highway a broad avenue half a mile in length led up to a gate below the bluff in front of the. mansion of Roebuck. On each side of the avenue was a row of lombardy poplars— tall, pointed, steeple-like trees, but already stricken at top with that early decay which afflicts those aspiring favorites of the last generation. When Julia touched Arab with her switch two young gentlemen were meeting at the entrance of the avenue.

"Good morning, Mr. Palmer."

"Good morning, Mr. Fitzhugh."

At the same moment they turned the heads of their horses and rode together between the poplars. . At first they talked of the weather, their horses and other trite or trivial matters, and, while their conversation is unimportant, there will be time to describe them. They were about the same age, of twenty-six or seven, and were both handsome and tall; but Fitzhugh was not quite as tall as his companion; the former had dark hair, eyes and complexion, and those of the latter were light. The dress of Palmer was fashionable and precise; that of Fitzhugh genteel but negligent. As horsemanship is the passion of all classes in Virginia, but especially of gentlemen, they were both well mounted. The horse of the dark-haired rider was black, of moderate size and evidently of fine blood, while he of the fair complexion rode a stouter animal of chesnut color. Palmer's features were exactly regular and without an apparent blemish, except that his light blue eyes displayed rather too much white. They expressed no decided character, and even the doubtful negation of expression might signify either apathy or prudence, and his face might be a mask or a mirror. That of Fitzhugh was less regular and more flexible in feature and it was more responsive to mind and heart. Its habitual expression was one of dreamy idleness. But it caught the change of every passing influence so readily that a stranger might have suspected his character of levity if another nature more profound had not been indicated by the breadth of his forehead, the depth of the eyes and the firm lines of the mouth.

"There goes Miss Fairfax towards the house," said Palmer.

"And her uncle with her," added Fitzhugh.

"But he shall not assist her to alight. I intend to perform that service myself."

"If you are at the house before me, you may."

"Agreed."

"Show him your heels, Sultan," said Fitzhugh, and, at a touch of the cane, his horse bounded away. Palmer also, humoring the banter, put spurs to the chestnut. If they were seen at all by Julia and her uncle, they were soon out of sight as they approached the bluff. For a short race there was not much difference in speed between the horses, but the black held the start he had taken. As no person was seen at the gate, it appeared that the necessity of stopping to open it would end the race and set the riders even. But from each side of the gate ran a stone wall or fence, about four feet high. Fitzhugh, swerving his horse from the middle of the road to the sward at the side, came up to the fence and Sultan cleared it at a leap. Palmer declined to follow, and his companion halting, turned and waved his hand with a good-humored laugh. He waited for Palmer to pass through the gate and then they rode together up the bluff. Miss Fairfax had already dismounted and was not to be seen. The gentlemen, giving their bridles to a servant, entered the house. They had not sat long when the young lady made her appearance.

For some minutes the cost of the conversation was defrayed almost exclusively by herself. The thoughts of her visitors were so engrossed with admiration of her beauty that they talked but little. They had often seen her before. Fitzhugh had known her from her infancy. His family and hers had long been neighbors and intimate friends. The acquaintance between her and Palmer was of some years' standing, though it was little more than formal. Neither of the gentlemen professed a warmer feeling for her than friendship; but, in her presence, they felt the fascination of a kind of beauty always new and surprising. At length they found their tongues and for half an hour the conversation flowed fluently enough. They talked of neighborhood news, recent publications, new music and a variety of other topics of transient interest. Julia had the pleasing talent of her sex, and her conversation, like her dress and manners, had the unobtrusive charm of simple elegance. Not from any parade of learning or accomplishments could it be discovered that her education had been as complete as wealth could procure for her. She had received also that better education which girls acquired in those happy homes in Virginia (happy now no more!) where gentle manners were framed to modesty and purity, and where characters were attempered to the duties of life. Palmer, in conversation, was sensible but formal. It was apparent that his moderate faculties had been carefully cultivated in schools. He was versed in the fashions and affected the manners of cities. His imagination was dull and he lacked the versatile and various ease of an agreeable talker. In that respect he was excelled by Fitzhugh when he was in his lighter mood and was excited by congenial company.

Julia, being requested to sing, sat at the piano and sung an Italian song with brilliant operatic music, at the desire of Palmer, whose musical taste had received as elaborate culture as his intellect; and then she sung an English ballad to gratify Fitzhugh, who was an enthusiastic lover of melody, but without much musical science. Her skill satisfied the judgment of the critic, and her sweet voice thrilled the nerves of the enthusiast. One of the gentlemen then requested her to sing something of her own selection. "Then hearken," she said, "for I am going to sing you a song with a moral—a homely little song that was sent to me the other day." Whether she took it up by accident, or chose to amuse herself with the part of a playful moralist, or was influenced by some thought of Fitzhugh, who was settling into an attitude of indolent dreaming, may have been uncertain to herself. She esteemed Hugh Fitzhugh very highly, and treated him with as much familiarity as life-long friendship might warrant between young persons of different sexes. She shared the regret of his friends that, after leaving the University with a

brilliant reputation, and traveling in Europe a year
or two, he seemed to have given himself up to listless idleness.   Not even the estate which he inherited,
and on which he resided with his widowed mother,
appeared to engage his serious attention.   Julia often
heard her father express a fear that the bright promise which his young friend Hugh had given would
be disappointed through mere indolence and a love
of idle pleasures.   Whether she remembered this or
not at the moment, she sung her song "with a
moral"—

THE SONG OF THE BEE.

In sipping sweets and kissing flowers
    The nimble-wingèd bee
From morn till night beguiles the hours—
    And who so blithe as he?
O, might we pass this life of ours
    As gaily as the bee!

From every flower, with every kiss,
    A treasure sucks the bee,
Nor wastes an hour in idle bliss—
    And who so rich as he?
Thy roaming revels come to this—
    To fill thy hive, O bee.

So love and song, and all delights
    That clear the spirit free,
May sweeten toilsome days and nights
    That store the hive for thee;
But life is naught if pleasure blights
    Its fruit—for man or bee.

"That song, I am sure, was sung for me," re-marked Fitzhugh.

"Does it please you?" asked Miss Fairfax.

"The moral, not the music, was meant for me."

"Do you suspect me, then, of preaching to you or at you?"

"Perhaps it may turn out a song,
Perhaps turn out a sermon."

"And why do you take it as a sermon rather than as a song?"

"I will think of it," he said, musingly.

"Do, Mr. Fitzhugh," she replied, in a tone which seemed at once to apologize for the candor of her sermon, and to insinuate an interest in his career.

"I wish so fair a preacher would level a sermon at me," said Alfred Palmer.

"If I am suspected of such presumption I must never transgress again, Mr. Palmer. But here comes papa—and Uncle Dick with him, too. Between them they shall teach you all wisdom, whether the amiable or the satirical."

Colonel Fairfax met the young gentlemen with a hearty greeting, and the doctor said, "Brother Fred and I have just had a pretty quarrel about the comparative merits of your horses, gentlemen; take care that we don't finish it over you."

"You must not call it a quarrel," said the colonel.

"Well, a discussion—the milder synonym."

"I would like to show the gentlemen a horse of mine;" and the colonel was about to dilate upon horseflesh, for it was one of his vanities, and the number of fine horses on the plantation formed one

2*

exception to the judicious economy of his management. But he checked himself, and, gliding with
easy urbanity to a more appropriate subject, he led
the way in an animated conversation, to which all
present contributed. Julia, who always showed most
vivacity in the presence of her amiable and cheerful
father, talked with sparkling gaiety; the guests imi-
tated her vivacity, and Doctor Dick let off some
squibs at intervals. Colonel Fairfax was fond of the
society of young people, and they enjoyed his frank,
entertaining and intelligent conversation. The young
men of his acquaintance loved him, and admired his
character. Hugh Fitzhugh had been accustomed
from boyhood to look upon him as his best friend,
almost as a guardian. His mother, left a widow with
no other child when Hugh was very young, was his
legal guardian, but Colonel Fairfax was her constant
adviser. Albert Palmer was born in New England,
and, though he had lived a great part of his life in
Virginia, had no intimate acquaintance with the family at Roebuck.

At length the current of conversation was interrupted by Doctor Fairfax, who remarked abruptly, "that
is a Yankee horse you ride, Mr. Palmer—a Yankee
Morgan."

"You would not imply," said Julia, "that he is
the worse for a Northern origin, Uncle Dick."

"By no means; I like the Yankee-bred Morgans."

But the irritation of sectional controversy had made
men sensitive to every comparison between the North
and the South, and the most inoffensive allusions
would sometimes rub the raw and provoke resentment. Palmer had certain reasons for being more
sensitive than others when he suspected that a slight

was cast upon his Northern birth, and the abrupt manner of the doctor, which startled even Julia, had irritated him. He said with asperity: "you are mistaken, sir. I am a true Southerner. I use nothing from Yankeedom that I can obtain in the South. In fact," he added with a rising voice, "I despise the Yankees."

There was silence, for all present were shocked and embarrassed. Virginians cherish the love of native-land with romantic fidelity. They could tolerate in a stranger the utmost devotion to the country of his birth, though it might be the country they most disliked. They could not comprehend the contempt expressed by Palmer for the land of his nativity and the people of his blood. After an awkward pause the doctor, who delighted to abuse the "Yankees," broke the silence.

"Well, since the Yankees have no friends here, I will air my opinions of them."

"Come, Uncle Dick, be charitable. We know you keep the North as a woman keeps a pin-cushion, to stick pins in."

"*Acer tetigisti*, Colonel Julia, which, being interpreted, signifies that you are as sharp as one of your needles this morning. But I'll balk your penetration this time. I shall use none but a blunt instrument— a mere maul. I shall simply take the liberty of saying that the Yankees are the meanest, the most arrogant, the most hypocritical, the most meddlesome and the most corrupt branch of the human family—if I must acknowledge them as men and brothers."

"O fie, Uncle Dick, they are a religious people."

"Their religion is fox-fire, a superficial light from rottenness—their morals a science of fraud. Their

credo is a long face on Sunday and a long purse on
week days. Their water of baptism is water of pe-
trifaction, turning their hearts to stone. Look at
those three thousand preachers who petitioned Congress recently—their petition was a howl of hate
against the South. When they stretch out their holy
hands over this half of the country, their benedictions
are bans and their very halleluiah is a doxology of
devils. They have almost canonized the bones of old
John Brown, a robber and assassin, because they were
Southern women and children whom he would have
incited negroes to murder in their beds. Like priests,
like people. The better class of preachers at the
North are ransacking the Apocalypse to prove that
the end of the world is at hand, and they confirm
their predictions by citing the unparalleled depravity
of mankind—a depravity which they actually see at
their own doors, though it is not seen in the South."

"But, brother Dick," interrupted the colonel,
"those are only their fanatics whom you describe."

"They drown the voices of all others. And then
Yankee politics—a corrupt despotism of demagogues
—professing but one principle, the rule of a majority,
and practicing but one, public plunder. Fanaticism,
however, will soon dominate politics. Already most
of the religious societies there are political clubs.
Priests are sure to be the tyrants of a land where
pure religion does not prevail."

"The spirit of caricature runs away with my big
brother to-day," said Colonel Fairfax, laughing.

"Caricature! What I say is as true as daguerreo-
type."

"And not more life-like, I dare say, Uncle Dick."

"Julia, a good girl like you cannot imagine such

evils as polute Northern society. Their cities are
sinks, their towns ape their cities and they poison the
country. They abound with haunts where men have
exerted their ingenuity in perfecting vice as they have .
elsewhere in improving machinery. What is their
society—what must it be from its structure, even
aside from religion and politics? A confused populace struggling for wealth or life—a perpetual prize-
fight, with millions in the ring—a mob without gentlemen "——

"Hold, there, brother Dick, you won't say there
are no gentlemen in the North," cried the colonel,
laughing at the doctor's notions.

"Gentlemen—yes, many of them, as there are
many good Christians. But there is no class of gentry with a recognized position and influence. Here,
you know, the gentry, rich and poor, without the
support of unequal laws, exert a direct and legitimate
influence upon the movements of society with the
open approbation of the people, and with open responsibility, under the correction of public opinion.
There, gentry is ostracised. Wealth, everywhere a
power, rules there by indirection and corruption. It
buys the press. It subsidizes the pulpit. It bribes
the demagogues. It corrupts all leaders of the public. When fanaticism is quiet, the force that rules
the Yankees is money and a mob. In fact, there can
be no gentry, where nothing is stable, and gold is
the standard of all worth. Gentry is the peculiar
flower of an old agricultural community, where nature
shines on agriculture. How"——

"Pardon me, Uncle Dick, you are making a
speech."

"Heaven forefend, Colonel Julia; if I get to

speech-making, I shall become as great a bore as a Yankee professor, a superficial coxcomb who lectures always, about everything and—nothing."

"Breathe a while, Uncle Dick. Papa, I have not told you that I saw Mr. Ambler this morning, and invited him to dine with us to-day. The carriage has been sent for him, and he should be here soon."

"I am glad of it, daughter. Our venerable pastor is always a welcome guest. You must remain and dine with him, gentlemen. Do not refuse. You know the good old clergyman, and you must enjoy his society."

Fitzhugh accepted the invitation, but Palmer, with a polite apology, declined it, and took his leave. When the conversation was resumed, Fitzhugh said—

"It gratifies me to infer, Doctor Fairfax, that you think the time has arrived when we should dissolve our political connection with the North."

"What! follow South Carolina in secession?"

"Certainly."

"No."

"No?"

"Never."

"You amaze me. Would you prolong our association with such communities as you have just depicted?"

"I have not read in any book of surgery that to cut off the head is a safe cure for tooth-ache."

"Do you think, then, that to cut off the North is to cut off the head of the South?"

"No; you are too literal in spelling a metaphor. But secession will be fatal to the Southern States. The North will subjugate them, and then where will be your remedy?"

"How can such a people, fighting for independence, be conquered? They would be exterminated first. See how their patriotic zeal already burns with martial fire. Many men pant for war with the North."

"I have heard such men talk. They will serve as light-wood to kindle a revolution, but we shall need more durable fuel to keep it up. The South is not fanatical, or malignant, or corrupt like the North, but, what is worse in view of such a conflict, it is weak. It is weak just where many imagine it is strong. Besides the obvious disparity of numbers and material between the North and South, consider that you would link Virginia with States that must fail her in a long and exhaustive war. One of them has a gentry and no people; another, a people and no gentry, and a third, neither people nor gentry—neither body nor spirit. The very vices of the Yankees will contribute to their cruel success in such an enterprise as the conquest and plunder of the South. Think you I would provoke a horde of Northern barbarians to overrun Virginia with fire and sword?"

"Shall we, then, submit to oppression through fear? The Northern States, as you have described them, are unfit associates of a Commonwealth like Virginia. They have repeatedly nullified the laws, and broken the Federal compact in points essential to our security. By a perversion of constitutional forms they have seized the common government with an avowed design of wresting its tremendous powers to their aggrandizement and our oppression. The wrongs they have perpetrated would justify war—much more simple separation. The danger that we shall lose all the rights of our States if we acquiesce

in their aggressions is manifest and imminent. There
appears to be no way of escape from it, but by secession. The right of secession is clear. The right of
self-government is inalienable. By seceding, we
shall give no just cause of war. I hope war will not
come. If it should come, I believe the South will
not be conquered. But, whatever may be the possible event, it is better in such a cause to invoke the
justice of the God of Battles, than tamely to await
our inevitable doom in the Union."

Fitzhugh had risen, and while he spoke his eyes
beamed with enthusiasm, and his rich, mellow voice,
swelled into a tone rather too oratorical for private
conversation. Suddenly becoming conscious of this,
he paused and turning to Julia said—"pardon me,
Miss Julia, I am making a speech."

"It is easy to pardon the warm expression of patriotic feeling," she replied.

"Ah, Hugh," observed Colonel Fairfax, "you agi-
tate a perilous question, that requires for its solution
eminent wisdom and sobriety of judgment. A young
gentleman of your spirit and principles naturally
feels indignant at the wrongs and insults which our
States have suffered from a portion of the Northern
people, and alarmed at the danger which threatens us
from that quarter. The amusing caricatures of
Northern society which have been sketched by my
brother are not without a partial resemblance to truth.
I do not doubt the right of secession, and I regard it
as the only effectual check upon the Federal government whenever it shall become—as all governments
are liable to become—dangerous to liberty. But this
is not our whole case. Is it necessary or wise to
secede now? Will secession cure the ills we suffer or

avert the dangers we fear? Is there no remedy within the Union? Shall we relinquish all the advantages of the Union without further efforts to preserve it while saving also our rights, honor and security? The Union is very dear to me. I have been taught to love it from my cradle upward. As Virginians, we should cherish it as especially the work of our fathers and the monument of their glory. Secession may not bring war but war is probable. Subjugation may follow with its train of indescribable horrors. War at best—civil war above all—is terrible. Let us not be rash. Let us confide a little longer in the returning reason of our Northern brethren. Let us look and wait for some milder remedy than secession. Let us, if possible, preserve this great country entire and not afflict mankind with the destruction of our Union."

"Ought Virginia, then," inquired Hugh Fitzhugh, "from timidity or sentimental recollections to lag behind her sister States in the assertion of right—in a contest for independence and freedom?"

"Prudence, my dear sir, is not dishonorable; neither is reluctance to abandon a system which has produced vast benefits. I have no fear that our venerable Commonwealth will ever be dishonored by any act of her own. If she should—as I trust she may—restore to the Union the seven States which have seceded, and, at the same time, secure the rights of all for the future, that will be a work worthy of her ancient renown."

"But will the fierce passions of the North permit it to be done?"

"Forbearance, statesmanship, and patient, persevering effort must prove whether it is possible. At all events, I shudder at the thought of breaking up the

Union until every honorable experiment for its preservation has been tried in vain."

"But suppose, Colonel Fairfax, that while Virginia
is endeavoring to restore the integrity of the Union,
the Federal government should attempt to reduce the
seceding States to obedience by force?"

"Then we must fight. An attempt to subjugate
those States by arms after what has happened will
annul all claims of the Federal government upon the
support of any Virginian or any friend of Republican
liberty. Liberty cannot survive a triumph of Federal force in such a contest. No State can be neutral.
If the North constrains Virginia to fight for or against
the South, she must fight for the South at every hazard. Then secession will become a secondary question. War will be the first. We cannot aid in the
subjugation of our sister States."

CHAPTER IV.

TABLE-TALK AT ROEBUCK.

THE carriage returned, bringing the Rev. Charles Ambler. He was nearly fourscore years of age. His hair was white and his appearance venerable, but his form was erect and his step firm. His keen grey eyes, dimmed but not bleared by age, his aquiline nose and his square chin expressed decision of character, and saved his mild demeanor from a charge of apathetic dullness. In early life he was a successful lawyer. Then he served as a captain of volunteers in the last war with England. Afterwards, from conscientious motives, he became a student of divinity, and, in due time, a minister of the gospel. For more than forty years his life as a clergyman was one of apostolic poverty, of active usefulness and modest godliness. He shunned the sanctimonious affectations by which some preachers advertise themselves as ready-made saints. His goodness became known by its fruits.

Soon after he had been received with respectful salutation by Colonel Fairfax, and the other persons present had exchanged greetings with him, Mrs. Fairfax joined the company. After expressing to the clergyman her pleasure at his visit, she said— "Julia tells me that you would hardly leave your garden to dine with us."

"I confess, my dear madam," he replied, "I was

inclined to linger among my plants and flower-beds
this fine spring day if I could have resisted the fair
Julia. But, you know, from the beginning the
woman has had a knack of turning the man out of
the garden."

"When I tempted you with mamma's dinner," said
Julia, "I felt sure that you were well acquainted with
the way back to Paradise."

"I see," said the doctor, "it is now as it was of
old—the man lays the blame on the woman."

"And the story runs," replied Mr. Ambler, laughing, "that you, doctor, are more impartial, and lay
blame on everybody."

"My big brother was fairly hit then," said the
colonel.

"What! Have I the character of a common
scold? I will reform forthwith, under the rebuke of
my pastor."

"Nay, brother Dick," said Mrs. Fairfax, "that
character is one which your gallant sex assigns to
ours exclusively."

"But that, I maintain, is a slander," cried Hugh
Fitzhugh.

"You shall be the favored champion of dames and
damsels," said Julia.

"When I have learned the lesson of the bee?"

"Forgive me; I did not think the bee could leave
a sting. I see to-day that you anticipate stirring
times, and your soul is already stirred."

"I would not be idle when my native State is in
danger."

After some further conversation dinner was announced. The good cheer and generous hospitality
of Virginians are proverbial. Of course, they were

not dishonored by the Fairfaxes of Roebuck. The table exhibited the tempting abundance common to the country, and a costly elegance peculiar to the rich. Colonel Fairfax was an observer of all generous usages, and considered the honor of his family engaged to excel in hospitality. He valued the silver upon his table chiefly because the greater part of it had been upon the tables of his ancestors. He was himself temperate in all things, but he dined with a healthy appetite, stimulated by active employment, and he took his wine, not exclusively for the stomach's sake, but to make glad the heart. So far was he from moroseness, that he thought pleasure to be the playmate of virtue, though excess is the handmaid of vice.

When the viands ceased to hold the first place in the attention of the company, and conversation began to range, a remark of Mrs. Fairfax gave occasion to some reflections of Mr. Ambler upon the social condition of Virginia. "I believe," he said, "there is not a happier or better community. Nature has been bountiful to our people, but not prodigal; rewarding industry, but not dispensing with exertion; bestowing health, and requiring vigor. Fortunate circumstances make agriculture our chief occupation, but also render commerce and the arts profitable to those who prefer them. There is wealth enough for leisure to cultivate the higher faculties, and yet even the rich among us are incited to lead active lives under the open sky. Property is so diffused that the scale is gradual from the richest to the poorest. Even the poorest seldom turn beggars or thieves, for poverty here is neither extreme nor hopeless. Contentment is almost universal Perhaps the pressure of necessity is scarcely sufficient to stimulate as rapid improvement in useful arts as we might rationally desire. Morals are generally simple and pure. Truth, honesty and mutual good-will—the main elements of morality—are generally enforced by usage and opinion. Even the blacks have been raised to a degree of well-being and of virtue hitherto unknown to their race. They really seem to be happier in their way than their masters. Most of the evils which exist appear to be common to mankind, while many of our blessings are peculiar to Virginia."

"And yet," exclaimed the doctor, "the Yankees are eager to subvert our social system and foist upon us their superior civilization! A sordid cizilization, glittering with a thin surface of gold-leaf—having circulating gold for its life-blood, a golden calf for its God, and a material New Jerusalem with pavements literally golden for the heaven of its hope. A cizilization in which men, with fierce and grasping competition, grovel and jostle each other as men do in the gold-diggings. Every man in the North is let loose against his neighbor to become victor or victim in a struggle for life. Of course, all society becomes mercenary, and honors, laws, verdicts, religion, everything is on sale in the vast auction-mart. But because the general scramble of sordid selfishness assists the teeming fertility of a new continent to produce cities and palaces, they vaunt their vicious civilization as the final product of consummate wisdom."

"Let us be cautious as well as candid, my dear doctor," replied Mr. Ambler, "in passing judgment upon entire communities. In those of the North, as in others, there are conspicuous evils which are easily censured. Some men there flaunt their follies and vices before the world with singular hardihood. But my acquaintance with the Northern people has not been general or intimate and we cannot judge them rightly without knowing them thoroughly. Without such knowledge, it is fair to presume that, in the main, they are like other men—like ourselves. Remember how we have been traduced among them when accidental anomalies have been culled and caricatured as characteristics of our social system. Thus deplorable animosities have been kindled and fanned into a dangerous flame. We should not repeat the error in censuring them. Charity forbids it, and, since mistakes here endanger the public tranquility, prudence and patriotism enforce the lesson of charity."

"Is it wise then," inquired Mr. Fitzhugh, "to shut our eyes to the faults of our associates when they affect our safety? Should we not consider whether the corruptions, or the passions, or the policy of the North requires us to dissolve our connection with that country?"

"A truce;" cried Mr. Ambler, "since the conversation is drifting into a political discussion, I must retreat from it. Will you not help me out of the scrape, Julia?"

"I hope to have Miss Julia for an ally in supporting my political opinions upon a proper occasion," said Fitzhugh.

"I refer you to papa for my politics. He is my political conscience-keeper. But I am glad to second Mr. Ambler's desire to converse upon less exciting topics; especially as I have wished to hear the conclusion of an incident which he had begun to relate when dinner was announced. You were speaking,

Mr. Ambler, of a companion you had in the carriage this morning."

"Yes; you, Colonel Fairfax, know Abraham Marlin, the cooper?"

"Very well; an odd character, but a good man and a good mechanic."

"Have you ever heard him preach?" asked the doctor.

"Preach!" exclaimed Mrs. Fairfax.

"Preach or exhort, as you prefer. He is an illiterate enthusiast who has stumbled into a sect of New-Lights and forthwith taken to exhorting his neighbors. They are beginning to style him *passon*, I am told."

"I dare say he is a worthy man," mildly observed Mr. Ambler, "though he may be presumptuous. In all times there have been honest men who felt themselves called to preach religious truth because their souls were fired with religious zeal."

"They mistake the fever of fanaticism for inspiration," said the doctor.

"Uncle Dick, I fear your late reform needs reformation."

"True, Colonel Julia; you are as good as a second conscience to me. Since you are not satisfied with my reformation, I promise not to reform any more—reform myself, I mean."

"However," continued Mr. Ambler, "it was not of Marlin, the cooper, that I was about to speak particularly, but of his son, Mark."

"Mark Marlin—I know him well," remarked Hugh Fitzhugh; "he is a fine young fellow. I met him first in hunting. His father lives in a cabin on a small piece of land at the foot of the Ridge."

"Well, as I came from the village to-day I overtook a youth walking on the road-side. My attention
was attracted by his fine athletic form and his elastic
step. When he turned his face to me, and, raising
his hat, saluted me with the title of *passon* (my dear
doctor) I thought his countenance displayed more intelligence than we are used to find in such homely
garb as he wore and at his age, for he could not be
more than seventeen. Curious to learn something
about him and willing to give the pedestrian a lift at
the expense of your horses, Mrs. Fairfax, I invited
him into the carriage. He courteously declined at
first, but when I asked him to grant me some conversation as a favor to me, he came in. I soon learned
that his name was Mark Marlin, whose father I knew
slightly, and I drew him on to such other disclosures
as might enable me to judge of my duty to my young
neighbor."

"We, young men," interposed Hugh Fitzhugh,
"have to thank you for treating us all as sons rather
than as neighbors only."

"It is one of my pleasant duties, Hugh. I discovered that Mark had an acute intellect, and that he
had reflected much on some of the knotty problems
of life. From defect of education his ideas were
somewhat confused and imperfectly expressed. I saw
that he had some ambition, and I asked him what he
aimed to make of himself as a man. 'A gentleman,'
was his brief and ready response. I endeavored then
to gather from his talk what conception of a gentleman had fired his youthful ambition. He neither de-
fined nor described the character, but simply said—
'Colonel Fred is the sort of man.' Thus, you per-

3

ceive, my friend, that you are the model of our youth —even of the sons of our mechanics."

"And I am sure," Mrs. Fairfax began—

"Hush, my dear," cried the colonel with his cheery laugh, "if you open your lips about your husband, Mr. Ambler, as a faithful pastor, will have to rebuke us both for my manifold perfections. At present I stand charged only with being a gentleman, as, of course, I am bound to be."

Mrs. Fairfax replied with a look such as loving wives have often bestowed on worse husbands, and the clergyman proceeded—

"I reminded Mark that Colonel Fairfax had an ample fortune, which secured to him the social position of a gentleman. He looked at me, and said with some hesitation—'you are not rich, but you are a gentleman.' I could not, of course, repel this *argu mentum ad hominem*. But I observed that the colonel sprang from an ancient family. He did not shrink from the reflection implied upon the humility of his own family, but, in awkward phrases, went on to say that birth obliged Colonel Fred to be a gentleman in character and conduct, while it secured to him the consideration due to a gentleman without effort on his part in the beginning. 'But,' he added, 'a poor man, and the son of a poor man, in a free country, can rise to a gentleman's place if he behaves like a gentleman.' He thought that wealth would help him to his object, but he had a suspicion that the ways by which men get rich suddenly are unfriendly to the sentiments and habits that should distinguish a gentleman. He believed it would be better to aim at one of those professions which people look up to as carrying the idea of social rank. If we should have a war in which it would be creditable to volunteer, he would be inclined to go as a soldier, and fight his way up to a commission, as that would entitle him to the position of a gentleman, and, for the character of a gentleman, he would keep Colonel Fred in mind as his model. Besides, he said, he was studying books at home every evening after his day's work was done. The conversation by which these thoughts were brought to light, one after another, occupied the time until we came to the end of the avenue. Mark then left me, after promising to visit me at the parsonage."

"I hope," said the Colonel, "he will prove to be worthy of the care which I foresee you will bestow on the development of his character."

"Can you doubt it, brother Fred, when you remember his model?"

"I will be surety for him," said Hugh Fitzhugh, "though I believe Mr. Ambler, after a single half-hour's ride with him, knows him better than I do. In tracing the springs of his conduct, Mr. Ambler, you have shown an art which I do not possess."

"I learned something of that art in my first profession, the law, and I have learned the best uses of it in my present profession."

"Have you heard what happened last night to our neighbor Eckles?" inquired Colonel Fairfax.

"I have not. What was it?"

"Eckles, you may know, has for some time been excluded from society by the gentlemen of the county on account of his cruel treatment of his slaves."

"He came from Massachusetts," grumbled the doctor; "those Northern men, when they settle among us, do not know how to treat negroes, because they have not been bred as slaveholders. They, with a few native reprobates, give the only color of truth there is for the enormous calumnies upon our society that are circulated at the North."

"Yesterday," resumed the colonel, "he maltreated one of his slaves, and, to punish him for it, some young men of his neighborhood went to his house in the evening, and, inviting him out, they ducked him in the river—by way of a warning, they told him."

"I hope he was not seriously hurt," observed Mrs. Fairfax.

"No; he got a thorough wetting only, I understand. It is probable, however, that he will sell his property and leave the country."

"No doubt," said the doctor, "he will return to the North, turn abolitionist and deliver lectures on the horrors of slavery—admittance twenty-five cents a head."

"Might we not, Colonel," asked Mr. Ambler, "protect the negroes by law more effectually against such masters?"

"It is doubtful. Good as well as evil results from the large discretionary authority allowed by law to the masters, as in the case also of parents. Opinion, religion, custom and time are safer as well as surer forces than law for the melioration of such social institutions. *Quid leges sine moribus proficiunt?* During the last two centuries the condition of our slaves has been greatly improved without much aid from legislation. The authority of the masters, in point of fact, is seldom abused in Virginia. We may expect improvement to be progressive. The trenchant operation of positive law upon the intricate and delicate relations of society is apt to be mischievous, unless the law merely sanctions or completes what time has proved and usage enacted: Then, though law does no harm, it is almost superfluous. Thus, when time had left little for law to do, slavery was abolished by law in the Northern States. In England it was abolished insensibly by time alone, without law."

"At all events, colonel, perhaps our legislation might be amended with respect to the marriage of slaves and the separation of their families."

"Possibly, if the pestilent agitation of more vital questions connected with the institution did not prevent a calm consideration of such subjects, some practicable amendment might be devised. But it would be difficult to frame a law that would not do more harm than good. The practical evils to be corrected have been in a great measure removed already in Virginia by the silent influences to which I have adverted. Families are seldom separated without their consent, except in circumstances of necessity, such as must separate families in all communities and under whatever laws. Marriage is more generally enforced by the authority of the masters than willingly observed by the negroes. Their natural indifference to marital and parental obligations is more in fault than our laws. If you absolutely forbid the separation of families, will you not condemn both masters and slaves to unavoidable suffering in many cases?"

"But a Christian State should protect the sacred bond of matrimony."

"The purely religious idea connected with marriage by many Christians is not a proper subject for legislation. It is to be inculcated and enforced, as it is now among whites and blacks, by the teaching and discipline of religious bodies. I believe that, whenever the slaves are prepared to perform the duties of the family, there will be little need of law to protect their family ties. Probably they are better protected and more faithfully observed now in Virginia than such ties are among free negres anywhere or among the poorest classes in other countries."

"Now, my dear husband, I think we may lay these grave themes aside. Julia and I have been silent a long time."

"Place aux dames. I yield the floor to the ladies. Shall we talk of a wedding?"

"I can tell you something about a wedding nearer home than you think, perhaps, papa, and not so foreign to your own grave discourse as your mode of putting that question implies," said Julia.

"A wedding it shall be then, daughter "

Julia gave a slight and humorous description of the last grand wedding among the servants when her maid, Grace, had been taken for better for worse by carpenter Dick, with every vow that should bind two lives together and with a disinterested contempt of marriage settlements; when all Africa of Roebuck held high festival; when the women, "black but comely like the tents of Kedar," arrayed themselves in gorgeous colors, and when Mrs. Fairfax, having supplied a great supper, gave a smiling care to the entertainment of her servants. The slaves had jollity and sensuous pleasures which a negro loves; master and mistress assumed the cares which a negro abhors. The children of Ham were cursed with servitude but their nature was adapted to make it easy. The rose of a blessing often blooms on the thorn of a curse.

CHAPTER V.

ROEBUCK THREATENED.

ONE evening, a few days later, Albert Palmer sat at home with his father and mother. The parlor in which they were had costly furniture, and the house was large and commodious. The father, Mr. Israel Palmer, was a little over fifty-five years of age, and, in appearance, might have been his son grown older, rich and wary. Some score of years before that time he had come from New England with a little capital, and settled in Virginia as a merchant. He had thriven, and, a few years ago, he purchased land in the county with a hope of crowning a life of successful business with the respectable enjoyments of a wealthy planter. He now coveted, as he had once envied, the social rank which he regarded as aristocracy. He was hospitably received in the county, but, by degrees, a difference of manners and tastes rendered the intercourse between him and his neighbors more constrained and less frequent. Being jealous and suspicious, he imagined offence where none was intended. Estrangement and then dislike ensued. Stung by fancied insult, he meditated retaliation. He was not a man to yield to a real or imaginary conspiracy to exclude him from the society of the "aristocracy." He was resolved to retain his estate and reside on it. He would watch for opportunities to elevate his own family and to avenge

himself on others. His feelings had become almost
morbid when the prospect of secession and war set
his shrewd and active mind to calculating what advantages he might derive from those events. He
was so cautious and secret that his thoughts were not
freely disclosed even to his family.

His wife was a tall, slender woman, with many an-
gles and no curves. She wore her hair, her eyes, her
lips, her limbs and her gown with formal precision.
She sat erect in a square, high-backed chair. She
placed her hands on her lap smoothly along, palm to
palm. She set her feet flat on the floor, near together, and making with each other the very angle
which, according to her notion, was proper. When
she moved from one seat to another, she elongated
her figure in rising with the jointed, hinged and
oiled exactness of a mathematical instrument, glided
away on a straight line, with mechanical regularity
of step, and let herself down like a jointed instrument
again. When she talked, her voice ran out in a level
stream without break, emphasis or cadence. The
sentiments she uttered were always frigid, but never
wrong, according to the standard of right which she
had studied. The warmer and nobler emotions were
represented in her discourse by eulogies of them.
She deprecated their opposites with little hitches in
her utterances that were hints of horror. She passed
for a saint in her family and in her conscience too.
She practiced the politeness of elaborate flattery. She
was a woman of learning, for she had been educated
in Boston, and talked rather "like a book" than like
a lady. She remembered some scraps of Latin, which
she lugged into her conversation in season and out
of season.

Husband, wife and son were discussing the latest news. The same subject was discussed that evening in every habitation of Virginia where the intelligence had been received. The commissioners deputed by the Confederate government to visit Washington and solicit an amicable adjustment of the questions incident to secession, after being detained with delusive art until certain warlike preparations, were secretly made, were rejected. A defiance and provocative of war was offered to the South by sending vessels to Charleston harbor to be fired upon, and finally it was announced that the President of the United States had, by proclamation, called forth an army to be employed against the Confederate States, and that, in consequence of this proclamation, the Convention of Virginia had passed an ordinance of secession, subject to ratification or rejection by the people at the polls. It was also rumored that the State authorities had dispatched a volunteer force to seize the armory at Harper's Ferry.

"This means war," pronounced the paternal Palmer.

"Undoubtedly war," echoed the son.

"The ordinance of secession will be ratified by the people."

"Almost unanimously."

"We should be prepared for those events," said the father.

"We must choose a side, no doubt," replied the son.

"Or sides."

This brief, ambiguous qualification, added by his wary father, was not quite intelligible to Albert, but he asked no explanation and none was offered. The

3*

old gentleman sat for some minutes in silence looking
at his son, as if cautiously pondering how far he might
trust his own flesh and blood with his thoughts. At
length he quietly remarked—

"The North will subjugate the South."

"Do you really think so?"

"It is mathematically certain."

"You scarcely appreciate the Southern people,
father."

"I appreciate statistics."

Again there was silence. The thin lips of Mrs.
Palmer parted, as if to open a passage for the steady
little breeze of words which usually flowed without
apparent impulse from her mouth, whenever it was
open, like the breath of the Blowing Cave. But she
saw that the gentlemen, while gazing at each other,
were revolving thoughts which might not brook
interruption from her just then. So the lips were laid
together again in a straight seam. Her husband resumed the conversation in the same quiet tone.

"This war will destroy slavery."

"I do not foresee that as a necessary consequence,"
replied Albert, "even if the South should be conquered, still less, if the independence of the South
should be successfully maintained."

"As hostility to slavery was the origin, the destruction of slavery must be the end of the war. If it
should have the magnitude and duration which I
anticipate, it will destroy slavery even if, in the final
result, the South should retain its independence."

"My dear husband and my beloved son," Mrs.
Palmer slipped into a slight pause in the conversation
of the gentlemen, "my conscience prompts me to
observe that we ought not to grieve at the release of

millions of our fellow-beings from the shackles of
bondage and the lash of cruel task-masters; all men
are created free and equal; man cannot lawfully hold
property in man; traffic in human flesh cannot be
blessed with the approval of heaven; this reflection
occurred to my mind, my dear husband, when you
sold Tom, to be carried to Lousiana without his wife
and children, but it was true, as you said, that he was
quite disobedient and he did not want his family to
go with him and his wife did not want to go, and that
last family you bought you got at a low price, because
the owner did not wish to separate them and could
not find another purchaser for them all; it was very
humane in you; I hope the day will soon come when
the whole family of man will enjoy the sunshine of
universal freedom under "——

"We should be prepared for these events, Albert,"
repeated the father.

"Prudence requires it," prudently echoed the son.

"I will sell my slaves."

"The money might be more secure in any event of
the war."

"But, my dear husband, would it not be more consistent with our principles to emancipate them?"

"To be denounced as an abolitionist?"

"True; that is an insuperable objection; we must
preserve our respectability in society; my sensibility
is deeply wounded when I think of the painful necessities of our position here; I sometimes regret that we
left New England, *coelum non animum mutant qui trans
mare currunt;* to be sure we have improved our worldly
condition here, but nothing is so sweet as a calm
and quiet conscience; I suppose me must sell the
negroes "——

"I will invest the money abroad," added Mr. Palmer.

"Would it not be prudent to sell your land also and invest the money abroad?" asked Albert.

"Never!" exclaimed the father, rising and walking about the room in evident excitement. It was part of a cherished plan to retain his land as the territorial foundation of that social supremacy to which he aspired. The proposal to sell it pricked his most sensitive nerve. But, with habitual self-control, he restrained the expression of his thoughts, and, after some time, resumed his seat and his composure.

"You have said, Albert, that we must choose a side in this war."

"'Or sides,' you added, father."

"Why should a man risk his fortunes with one party exclusively? Or why should you and I both appear on the same side?"

These questions surprised Albert. He had taken for granted that, in such a contest, it would be necessary for him to act a decided part, and he had not dreamed of acting in opposition to his father. He had made some progress toward a decision for himself, but with a mental reservation that his father was to approve his final choice. He had been educated at a Northern University, but even there, he had affected to play the Southerner. The young men of Virginia always treated him with cordial friendship, and, by their frank manners, high spirit and honorable conduct, they won his esteem and excited his emulation. From them he borrowed some sentiments of local patriotism, such as the young always cherish, and he was ambitious to appear among them as a true and ardent Virginian. He adopted his father's aspiration to improve the social position of the family, and thought his own marriage. might promote that object. He was not insensible to the charms of Julia Fairfax, and, with hereditary thrift, had calculated the advantages which the hand of that heiress could bestow. Under the influence of various feelings and calculations, he had accustomed himself to make loud professions of violent Southern sentiments, and he could scarcely have told how far they were sincere and how far affected. He was inclined to range himself still on the side of Virginia in the war that was now imminent, but he was ready to weigh all advantages on each side before taking an irrevocable step. It had never occurred to him that he might secure the advantages of both sides or of neutrality. Perplexed by his father's questions, he looked at him as if he would read an explanation in his face, but that was not to be read like the face of a clock. Mr. Palmer, instead of explaining asked another question—

"To which side do you incline, Albert?"

"I have believed that it was your desire to identify our family with this community, and it would seem most consistent with your views that I should embrace the cause of Virginia," cautiously replied the son. After another pause the father said—

"You have visited Miss Fairfax?"

"Not often."

"What course will her father pursue in the war?"

"Doubtless he will adhere to Virginia."

"He owns a fine estate?"

"Yes, sir."

"It will be confiscated."

Again there was silence. The suggestion of confiscation was new to Albert, and both gentlemen were interested in trains of thought connected with it, but neither communicated his reflections to the other. At length the father briefly announced his conclusion.

' Go with the South, Albert. I will adhere to the North."

" Really, father, you will oblige me if you will explain the reasons which lead you to a decision so extraordinary."

" Is it not natural for me to prefer the land in which I was born and in which I lived until I was too old to discard the attachments of youth, and that you should prefer the land in which you have grown up ?"

" Possibly; but"—the young man hesitated. He was about to insinuate that his father had put forth a mere pretext to cover deeper reasons. He was understood. The father replied to his thought.

" I choose, then, the party that is most likely to prevail. I expect thus to save my property. You have none to lose. By the sale of negroes I may obtain means to purchase confiscated estates. All will enure to the benefit of yourself and your mother and sister. This is preparation for one event and that almost certain. But if the South should happen to succeed you can save my property, and, by marriage, you may obtain another estate. Now do you understand ?" he asked with asperity, as if he was angry with his son for requiring him to disclose his secret plans. The latter inquired—

" May not your property or perhaps your person be in danger here, when it becomes known that you embrace the Northern cause ?"

" It need not become known *here*."

As the gentlemen ceased to converse, Mrs. Palmer deemed this a favorable opportunity for herself to talk, but she had to soliloquize. Her keen scent of the family interest made her a safe confidant of all domestic debates, and the instinct of unwavering selfishness had sometimes carried her on a bee-line to the stores of fortune when reason would have stumbled in the search. But when business had been settled, the gentlemen did not deem it necessary to hear her homily.

"It is a good thing to see brethren dwell together in unity; it is a great crime to destroy the glorious Union established by our fathers and cemented with their blood—liberty and union· now and forever one and inseparable—every man should do his duty to his country; *dulce et decorum est pro patria mori;* we should be willing to die for our native land; your native land is New England, my dear husband—'lives there a man with soul so dead who never to himself hath said, this is my own, my native land;' you did not cease to be a true New Englander by coming to Virginia to make a fortune; even a poor banished exile carries with him the sentiments which he inhaled with his native air; *patræ quis exul se. quoque fugit;* the North is the strongest; why should the dear children lose their patrimony in a quarrel between Northern fanatics and Southern fire-eaters; a man who don't provide for his family is several degrees worse than an Infidel; if poor Colonel Fairfax's estate should be confiscated you may be able to buy it with the money you get for the negroes; I abhor the traffic in human flesh; I was brought up in pious principles; if the South should succeed, Albert might marry Miss Fairfax, and save the estate all the same; it would be so kind of us to keep it in the poor colonel's family; we need not talk about these things; nobody need ever know, Albert, whether your father is North or South; he is a very wise man."

"Mother, where is sister Jane? I want some music."

Sister Jane was called, but her music only served to remind Albert of Julia Fairfax, whose image lured him along a chain of logic that ended in a conclusion favorable to the Southern cause. He resolved to adhere to it for reasons rather more reputable than those which his father had suggested. But he found it satisfactory to know that a course of conduct which was right was also, in the judgment of his wise father, prudent in all aspects.

When the music ceased, Mr. Palmer drew forth his watch and intimated that the hour for family worship had arrived. All the daughters were summoned, and Mrs. Palmer placed on a stand beside him a Bible, a hymn book and a candle; for, in every external observance, as in every prudential virtue, Mr. Israel Palmer was the model of a Christian.

CHAPTER VI.

WAR.

ON the next day sat the County Court. At an early hour the court-house green and the village street were thronged with men. Horses filled every stable and shed, and stood along both sides of the street from end to end. The county had turned out, for the county was deeply agitated.

The village had but a single street. On one side of it stood the court-house, with its adjacent offices and neighboring jail. Opposite was the Swan Tavern, an ancient inn, famous for good cheer. Scattered along either side of the street were two rival stores, the shops of the blacksmith, saddler, wagon-maker and shoemaker, the offices of two lawyers and two physicians, and the dwellings of half-a-dozen mechanics. At one end of the street stood a wooden building, of which the lower story was occupied by a wool-carding machine, propelled by horse-power, and in the upper story was a printing office, from which a weekly newspaper entitled the "Tobacco Leaf" was issued about twice a month, and in some months thrice. At the other end of the street was an old church, built in Colonial times, with a parsonage of less antiquity. The church-yard contained many monuments that were moss-grown or crumbling with age. On some of them could yet be dimly traced heraldic or literal mementoes of the pride of a former generation, and on others were inscriptions so quaint that nothing but antiquity could save them from from a suspicion of drollery. With these, of course, were decent but tasteless tombstones of modern date.

Such was the village which had once been endowed with a proper name—some name already famous, or one which the village was expected to render famous. But it was almost forgotten and never mentioned in the county. People always spoke simply of "the village," as if there had been but one in the universe. In fact, there was not another of equal importance in the county, and there were but few in Virginia. Except those whose professions or trades bound them to towns, people in that fair, bright county preferred rural residences. In the wide suburbs of this village resided, among shady groves and on small farms or large lots, the merchants, professional men and principal officers of the county.

On the court green—a shady lawn of considerable extent—the citizens of the county were accustomed to meet on all public days for the transaction of business, to hear and tell news, or to discuss the affairs of the county, the State and the Union. Never before, perhaps, had so many of them been assembled there as on this April court day, in the year eighteen hundred and sixty-one. A glance at the assemblage would have discovered that there was intense popular excitement, but it was silent and stern.

When Colonel Fairfax went upon the green that day, and even before he had left his horse, he was surrounded by different knots of men, successively grasping his hand and seeking his counsel. He was always received there as a favorite citizen, for he was very popular. But on this occasion it was not mere popularity, it was a profound respect for his wisdom, integrity and patriotism that drew the people around him, as their counsellor in a crisis of public danger. To their eager inquiries he replied, sadly but firmly, " the hour has come—we must fight." His words flew from mouth to mouth, and the whole multitude soon knew that " Colonel Fred thought we must fight." This opinion accorded so exactly with the previous conviction of every mind and the impulse of every heart that it was accepted at once as a conclusive judgment. When it became generally understood that the question of war was determined, and that the people were all of one mind, the hushed excitement was succeeded by murmurs of mutual encouragement. Most of those present were thoughtful and resolute men, who were well aware that the war which they accepted as unavoidable was for them a calamity. They felt as brave and rational men may feel when they are forced to choose between the risk of death and the loss of something held dearer than life. There were no desperate wretches to whom war might bring relief. There were no mere " food for powder." But when the feelings of the crowd began to find vent in words, some enthusiastic young men evinced the animal joy of youth at the prospect of glorious strife. Among the boys excitement, as usual, effervesced in hilarity. Their spirit of glee was caught up as a multitude catches any emotion, no one can tell how or why, and in a little while smiles were seen on the lips of men whose brows were yet stern. Their hearts were heavy but not dismayed. The spring of courage supported the weight of war.

Hugh Fitzhugh stood upon the steps of the portico

in front of the court-house. A crier of the court, standing beside him, solicited attention by shouting with stentorian voice—" Oyez, Oyez! silence is commanded, on pain of imprisonment—beg pardon—I take that back—Oyez, Oyez! Hugh Fitzhugh, Esquire, will now address the people, and God save the Commonwealth and this worshipful court—I beg pardon again—but I will say, God save old Virginia, and I'll never take it back, pardon or no pardon."

Whether the crier had a design or merely blundered into an accustomed formula of his office, his final prayer for the Commonwealth, uttered with earnest emphasis, sent a thrill through the crowd. A score of voices cried, "three cheers for old Virginia — God bless her!" and all the people responded with a tumult of cheering. When there was silence, Fitzhugh said:

" It is proposed to raise a company of volunteer cavalry for the defence of the State. I hold a paper prepared for the signatures of those who wish to volunteer. Let them now come forward. If others will pardon me for taking the start of them, I will set my name down first."

" Well done, Hugh !" exclaimed the older citizens. " Wait for me ! Wait for me !" shouted many of the younger. " Three cheers for Hugh Fitzhugh !" cried one—" three cheers for the cavalry !" added another, and " three cheers for the Old Dominion !" was a general call. All the cheers proposed were given with a will, and while the mass fanned itself into a flame with its own breath, the young men were stepping forward and enrolling their names. But it became necessary to retire from the portico, for within the temple of justice the voice of the crier was heard commanding silence in the formula with which the sessions of the court were opened. The court was held by five justices of the peace, respectable farmers, and the presiding justice was Captain Walker, a venerable man of ninety. He was remarkable for vigor of mind and body at that age. ' Few men of seventy carried their burden of years with as unbending firmness. In the earliest years of the century he was a leading citizen of the county, respected for his uprightness, his energy and his ability. Increase of years added all that should accompany old age. Having once served as a captain of volunteers, he was still called "captain." The fictitious title of colonel, often courteously or jocosely conferred on conspicuous citizens by popular brevet, could not supersede the real rank of actual service. A fiction fastened upon his name would have offended the genuine esteem felt by his neighbors for a character so ruggedly sincere.

It was apparent that no judicial business could be transacted that day. The Commonwealth's attorney, Mr. Williams, rose to address the court, and, after alluding to the commencement of war, observed that in the first instance the counties would probably have to provide for the immediate expenditures required for the public defence, for the equipment of volunteers and for the support of their families in the cases of poor men during their absence from home. At his suggestion, the court ordered all the justices of the county to be summoned to the next monthly term for the purpose of considering this subject. He then stated that the people desired to hear a discussion of public affairs, and particularly of the question submitted to them by the convention—that of secession. In order that the court-house might be occupied for this purpose, the court, on his motion, adjourned for the day.

Proclamation having been made at the door, the people gathered into the court-house—all except those who were too intent upon the formation of a company of cavalry. The question of war had been determined, or rather, as they thought, it had been forced by their enemies. The question of secession remained to be discussed and decided. The house was soon brim-full. The dense assemblage included citizens of all ages, classes and conditions. High and low, rich and poor, learned and unlettered, were packed together. The upturned faces expressed every degree of intelligence and a great variety of character; but all were earnest faces, and not a dozen men were there who would have told a lie under any temptation.

According to custom, a chairman of the meeting was appointed. The person selected for that office was Captain Walker, the presiding justice of the County Court. When he stepped forward on the justices' bench to take the chair the whole assembly rose in token of respect for him and stood until he was seated. Before taking his seat he spoke a few words.

"My countrymen: I thank you for this honor, but I accept it with sadness. I rejoiced at the birth of the Union. Now, on the verge of the grave myself, I am summoned to its death-bed. Would to God I had died first! But it is better to have liberty without union than union without liberty."

CHAPTER VII.

SECESSION.

SOME of the speeches delivered to the meeting were long and elaborate, but they have not been preserved in full. Brief notes, taken by the editor of the " Tobacco Leaf," were published in the next issue of that journal, and thus the heads of argument can now be reproduced. They will be given with their imperfect brevity, but in the connected form of speeches rather than in the manner of detached memoranda, as they appeared in the newspaper. Mr. Williams first addressed the meeting :

"You are yet a free people," he began, "you are assembled, not as conspirators concealed by darkness and bound by clandestine oaths, nor as subjects overawed by bayonets, but as free citizens deliberating in open day according to ancient usage upon the affairs of your country. Whatever may be your decision this day or at the polls, you will, in deciding, exercise a hereditary right in a lawful manner. You will perform the gravest duty that ever has devolved upon you as citizens. Decide for your country.

"You love the Union. Only a few weeks ago, at the election of members of the convention now in session, you gave a new and conclusive proof of your devotion to it by your votes. Even to-day, though your judgments may be convinced that secession is necessary, yet in advocating it I may shock the sensibility of your life-long attachment. In no State has the Union been cherished with more sincere affection than in Virginia. But you will not shrink from duty because it is painful.

"The right of a State to withdraw from the Union whenever, in her judgment, it has become oppressive and she has no other adequate remedy, is a right which our fathers have taught us to venerate as essential to the preservation of our liberties under the Federal system. You are familiar with the reasons by which it has been vindicated. I need only remind you of some of those reasons. According to an acknowledged principle of natural justice and of public law, a sovereign State has a right to dissolve her compacts with other States whenever, in her judgment, there is just cause to dissolve them. If this right were not allowed, a State would often have no just redress for the violation of a compact by another party. She is held to be justified in annulling it in morals as well as in law, when it has been wilfully violated by the other party in points essential to her security or welfare. The application of these principles to the Federal Union will not be denied by any one who admits that our States are sovereign and that the Constitution is a compact between them. But these were the propositions established in a memorable contest—the first great Constitutional controversy in the Union. Virginia had a conspicuous part in that controversy, and has preserved for the instruction of future ages the unanswerable proofs she then arrayed to establish that the States are sovereign and the Federal Constitution is a compact between them.

"When the Colonies threw off their allegiance to Great Britain, they assumed the character of States. In that character they were recognized by each other, and by all nations. In that character they framed and adopted the Federal Constitution, retaining in it the name of United States. Important provisions of that instrument recognize their continued existence as States, with the equality of sovereigns, and with a large and undefined reservation of independent powers. By the most solemn acts of Massachusetts and of other States, the sovereignty of each State in the Union has been affirmed. Our political and judicial history is full of documents supporting the same doctrine, associated with the fundamental principle that the Constitution is a compact. The right to dissolve the compact, inherent in the • States was not surrendered in the Constitution. On the contrary, it was reserved by Virginia in her ordinance to ratify the Federal compact.

"If we ascend above Constitutions and historical documents to the sources of natural and eternal justice, a natural, inalienable, indefeasible right of self-government belongs to great communities like these Southern States—civilized, organized communities, capable of fulfilling the duties of a nation. This is a right which no constitution or compact can annul, and no power can take away.

"Having the right, Virginia ought to secede. The Federal compact has often been nullified or violated by many of the Northern States, wilfully, wantonly, persistently in matters vitally affecting the Southern States. The power which the North has acquired, and its persistence in wrong, have destroyed all hope of redress in the Union. Many acts of Northern aggression are fresh in your recollection. Each one has been met with solemn protest by the South, and every protest has provoked a new outrage. I shall not now recite the long and dreary catalogue of aggressions, for the most recent events demand our exclusive attention. History will keep a record of all.

"The framers of the Federal Constitution guarded against abuse of power by the government in every way that their wisdom foresaw to be necessary; for they knew that all governments tend to tyranny. They protected the small States against the ambition of the larger. But the problem of binding two powerful and unequal nations together under one government, without permitting either to oppress the other, was not present to their minds. They did not foresee that a confederacy of the most populous States would be formed within the Union, constituting a distinct nation, animated with the usual passions of nations, and with animosity against the whole body of the States not embraced in that Confederacy. But this is what has happened. The Constitution, so far from providing security against oppression in such a case, has unintentionally facilitated the design of the Northern Confederacy to op-

4

press the South.   By a combination pursuing the forms of
the Constitution; a minority of the people of the Union have
concentrated the whole power of the North and seized the
government, electing a President upon principles so unjust
that he could not receive one Southern vote.   Those who
persuade themselves that the dominion thus usurped by the
North over the South will ever be relinquished, or that it
will be exercised with justice, forget history and ignore
human nature.   Since a Northern Confederacy has usurped
the authority of the Union for our oppression, we must
save our liberty by a Southern Confederacy beyond the
Union.

"If any doubt heretofore remained of the necessity for
this action, it must have been dispelled since the North has
claimed the right, through the Federal government, which
it controls, to reduce the South to obedience by arms, and
has drawn the sword for that purpose.   We might easily
refute that pretension by Constitutional argument, but the
sword can be answered only with the sword.   The framers
of the Constitution distinctly refused to confer on the Federal government the power to compel the submission of a
State by military force.   The last President of the United
States officially disclaimed the power.   It could not exist
without transforming our Federal system.   It cannot be
exercised without establishing a military despotism at
Washington.   But reason is silenced.   The voice of can-
non, and not the voice of the people, must decide these
controversies.

" We must defend our sister States of the South.   We
cannot be neutral.   We will not make war against them.
Honor, affection, self-preservation, compel us to take arms
in their defence.   If we are to fight we must secede.   Unless the State resumes her separate existence, and reclaims
the authority which she has granted to the Federal government, her people will incur the penalties of treason by
fighting against that government.   If she secedes, she can
unite with the other Southern States and make their joint
resistance effectual.   Her example will be followed by
States yet adhering to the Union.   The formidable array

of all the Southern States may even yet deter the North, and arrest the war. At all events, it will assure success."

The address of Mr. Williams was heard with silent attention. At the conclusion of it he proposed a resolution to declare the sense of the meeting that the ordinance of secession should be ratified by the people. Then there was a pause in the proceedings, to afford any who might wish to speak an opportunity. No one came forward until the chairman was about to take a vote. Then Doctor Fairfax rose, and with some trepidation in his voice, signified a desire to address the meeting.. The solemnity of the occasion and of the audience repressed his propensity to sarcastic levity and braced his nerves—for he was a man of nerve—to the unaccustomed task of addressing a public assembly. He spoke thus in substance :—

"I am opposed to secession. I concur in the opinion that we are now obliged to engage in war for the defence of the South. War supersedes other controversies, and, therefore, I shall not discuss the right of secession or the causes of secession. Certainly, we shall be justified in seceding, if secession is advisable as a measure of war. But it is with reference to the war that, in my judgment, secession is not advisable.

"If we remain in the Union we may reasonably hope to terminate this war with an honorable peace; for we shall fight upon no pretension that our enemies may not ultimately concede for the sake of peace. If we secede, we can never return to the Union without a surrender of the main point of contest—that is, without acknowledging ourselves conquered. The North will never concede our separate independence. The war must be fought to extremity, and, in the extreme event, the South will be subjugated. By staking all upon a desperate venture, we shall lose all. By moderating our pretensions, we may se-

cure important rights, which may be respected hereafter,
because we are ready to defend them with the sword.
If Virginia adheres to the Union the States which have seceded may, under her example and mediation, return to it,
and there may be a peace honorable to all.

"That the war, if prosecuted to extremity, will result
in our subjugation, appears to my mind painfully certain.
The fighting population of the North is as three to one of
our own at the beginning, and with every hour of war this
disparity will be widened. Emigration from Europe will
replenish the North. All the adventurers, paupers and
vagabonds of the Old World can be hired to fight against
us. Casualties and the curtailment of our territory by invasion, will diminish our numbers and no foreign supply
will restore them. We shall lose Delaware, Maryland,
Kentucky and Missouri certainly. War is in a large
measure a work of money and machines. The North has
both. We have neither. The North can soon set afloat an
unequalled navy. The South can have none. Commerce
will continue to enrich our enemies. We shall be cut off
from all the world beyond our own shores. The Federal
government has unbounded credit. Our government must
establish itself before it can enjoy the credit through which
it should be established. Our vast rivers will divide our
power and admit the forces of the enemy into the heart of
our territory. With a population thinly scattered over an
immense area, we have no adequate means of concentrating
our wealth, our men or our policy. Natural and artificial
means of concentration, the most varied and complete, will
be in possession of the enemy and despotism will concen-
trate their policy.

We must not rely upon dissensions in the North. Poli-
ticians there have encouraged us to resist, and have declared that the army which marches to conquer us must
first pass over the corpses of themselves and their partisans.
Trust them not. When war rages we shall not have a
corporal's guard of determined friends in that country. You
will see that even so bald a pretext as that the South has
fired the first gun, so shallow a trick as that which drew

the fire of Confederate batteries on Fort Sumter, will con-
solidate the Northern populace in furious support of the
war. The North is divided into two parties, truculent Re-
publicans and truckling Democrats. No party there will
act upon the obvious truth, that when liberty is attacked
with the sword it can be defended only with the sword.
After it shall be lost, through their aid or apathy, some
Northern men may solicit your assistance to rescue it from
an iron tyranny by windy speeches and ineffectual votes.
But in the real struggle you will stand alone.

"Expect no aid from Europe. Imagine not that cotton
is king, or that the necessities of commerce will bring England or France or any other power to intervene for our
benefit. Intervention must be war, or it must be futile.
The old nations, taught by experience, dread war and value
peace. English cotton manufacturers, having excessive
stocks on hand, are now in a condition to be saved from
ruin by any event that will interrupt the exportation of cotton from this country for the next three years. English
commerce will flourish by any war in which England takes
no part. English policy demands the abolition of slavery
and the consequent abridgement of the cotton culture on
this continent—ends to be accomplished by the triumph of
the North. Though a division of the Union may be desirable to her, as reducing a formidable power, yet the impover-
ishment of the South by war and the necessity of employ-
ing Northern force to keep a conquered people in subjection, may be deemed almost an equivalent. England will
stand aloof, and without her, no other power will interfere.

"I will not attempt to appal you by depicting the horrors of war. It is not to cowardice that I would appeal,
but to wisdom. Indeed I would invoke you to welcome
all the evils of the most terrible war, if through them you
can be assured of independence of the North. But we
should understand, in advance, that this war will probably
be waged against us in the most atrocious spirit. The
Federal government, treating us as rebels, will deny to us
the rights of war and the rights of humanity. Their hos-

tilities will be havoc.   It will scarcely be surprising if they
are lawless and barbarous enough to arm our slaves against
us.   It is a mistake to suppose that secession will prevent
them from inflicting the penalty of treason on our soldiers.
They will not respect the ordinance, and, if they refrain
from that outrage, it will be through fear of our power—
a motive that will operate equally with or without seces- •
sion.

"A war of prodigious extent, waged by a superior
power in a savage spirit, will finally exhaust the endurance
of the South.   We shall, doubtless, make one brilliant campaign, through the superior courage of our people.   But
they cannot sustain, for more than two years at the utmost,
the constant pressure of such tremendous odds.   Virginia,
I trust, will endure, if necessary, until she shall be made a
wilderness.   Doubtless in this great struggle she will be
true to her ancient character.   But do not expect other
Southern States to emulate her conduct.   They will do
great deeds and suffer horrible afflictions before they will
surrender a good cause, but some of them will yield before
independence can be secured and long before Virginia will
be subdued.   Her sufferings and her heroism will be in
vain.

" Whose imagination can fathom the depth of our degradation when we shall have been subjugated by the North ?
The war upon us will never end.   A people who hate us
now and who then will have been rendered furious by resistance and arrogant by victory, will have irresistible power
to glut their hatred and revenge.   They will hold the South
by a military tenure.   They will be our masters.   They
will be conquerers and we the conquered.   *Væ victis!*
We shall be ruled by satraps, great and small.   Our government will be dissolved, our laws annulled, our courts
suppressed.   Garrisons, perhaps composed of our own
slaves, will occupy our towns to overawe a people who will
never again be trusted.   It will not be sufficient for them
to submit peacefully to the authority of the conquerers ; to
avoid suspicion and still sharper oppression, they must
fawn upon their tyrants and profess to be in love with their

chains. They must hasten to sacrifice their institutions, their civil rights, their manhood, in order to appease the jealousy of foreign rulers. Their country will be for them both a prison and a charnel house, and among the ashes of their sons and brothers slain in the war, they will brood over the hopeless bondage which the war has brought on themselves. The soldiers who conquer us will be pensioned; those who defend us beggared. Not a voice in all the North will then be raised to demand the restoration of our people to their ancient rights. The most favorable treatment proposed for them then by any Northern man of influence will be so cruel that, if whispered now, it would curdle your blood with horror. Those who will think that our rebellious people deserve hell will deem it mercy to consign them to purgatory. But I desist; I believe that no fancy can approach the actual wretchedness of a proud, brave, intelligent people, subjugated by such a power as the North."

When Doctor Fairfax sat down, Mr. Williams rose again and remarked that if no other person desired to speak he would make a brief reply to the last speech. As no one else rose, he proceeded:

"The right of secession has not been denied. That there are sufficient causes for it has not been denied. That it would render our resistance to the North more effective by uniting the South has not been denied. That independence of the North is the prize most worthy of our exertions when we are compelled to fight is admitted. But we are to be deterred from availing ourselves of these advantages of secession. How? You are told that we shall certainly be conquered. If this be true, yet subjugation will scarcely be a fate more dreadful than the perpetual despotism to which we shall basely submit by remaining in the Union. At least, a gallant struggle for indepedence will save our honor—the most precious heritage of a people. But it is not certain that the united South will be conquered by the North. It is possible, but it is not even probable. We shall stand on the defensive. We have only to endure, and time will exhaust the enemy. If our vast territory renders concentrated resistance difficult, it renders subjugation impossible. The native courage of our people and the spirit which the cause of liberty inspires will overcome an immense superiority of mere numbers. Our fertile country and our laboring population will feed and clothe our army, so that neither money nor foreign commerce will be so necessary to us as to the enemy. Machines and navies are less needful to us than to our invaders. Our white population can spare a larger proportion of fighting men than that of the North, because our blacks will remain to labor. If so many millions of freemen, fighting to preserve their liberty and resolved to sacrifice everything for independence, shall be subjugated, the lessons of history are false. Let us not throw away the rich prize of success through timid apprehension of failure. This enterprise is dangerous. It must put the endurance of all Southern people to severe trial. Let them be sustained by the hope of independence. Since we must fight, we must incur the hazard of subjugation. It is vain to expect peace until we show ourselves able to resist the North. For the sake of peace we have vainly forborne, yielded, solicited, until we are almost disgraced. Since we must fight, let us fight for independence."

After ascertaining that no other person desired to speak, the chairman submitted the resolution to a vote of the meeting. All the people responded "aye," except five or six who answered "no." Very soon after the result was announced the citizens began to move out of the door, but the movement was arrested by the voice of a boy who sat on a table within the bar, and who began to call out—"Marlin! Marlin! a speech from Abram Marlin!" Such a call always finds an echo in a crowd. Several voices took it up and cried—"Marlin! Marlin! Marlin!" The eyes of the youth who led this chorus were fixed upon a man who stood on the steps leading up to the judi-

cial bench with a leg and au arm over the banister.
He was dressed in coarse but clean homespun. He
seemed about forty-five years of age. His person
was rather tall and lank. His features were rough,
and his hair hung down, long, straight and thin
around his neck. Under shaggy brows his grey eyes
had a restless, vigilant motion, as if the brain was
active and excitable. When the repetition of his
name became emphatic, though still apparently made
in jest, he withdrew his limbs from the banister and
walked up the steps. Standing on the judicial plat-
form, he turned his face to the audience with unmoved self-possession. He then began :—

" I ain't a gwine to make a speech, my feller-sinners.
I couldn't say much about that ere doctrine of secession.
It ain't one of the doctrines that I'm used to preach about.
I stick to the doctrines in the good book, and them doctrines I always try to make so cl'ar that the women and
niggers can understand 'em. But I've been a ponderin'
over this ere war in the silent watches of the night when
my Betsy was fast asleep. I've looked up the prophets on
this subjec'. It rether looks to me like we're a gwine to
fight the great battle agin Gog and Magog. Leastways
that battle has never been fou't yit, and so it stands to reason that it's got to be fou't sometime. Now, in the thirty-
eighth chapter of Ezekiel, it is said unto Gog—'thou shalt
come from thy place out of the North parts, thou and many
people with thee, all of them riding upon horses, a great
company and a mighty army.' So it stands to reason ef a
man always keeps a fightin' agin the armies that come out
of the North parts, he'll be fightin' on the right side when
that big he-fight of all comes off. So I've been a ponderin'
that I'd take a chance in this ere war agin the North.
Anyways it will be a fight for Virginny, and that's a good-
enough fight for me. Next to my God, I'd go my death
for old Virginny. I'm rether dubous that I'm too old and
rheumatized to march in the infantry, but ef I had a hoss
4*

I'd jine the calvary. I ain't got only one hoss, and. that's
a mule. Ef any gentleman would swap a hoss for that
mule"——

"You shall have a horse," said a voice from the
crowd.

"Then count me in. Doctor Fairfax says the Yankees
will whip us. Well, the doctor ain't a prophet, nor the
son of a prophet. Leastways I ain't seed his name thar
among the prophets. But one thing I kin tell you, and I
have Scriptur' for it, the Yankees, even if they have Gog
and Magog to back 'em, can't prevail agin the Lord of
Hosts. Let us have Him on our side and we're safe, my
brethren, in peace or war, in this world and the world to
come. Ef we want him on our side now, we must go to
war with pure hearts and in humble reliance on Him. We
must ask His blessing. Let us pray."

He knelt down, and stretched out his hands. His
sudden and unexpected movement, and call to prayer,
took the people by surprise. Almost involuntarily
they rose up and stood in reverential attitude, while
Marlin poured fourth a brief invocation, so fervent
that his grotesque language could not prevent it from
touching the hearts of men, and when he ceased a
solemn "Amen" was murmured in all parts of the
house.

When the meeting was over it was found that a
sufficient number of volunteers had enrolled themselves to constitute a company of cavalry, according
to the laws of the State, and a time was appointed for
the election of officers. As it was near sunset, the
people began to mount their horses and start homeward. When Hugh Fitzhugh was about to pass out
of the green for the same purpose, a number of young
men surrounded him, and shouting his name, demanded a speech. The clamor drew others about
him, and men who had mounted their horses stopped

or turned back in the street. When he reached the top of a stile he saw a large audience standing in expectation, and he found it necessary to say a few words. He thus addressed the people:—

"VIRGINIANS:—By that title you are bound to noble thoughts and heroic deeds. The time demands them now. Discussion is ended. War is begun. The North has pressed the South to the wall. We must defend our liberty, arms in hand, or be forever dishonored and enslaved. If there is a man among you who would surrender liberty or honor in exchange for life, no blood of Virginia runs in his veins. The war may be terrific. The enemy is powerful and malignant. The soil of Virginia may be crimson with the blood of her sons and her foes. But her sons will bleed for the honor of their mother. Invaders may give your dwellings to the flames; but your children will inherit freedom. When the war shall be most dreadful, remember the alternative—bondage. Look to the end—independence. Honor and shame—liberty and slavery—choose between them. As you shall choose, wear your fetters or your swords. Pardon me, Virginians—I know your choice is made. You are resolved to live and die freemen!"

CHAPTER VIII.

DRINK.

WHEN the sun had set and all the citizens had left
the village, except a few who had qualified the spirit
of patriotism with the spirit of rye, three or four of
the latter class sat in the porch of the Swan Tavern,
upon a wooden bench against the wall. Before them
sat a young man on a large, split-bottomed arm-chair,
leaning back against the banister, with his feet elevated. He was genteelly dressed, though his soft hat
was crushed and drawn down over a corner of one
eye. He was small and slender. His hair and mustache were black. His heavy eye-lids hung aslant
over the pupils, half closing them, and there was a sen-
sual, fleshy fullness about his lower jaw. His name
was Baxter. He was the son of a gentleman of high
character, who was the clerk of the County Court,
and had held the office more than thirty years. The
son had been carefully educated, and had in youth
shown quick parts and that forward pertness which
partial parents sometimes mistake for precocious genius.
When he grew up to manhood he led an idle, reckless,
dissolute life, studying the chemistry of juleps in bar-
rooms, the mystery of horse-flesh at races, or natural
history at faro-banks, called in slang " tigers." He
had dauntless courage and a sort of wit that made him
a favorite in low company. He was looking out from
under his heavy eye-lids at the faces before him with
an expression that might have been serious if he had

been sober, but as he was not, it was comical. At length he said, abruptly—

"Bill Ankrom, I have been wondering why a fellow like you volunteered to fight in this war. You would oblige me by telling me if you know, yourself."

"To keep the Yankees from abolishing slavery, of course."

"How many niggers do you own?"

"None by ——. You know that as well as I do. But if they set the niggers free, who'll be below me?"

"Nobody can be lower, I believe. You think, as matters now stand, a white skin is a patent of nobility granted by God and sanctioned by law?"

"Something that a way, I reckon. Do you think I want my son to black your boots or my darter to cook in your father's kitchen?"

"Your theory is that society must rest on mudsills, and if the black ones are torn away white ones must be stuck under. You are a philosopher, Bill; did you know that? It would be a pity that a Yankee bullet should crack your craniology. But stick to your patent of nobility—you have no chance to get another. And you, Bob Faris, are you going to fight for the same reason?"

"Well, I ain't jined yit, but I reckon I'll go in for the principles of free government."

"Bully for you, Bob. You call a Democratic government free, don't you?"

"Yes, I was born a Dimmicrat."

"Wouldn't you think me a fool if I went out to fight for the privilege of having a batch of drunken nincompoops like you fellows on that bench to govern me? That's your principle of free government. It has brought us into a pretty muss in the United States.

We have tried to run a machine that can't go right unless you make thirty millions of people understand the art of government. It requires all those Yankees away up in Maine to understand the interests of all those Creoles away down in Louisiana. You see the end of it, and now you want to fight for a free government of the same sort. You must be very drunk to-day, Bob. Now, Sim. Franks, you ought to be a soldier. Your skull is a life-insurance."

"You take care of your own skull. Why don't you volunteer?"

"Oh, I intend to be a commissary. I want to be in the eating and drinking department. I'll make one big continental spree out of this war."

"I never thought you was a coward afore."

"Because I am not a coward, must I fight merely for fun?"

"I've seed you do it."

"Well, here is fun," said Baxter, turning to look into the street. Two men there sat on horseback, facing one another. They had the appearance and dress of middling farmers. One had a red head and the hair of the other was whity-brown. They had evidently tasted the cup which does inebriate. Halting at the same moment, they eyed each other with drunken defiance, and then engaged in a polite and obliging conversation, which attracted the attention of Baxter.

"Sir," said the man of fiery top-knot, "you must excuse me, sir, but I have been credibly informed, sir, that you said, sir, you would whip me, sir, the first time you laid eyes on me, sir."

"Yes, sir; your information is correct, I am happy to inform you, sir."

"If you are not blind, sir, you can lay eyes on me now, sir."

"If you will do me the favor to get off your horse, sir, I will now do what I promised, sir."

"With great pleasure, sir."

They dismounted, and giving their bridles to a servant from the tavern, took off their coats and squared themselves for a duel of fists. They approached each other with a parade of fairness and civility, though with unsteady gait.

"Now strike me, sir, if you please," said Whitybrown.

"No, sir, you are under promise to whip me, sir. Strike first, sir."

The man of threats accepted the invitation, and after a flourish of fists, discharged a blow with all his might. But he missed his antagonist and fell upon the ground.

"Get up, sir, if you please," said he of the red hair, and he waited until his request was obeyed and the other belligerent was ready for a second round. Then, with more fortunate aim than the latter, he sent the whity-brown head to the ground again. After looking at him in the dust a moment, the other walked off toward a grass plot beside the road, and said—"Come here, sir; that street is dirty, sir." The fallen belligerent arose and followed him. Then the fight continued for some time with various fortunes, but as both combatants were easily upset and neither would strike a dangerous blow, very little damage was done. At last, when both were weary, and the challenger or threatener was down, his adversary stood over him and said—

"Now cry enough, sir; I'm sure you've got enough."

"Never."

"Then, sir, you are drunk or a fool, sir. I scorn to fight a man, sir, that's too drunk to know when he's whipped, sir."

Having thus spoken, he walked away toward his
horse, while the prostrate combatant called after him—

"Maybe I'm too drunk now, but I'll keep sober at
next court. I'll thank you to meet me then|."

Baxter and the other persons on the porch, who had
been amused spectators of the bloodless battle, now
descended into the street, congratulated the gentlemen
on the honorable termination of their difficulty and insisted that they should shake hands and 'be friends.
Baxter, suggesting a peace-maker perhaps on the principle of an adage touching a "hair of the dog," urged
them to come into the tavern and take a drink with
him and his companions. Protesting against the
peace, they assented to the drink. Once in the bar-
room, the participants and spectators of the recent
conflict discussed that affair in such fashion that
another fight became imminent. Consequently another cup of conciliation became necessary. So they
wrangled and drank or drank and wrangled, while
Baxter urged peace or war or whiskey, according to
his fluctuating humor, until darkness had long settled down upon the village.

"Here comes Blind Pete," exclaimed Baxter, as a
pale, thin man, led by a little boy, entered the bar-
room; "come in, Pete; we'll make you see stars
without your eyes. Take a drink."

The new-comer, nothing loth, condescended to
perform that ceremony of initiation, and while he
was imbibing the liquor, Baxter said:

"Who's your bail now, Pete?"

"Oh, sir, I always gives the best bail in the county."

"Yes, you go to jail like a rogue and are ransomed
like a gentleman, thanks to your blindness. Your
blindness is catching, or the gentlemen could not

wink so·at your rascalities. But who's your bail
now, Pete ?"

" Colonel Fred."

" Why, it was for stealing his bacon they put you
in. jail."

" That's the reason he was bound to attend to the
case. You see it was his own case, like."

" You are a lucky thief, Pete. If you had your
eyesight you would be in the penitentiary. But now
when you steal, all the gentlemen feel bound to let
you off, though you own land and steal for the love
of larceny. Whose corn is to load your cart to-night,
Pete ?"

" You always will have your joke, Mr. Baxter."

" I believe I will to-night. Where's your cart?"

" At the upper end of the village."

" And the blind mule with it? Ready, I suppose,
for·your nightly tramp to collect provisions and forage
that the negroes steal and sell to you for whiskey."

" Night, you know, Mr. Baxter, is the same as day
to a poor blind man."

· " Well, I am going to take a ride with you to-
night. Come along, boys. We'll escort you two
fighting horsemen on your way home. It is time
for you to go. We'll celebrate the restoration of
amicable relations between you by a nocturnal procession, with that red head for a torch-light. Pete's
a dark lantern and shines only in corn-cribs and
meat-houses. Come on."

After one more drink they all sallied out into the
dark. When the horsemen had been helped into
their saddles, they all followed Pete to.his cart. The
little boy, who was Pete's son, being young and puny,
was carried along by his father, because his tender

years and feeble health secured to him impunity like
that which Pete himself derived from blindness.
Baxter mounted the mule and ordered the rest of his
procession; except the two horsemen, to get into the
crazy vehicle. "Hillo, Pete," he cried, "the spine
of this mule will split my spine North and South, as
those other mules are splitting the Union. Why
don't you feed him better when corn costs you
nothing but the stealing? He has more ears on his
head than you ever put into his trough." However,
he adjusted his posture as well as he could to the
spinal ridge of the mule and began to belabor that
patient animal with a heavy stick which he had
picked up. "Go to the front, Torch-light," he cried,
"the procession on wheels will follow." It did follow, but at a slow pace, for the mule did not resent
the heavy thwacks he received. Baxter, hoping to
accelerate his gait, ordered his passengers to whoop
and yell in his rear. But the mule never wagged an
ear. With such freaks as drunken folly prompted,
they diversified the enjoyment of their snail-like journey, until at last they began to descend a hill. The
force of gravity was too strong for the knees of the
stubborn animal, and he started off at a trot, to keep
out of the way of the cart. Faster and faster he went,
while Baxter whipped and the cart jolted and bounced.
"Look out, boys," shouted Baxter, "I'm going to
make sausage-meat of you." This benevolent warning
was scarcely uttered when mule, cart and passengers
were tumbled over in a promiscuous wreck at the foot
of the hill. "Halt in front! Bring us the torch-
light," cried Baxter. Upon a careful analysis of the
mass of animate and inanimate matter, it was discovered that no person was hurt beyond some slight

bruises. A mule is more invulnerable than Achilles. The repairs of the cart detained the party some thirty minutes. "I am glad it is no worse," said Baxter; "I thought I was sending you all to Baxter's Saints' Rest."

The procession moved on until the mule stopped near a barn and refused to go farther.

"Whose barn is this, Pete?" asked Baxter.

"I can't see, Mr. Baxter."

"Neither can your mule see; but he knows the barn. Can't you tell whose corn you stole on this road? I'm sure the mule got a bite here."

"Really, Mr. Baxter, I've been at so many places with my cart "——

"Never mind; I know this place myself now; it's old Palmer's. I see we must stop with him. Come, boys; let's rouse him up. He is an old Yankee. We'll make him drink to Jeff. Davis in some of his own liquor."

"Agreed!" was the general response.

Leaving the boy with the cart in the road, the men walked to the house, and at their noisy summons a servant, half-asleep, came to the door, and admitting them, ushered them into the parlor, where they found Mr. Palmer and his wife. Their daughters had retired, but they were waiting for the return of Albert, who had gone to a distant part of the county. When they beheld Baxter and his retinue entering the parlor they were astounded. They stood in expectation of an explanation, which Baxter was rather slow to give, for the unexpected presence of a lady somewhat abashed him. In a little while he rallied, and advancing with an air that was meant to be both stately and courteous, he offered the customary salutation to the involuntary host and hostess. He added: "Mr.

Palmer, I was riding this way, and I could not think of passing your house without dropping in on you, indeed I couldn't. Knowing your hospitable disposition, I invited my friends to come in with me. Let me have the honor to introduce them." He proceeded to call the roll, and appended to each name a brief exposition, as thus: "Bob is a champion of free government; all he owns in the world is a principle, and he values it accordingly; he'd die for it. This man with a bonfire on his head—this woodpecker has been pecking that head there that looks like dead wood, but now, you see, we are all birds of a feather and flock together. This is a nobleman, and he carries his patent in his face, for it was once white, but the parchment is now brown, which shows the antiquity of his title; he is descended from one of those old sea-rovers who made a wharf on Ararat when the water was up, but it is not certain which of them, after Noah, was his ancestor. This is Peter the Hermit; he lives a retired life in day-time; he roams abroad at night, because he stands on equal rights, and he is equal to any of us in the dark; he has a way of equalizing property too, by the stars"—and so on.

Mr. Palmer bowed stiffly to the visitors and requested them to be seated, he and his wife setting the example. Baxter reclined at ease in a large arm-chair. His followers remained standing. Presently he said: "Mr. Palmer, I was telling these gentlemen you were as hospitable as a lord." Either this hint or the appearance of the guests, suggested to Mr. Palmer that they had come in to be treated and that the shortest way to get rid of them would be to treat them at once. He said: "Gentlemen, perhaps you will do me the honor of taking something to drink with me."

"Perhaps we would," said Baxter, "I think about ten drops of that fine old brandy would be good against the night air."

When the host rose to have the liquor and glasses brought in, the hostess went gliding out of the room. Fluttered, if not alarmed, she had once or twice risen to retire but resumed her seat. Her movements were still rectilinear but rather spasmodic. When she went out the small remainder of Baxter's diffidence also departed. When the liquor came and began to flow, his insolence flowed with full tide, "I like your brandy, Palmer," he said, slapping that gentleman on the shoulder, " fill again." He enforced the precept by his practice, and his companions, without much urging, followed his example. Mr. Palmer would willingly have refrained, but he still hoped that every glass would be the last, and thinking it necessary to keep the riotous crew in good humor by politeness, he did not refuse to drink with them. "Take more, old fellow, fill up; I assure you the liquor is good," said Baxter again and again. "Now, I'll give you a toast. A bumper, Palmer. A bumper, everybody, tag-rag and all. Here's the health of Jeff. Davis and success to the Confederate States of America. You'll drink that, old fellow."

" Certainly, Mr. Baxter, with pleasure," replied Mr. Palmer, and he drank with the rest. Throwing an arm affectionately round his neck, Baxter said : " I am glad, Israel, to find you are one of us. You must volunteer, indeed you must. To your tents, O Israel. You are no Yankee—d——n the Yankees."

" Of course, Mr. Baxter, I go with my State."

"How's that? Which State? None of your Yankee tricks. You must have another drink. Fill up. I have another toast to propose."

When the glasses were full ho proposed—" d ——n
the Yankees." Mr. Palmer set down his glass and
said, " you must excuse me, Mr. Baxter."

" What! turning Yankee on us?"

" No, but," he added demurely, "I never curse." ·

" Are you there, Israel? I beg pardon. No gentleman is obliged to curse; no gentleman ought to
curse, though profanity is not as bad as hypocrisy—
don't you think so, my jolly host? Well, I take back
the bad word and give you—down with the Yankees."

"I join you now with pleasure, gentlemen," said
Mr. Palmer.

" But it is time for gentlemen to retire," said Bax-
ter. "We have had a good time with you, Mr.
Palmer. Let us conclude with three cheers for Jeff.
Davis."

The cheers were given, and Mr. Palmer joined in
them. The irregular tumult of shouts roused the
ladies from their beds, and thus Mr. Palmer became
guilty of disturbing his family at midnight with riot
and rebellion. The visitors then shook hands with
him and with each other, having a confused notion
that they were about to separate. Even Mr. Palmer's
thoughts began to thicken and his lips to grow purple·
He followed the unmarshalled array to the door, and
finding Blind Pete in the rear, plucked his sleeve and
whispered, " come here to-morrow." He had some
previous knowledge of that darkling rogue, by repute
at least, and it suddenly occurred to him that his
peculiar qualifications might be rendered useful to
himself in times of confusion. ·

When Albert Palmer returned home that night,
discovering his father's condition and hearing of Bax-

ter's insolent conduct, he was mortified and enraged. Long afterwards he showed his resentful recollection of the insult.

Baxter, declining to escort the two mounted men further, turned the cart back toward the village. He took a seat in it with the others, and gave the line by which the mule was driven to the boy. Almost overcome with liquor and fatigue, he nodded as they jogged slowly along. But at the end of an hour he roused himself up and said—"boys we are consorting with a thief, and my mind misgives me that he has stolen something this very night while he has been in our company. Our character is at stake. Pete must be searched." That landed proprietor protested his innocence, but it was decided that a search should be made. His pockets were overhauled and very soon one of the party exclaimed, "here it is—silver sugar-tongs." The article was drawn forth and recognized as one which had been used to transfer some lumps of Mr. Palmer's sugar from a silver bowl to the glasses which he drank. "I knew it," said Baxter; "now, gentlemen, you shall sit as a jury in this case, and I'll be the court. To save time, I anticipate your verdict and pronounce sentence. Pete must be hung forthwith. If he goes to jail some gentleman of the county will become bail for him and that will be the last of the affair. Justice must not be balked any longer. No bail here—he is taken in the manner—hang him up with his own line."

Pete was dragged from the cart; the line was tied about his neck, and Baxter started to look for a tree. The criminal knelt, prayed, whined, wept, but his executioners seemed inexorable. The little boy cried pitiably. The tree was found and the line passed over a limb. By that time Pete lay on the ground, incapable of speech or motion. "Now," said Baxter, "you incorrigible scoundrel, you see the end of all your crimes. Nothing can save your life but the mercy of this honorable court. You have stolen corn by the cart-load. You have carried away pigs, and choked the innocent creatures lest their piteous cries should reveal your theft. You have robbed hen-roosts, treacherously tickling the toes of your victims to prevent them from cackling. You have debauched the niggers, wasting whiskey on their degraded revels. Worst of all, you have pilfered the sugar-tongs of a pious Puritan and compromised the characters of all these gentlemen who had condescended to ride in your rascally cart. What have you to say why the sentence of death shall not be forthwith executed?"

"Spare me, good gentlemen, and I'll never "———

"Make no promises, Pete. Nature will break them. You are a born rogue. But, with the consent of the jury, I will postpone this execution until to-morrow night, at twelve o'clock."

Pete sat up.

"More: we will let you go free of punishment altogether."

Pete rose to his feet.

"But upon this condition. You shall go to Mr. Palmer to-morrow, deliver the sugar-tongs to him, and tell him that you stole them, and that we compelled you to return them."

"I will, gentlemen, I will."

"I don't rely on your promise. But if you fail, you shall be hung to-morrow night. If you do as I command you, it will rest with Mr. Palmer to prosecute you, if he pleases."

CHAPTER IX.

POOR WHITES NEAR ROEBUCK.

WHEN Abraham Marlin returned home at evening from the village upon his mule, he found his wife, Betsy, preparing the homely supper, his son Mark closing up the cooper's shop, and his daughter, Eliza, a buxom, red-cheeked girl of fifteen, milking the cow. Betsy, the wife and mother, was a woman of large, lean frame, with a square head and features strongly marked. Plain truth and decisive energy were traced in every line of her countenance. Her dress was coarse, though neat, and her large hands were hardened by domestic industry. For forty years she had known poverty without repining for a single hour. She accepted her lot in life with cheerfulness, and encountered its difficulties with resolution. Her chief care, as it was her husband's also, was to train up her children in habits of industry and virtue. The parents were both illiterate, but the essential principles of a good life are learned without research, and taught without books.

Abraham was received in his humble cabin with as much respect and affection as if he had been the most illustrious of men. After supper he related to his family the events of the day at the village, but without mentioning the part he had performed, except the single fact that he had promised to volunteer as a private in the company of cavalry. When he stated

5

that circumstance, he looked at his wife as if he felt much anxiety to ascertain the impression it made on her mind. He was accustomed to consult her about every important step in life, but here was one, of the last importance to them all, which he had taken without knowing her opinion.

"You've done right, Abraham," she pronounced decisively.

"Well, Betsy, I thought you'd say so, from our talk last night, but I couldn't be easy in my mind till I'd tell you all about it, and hear how it would look to you then."

"You've done right, Abraham. It's very hard on us, but you ought to fight for Virginny."

"But, Betsy," he said with some hesitation, "I've got to furnish a hoss, and I've agreed to swap the mule for one."

"We can't well spare the mule. But," she added after some reflection, "the ground is nearly all plowed. We must git along with the hoe and the spade. It will be more work, but we'll do it."

"I reckon you could borrow a mule sometimes for half a day."

"We'll work, Abraham, while you fight."

During this conversation Mark was at first silent and attentive; then he became excited and even agitated. He sat on a rough stool near the chimney. Becoming restless, he rose and walked to the door; then he went back and sat down. His eyes fixed with eager interest now upon his father's face, and now upon his mother's, attracted her notice.

"Well, Mark," she asked, "what are you thinking about?"

"Can't I volunteer too?" he exclaimed with flashing eyes.

" God bless the boy!" said the mother, "if he was
a year or two older, we might have two soldiers to
fight for our country."

"Older! Why not now? I'm big enough, mother;
I'm strong; I'm healthy; I'm active. Why not
now?"

This was the first intimation the parents had received of Mark's vehement desire to become a soldier.
The certainty of war was too recent to have caused
much discussion in that secluded cabin, and he had
not disclosed to his parents his notion of fighting his
way up to the rank of a gentleman whenever a
patriotic war should occur. They looked at each
other in doubt, and sat revolving the question in their
minds. At length Abraham said—

"Mark, it won't do for you and me both to leave
your mother and sister."

"If our country needs you both," said Betsy, "I'll
take care of Eliza, and our Heavenly Father will take
care of us all."

"I wish I was a man," exclaimed Eliza, "I'd be a
soldier."

"But, Mark, we ain't got but one hoss," said the
father.

"Let's see, Abraham; don't the government give
hosses to the cavalry?"

"No; I larn the way is for every man to fetch his
own hoss, and the government to pay so much a day
for the use of him."

"Well," said Mark, after ruminating for a long
time on this obstacle, "I don't know how to get another horse. But, father, if only one of us can go,
don't you think you had better stay at home and let
me go? You will be of more use at home, and I can
stand a soldier's life better than you."

"You forgit, Mark, that I've promised to go. My word is out."

"I had forgot that. I reckon I'll have to give it up. Well, mother, I'll take care of you and Eliza. I'll be of some use if I help you to spare father for the war. But if I only had a horse!"   —

The next morning Mark and his father were in the little yard before the cabin, discussing a proposition which the son had brought forward, to the effect that he would volunteer for infantry service. The cavalry was so much more agreeable to the taste and views of the young man that at first he thought of nothing else, and in the agitation of the previous evening it had not occurred to him that he could be a soldier without a horse. But it came into his mind at night, while he lay in bed, wakefully turning the problem that had baffled him inside out in search of a solution. In the morning, although extremely reluctant to abandon the hope of serving in cavalry, he announced his new plan. While it was under discussion, Colonel Fairfax and his daughter Julia rode up before the cabin, followed by a servant, who led a saddled horse. They saluted the elder and younger Marlin with cordial kindness, and when Mrs. Marlin, hearing their voices, came out, they had many pleasant words for her. After a few minutes had been given to the chat of compliments, Colonel Fairfax said to Abraham:

"I heard of your remarks in the court-house yesterday, and of your offer to volunteer if you could get a horse. I am too old to be a soldier myself, and I wish you to ride the horse I have brought, as my substitute. We have long been friends, and I hope you will not refuse to use my horse. Lead him up here, John."

"Thank you, colonel ; you're mighty kind ; but I've made a bargain for a hoss."

"I heard of that too. It was when you offered in the court-house to swap your mule for a horse, and some one said you should have a horse. But your family cannot do without the mule."

"My word's out, colonel."

"Who was the person who promised you the horse?"

"I don't know. I didn't see him. I jist hearn his voice."

"Perhaps he will not come forward with the horse."

"Well now, colonel, do you think there's sich a person in the county? Is there any sich a gentleman as wouldn't make his word good?"

"We cannot tell. You had better make sure of a horse. You will do me a great favor by accepting mine."

"I must let the man have the mule, colonel, ef he comes up to his bargain, and then I'll have a hoss; much obliged to you, though, colonel, all the same. Ef he don't come I'll swap with you, that is; ef we kin agree."

"Really, Abraham, I feel much disappointed. I wish to do something for the war and for you."

While this conversation was going on, Mark eyed the horse that was in want of a rider, while he was in want of a horse, and his head was busy with the question how these two wants might be supplied honestly by one operation, beneficial to the cavalry service. Julia had no suspicion of his desire to obtain the horse for his own use, but she was always ready to say a kind word to every one.

"Mark," said she, with her sweet smile, "you will soon be old enough to fight for our country too, and I am sure you will be a gallant soldier."

" I am old enough now, Miss Julia." '

" Are you eighteen ? I am told that is the proper age."

" I'm only seventeen, ma'am, but I can fight in a good cause."

" You are a brave fellow, Mark. Do you hear him, papa ?"

" I do; but we must not let these brave boys go into the army too soon. The country may need them next year or the year after, and we must not grind the seed corn."

" I believe I can stand the service, colonel," said Mark.

" Do you really wish to go as a soldier?" asked the colonel.

" My mind is made up to go, sir, if my parents consent."

" But the authorities would not let a youth of seventeen be mustered in."

" Do you think so?" asked Mark, with surprise.

" I do indeed."

" Then," replied Mark, after thinking a moment, " I'll go and fight on my own hook. Some of the boys will let me mess with them, and I can always get a gun when there is to be a battle."

" Are you so resolved?"

" I am resolved to be a soldier in this war."

" Have you a horse ?"

" No, sir; for that reason I am going into the infantry."

" Would you prefer cavalry service?" ·

" Indeed I would, colonel; I would like it above all things."

" Then you shall have this horse, since your father refuses to take him."

"But I am not able to pay for him."

"I do not expect to be paid for him. You shall accept him as a gift."

"Thank you, colonel, but I cannot take him so."

"Why not, Mark?"

"We don't accept gifts of such value when we can make no return. It is a rule I've learned from my parents."

"Why, Mark," said Julia, "you are as independent as a—as"——

"As a gentleman, you would say, maybe, Miss Julia?"

"But consider, papa wants to give the horse to the public service, not to you alone. All his property belongs to our country at her need. You may surely help him to use it for our common defence."

"In any way consistent with my own honor—I mean no offence, Miss Julia—I would be glad to do so."

"Mark, you are an obstinate young fellow, and I have a mind to quarrel with you."

"Not for being honest, Miss Julia; not for being independent. What are we to fight for but independence?"

"Then let me sell you the horse," said Colonel Fairfax, "you may pay me for him when it suits you."

"But I may never be able. Would it be right, colonel, to take credit without a prospect of being able to pay? I may be killed or die in the service."

"Then the horse will remain," said the colonel, half provoked and half amused by these objections.

"Perhaps not," replied Mark, "and then you would get nothing, or my father would distress himself and pinch the family to pay you. There is no need of taking these risks, colonel, for I can serve in the infantry."

But Mark could not repress a sigh, and Julia saw glances exchanged between him and his mother that expressed the chagrin of the boy and the sympathy of the woman.

"Come here, if you please, Mrs. Marlin," she said, "I think you and I can arrange this matter. Men are so wrong-headed, you know. Mama owes you something for weaving?"

"Not much, Miss Julia."

"But we shall want more weaving done."

"I have a piece of my own in the loom that I would sell, Miss Julia."

"Then consider it sold. Now, there's your account against us for weaving, and there's the price of the piece in the loom, and there will be the weaving we want. Mark, the horse is as good as paid for already. Papa consents, your mother consents—don't shake your obstinate head. Your mother shall not be distressed about the little balance that will be due for the horse. You can send her your pay as a soldier, and it will amount to the price of a horse before you have a tempting chance to shoot or be shot at. Come, the whole business is settled between you and me, is it not, Mrs. Marlin?"

"Mother," said Mark, "do you think this would be right?"

"Yes, my son; I think we may do as Miss Julia says."

"Then I accept the horse with many thanks to you, colonel, and to Miss Julia."

"Oh yes, Mark, the women are worth more than

the men to carry on a righteous war. We have heads, Mrs. Marlin," she added, laughing and shaking her own pretty head.

"And hearts, too," said the colonel, smiling; "but now I must use what influence I can to have Mark accepted as a soldier."

When this sale had been negotiated with so much jockeying and feminine art, and the price—made small by more cunning mediation on the part of Julia—had been agreed on, Colonel Fairfax and his daughter took leave of the preaching cooper and his family. They spent a great part of the day in riding about among their poor neighbors, and distributing some of that property which the colonel held as a trust, and of that happiness which natures rich in cheerful goodness diffuse like the fragrance of flowers. In the course of their ride they called on Mrs. Fitzhugh, the mother of Hugh, at Willowbank, her place of residence. It was about two miles from Marlin's cabin, and if the reader consents to make that little journey with them, we too will go to Willowbank.

CHAPTER X.

WILLOWBANK.

The visitor, in approaching the old mansion of Willowbank from the highway, caught a glimpse of the white building through numerous trees, flecked with the opening leaves of spring. Near the house a few scattered survivors of the original forest, such as the great elm with triple trunk, the far-branching oak and round-topped walnut, stood among large old trees which, in the rings about their hearts, kept a calendar of the age of the family which planted them. At the foot of a sloping bank before the mansion grew a great weeping willow, with its long slender twigs and dark green leaves drooping in stately sadness.

The house was a long building of two stories, framed of wood, weather-boarded and painted white. There was a wide porch along the entire front. The old-fashioned chimneys were built outside, and at each end of the house. The rooms were large and the windows small. In a wide hall at the middle of the building was a flight of stairs starting at one side of the hall, and near the top, making a rectangular turn upon a broad landing, with massive, square posts, heavily capped. Over the spacious fire-places were high, wooden mantel-pieces, adorned with an infinity of mouldings and with rosettes and other figures which commemorated the taste of that Fitzhugh who erected the mansion in the last century. It was then regarded as a grand establishment, for it was finer than most

of its neighbors, and was the seat of one of the principal families of the county. Time gnawed silently
upon the woodwork, but in that community time
wrought few changes of ideas or social relations in the
lapse of only two or three generations. The family
retained its respectability, and the house was still regarded by all the county round as a grand establishment, notwithstanding that, since a railroad was made
through the county, some antique notions had been
put to flight, and some more costly and elegant dwellings had been erected in the neighborhood. The idea
of grandeur attached to the place descended as an
heir-loom in the family, excluding envy of modern
rivals and preventing projects of improvement. The
perfection even of the trees planted by a former generation, took its place among the domestic traditions,
and though new ones might have improved the prospect, they could not flatter the pride of ancestry. The
old furniture was retained, under the influence of similar sentiments. The tall, square, eight-day clock in
the hall, with iron weights, brass, wheels and lunar
face, could not give place to a modern time-piece, for it
had measured the ages of many members of the family,
second by second, from birth until death. The quaint
old bedsteads had been witnesses of the births,
bridals and deaths of several generations of Fitzhughs.
In the old presses were piles of home-made coverlets
and gay silk dresses that would stand on end, with
other relics of the thrift or fashion of a primitive aristocracy. A gourd hung over a cedar-bucket of drinking water on a shelf at the back-door, but there was
silver in the side-board. The many old things about
the old house could not be exchanged for shining
novelties without rending the very roots of the family
tree.

As Colonel Fairfax and his daughter saw Mrs. Fitzhugh, the widowed tenant of this habitation, walking in her garden with the support of a tall cane, she might have seemed a feeble woman of sixty or more, though she was several years under three score. She was pale and thin, but her form was not bowed, and her features were strongly marked with lineaments of pride. She had been for many years a confirmed invalid. But a vigorous and cultivated intellect, with indomitable will, resisted the inroads of disease, and from year to year she fought off death. The pride that was written on her brow seldom escaped from her tongue. It was neither boastful nor scornful. Within her breast it was strong in all forms, but especially as the pride of family. Her proudest and yet her weakest passion was her love for her only son, Hugh.

The place on which she resided—a plantation of considerable extent—with fifty or sixty slaves, descended to him at the death of his father. The widowed mother of an infant son, becoming sole guardian of his person and estate, devoted herself thenceforth to his nurture and education. She so managed his estate as to keep it entire and without debt, while defraying the expenses of his education and travels, but a woman and an invalid could do no more. The slaves, missing the authority of a man above overseers, became negligent and some of them dissolute. The plantation needed repairs, although the grounds about the house, being under the eye of Mrs. Fitzhugh, were kept with taste and care. Hugh, first as an infant, then as a student, and finally as a traveler, had been unable to attend to his estate in person, and after his return home, he neglected it. For two or three years he suffered all things to remain or to go backward, as if he were still absent, whilst he amused himself with books or hunting or fishing, or any idle sport that fell in his way. Thus it was that the expectation of his friends had been disappointed, and his name in the county began to wear the stain of thriftless indolence ; for it was thought that his inheritance imposed active duties. His mother felt that he was sinking below the requirements of his name, and that the son of such ancestors as his—ancestors whom her exaggerated family pride ranked only a little below   a line of heroes—should imitate their useful and honorable lives. But her affection was too indulgent to chide him and she could only wait, as she did, for the blood to show itself.

When she found that the prospect of war had roused his latent energy, and that he had volunteered as a soldier, she suffered a violent conflict of emotions. When he was to be exposed to the hardships and hazards of war, a mother's love for an only child, her overweening care for the son whom she had reared so tenderly, and her lonely widowhood, which might be rendered utterly desolate by the loss of him, made the sacrifice almost too grievous for her to bear. Yet she was conscious that to see him remain at home in ignoble sloth, while others less nobly obliged to duty, according to her ideas, marched to the field, would be intolerable to her pride. Then she exulted in the high qualities which she attributed to his action. She was proud to feel that the honor of his family was vindicated in him. Her devotion to Virginia, second only to her ruling passion, brought her patriotism to the support of her pride. Though every word was as a drop of blood from her heart, yet with unwavering resolution and tearless eyes she encouraged her son to pursue the path which he had chosen.

When she entered the house and received her visitors, she greeted Colonel Fairfax with high-bred but
rather antiquated courtesy, almost too ceremonious for
friends so intimate. But she kissed Julia with frank,
cordial, womanly warmth. "How very glad 1 am to
see you, my dear Julia," she said, "you always make
me happy, and you, colonel, are kind and thoughtful
in visiting me to-day. I regret that Hugh is not at
home to see you, but he is absent attending to the
business that now engages his time."

"Yes; his new company," replied the colonel; "I
may well call it his company, for he has been most
energetic and influential in forming it, and from many
things which I heard yesterday, I am sure he will be
its captain. Men begin already to recognize in him
the qualities which they demand in their leaders—
decision, courage, ability. I congratulate you, my
dear madam, upon being the mother of such a son."

Mrs. Fitzhugh did not reply at once. The subject
itself excited feelings which she could not easily control, and the praises bestowed by her most esteemed
friend upon her son melted her pride. Tears filled
her eyes, and in spite of her efforts to restrain them,
one or two trickled down her cheeks. But she checked
them and she did not again, during this interview,
give way to maternal weakness.

"I trust Hugh will do his duty," she said at last
with a firm voice.

"I am glad," said Julia, "to see you able to leave
your room."

"This is no time to be sick, Julia," she replied;
men and women, old and young, we are all needed for
the defence of Virginia."

"That is true," remarked the colonel; "Virginia

will be, no doubt, the chief battle-ground of this war, and it may be a war of many battles. I hope we shall be able to save our independence, but it must be at a terrible cost. From the superior power of the North, the South must be by far the greater sufferer. We must expect Virginia to be penetrated by invasion, and, perhaps, completely overrun. Our minds should be prepared for unlimited sacrifice."

"Let it be unlimited then," said Mrs. Fitzhugh, "if the North is cruel enough to exact it and if it is necessary to secure our independence. I am ready to begin with the dearest sacrifice a mother can make."

"Unfortunately," replied the colonel, "I have no son to offer to our country. But you and I and all who have property must be prepared to part with it freely. Even our homes may be lost for a time. Of course, if invasion reaches us, many of our slaves will leave us or possibly be enticed away. In other respects, we may hope that those who have been our brethren will conduct the war against us according to civilized and humane usage, but in respect to slaves, the origin of the war leaves no probability of forbearance."

"Your servants, colonel, will not leave you surely, so well treated and so judiciously ruled have they been. How can they be better off?"

"Yet many of them doubtless will hasten to the untried pleasures of freedom. They are easily deluded. If I thought them capable of judging wisely for themselves, I would not feel justified in holding them as slaves."

"I cannot consider them so ungrateful or so unwise."

"We shall see. But if we hold nothing too dear to be given up for the sake of independence, no misfortune of war can dismay us."

"No Virginian, I am sure," said Mrs. Fitzhugh, "will hold any species of property too dear."

"At least the women," added Julia, "must not shrink from the sad duties which war imposes on our sex. But, even yet, I hope and pray that some gleam of goodness or impulse of remorse will avert the doom of bloody conflict from our country."

"Well, Julia, you must not forget your old friend when war shall leave me lonely. Visit me often, and whenever you are with me I shall see sunshine in a shady place. Come, I will not frighten you away with my cloudy mood. Let me show you my flowers, though few of them are out yet. You shall be as sunshine to my garden, my sweet favorite. There's a speech you would rather hear, perhaps, from some gallant cavalier. But come along, let us be happy among flowers while we may."

The walk among the flowers, with gay garden talk, whiled away half-an-hour, in which the high-spirited old lady became lively and her visitors fell in with her cheerful humor.

CHAPTER XI.

THE VOLUNTEERS.

WHEN the company of cavalry was organized by the election of officers, Hugh Fitzhugh was chosen captain. The company numbered about a hundred, of whom a majority were young gentlemen, but men of all classes were included. There was one recruit whose name did not appear upon the muster-roll. Doctor Fairfax was resolved, as he said, to have a hand in the fight. But he conceived that, at his age, he might be excused from the rigid performance of all the arduous duties of a private soldier. He proposed, therefore, to conduct the war, for his own part, at his own cost and charge, as an independent volunteer, not enlisted, but under the command of Captain Fitzhugh. When he proposed this arrangement to the captain, that officer thanked him for the honor which it implied, but urged the doctor to permit his friends to procure an appointment for him which would enable him to be more useful, with less fatigue and exposure. But this suggestion was flatly rejected by the belligerent doctor. He declared that his sole purpose was to fight "the Yankees" in the most direct manner, hand to hand and to the death. Besides, he was going in free for a free fight, and would not endure the trammels of official obligation. The captain acceded to the arrangement, but he asked, with a smile—

"How is it, doctor, that you plunge headlong into the war, while you preach the policy of peace?"

"The chance of shooting at a pack of Northern wolves, captain, would tempt any man from his consistency. But you know I am really not inconsistent."

"You think the South is wrong in its present attitude?"

"Not wrong, but rash, captain."

"You believe that we shall be beaten.".

"A good reason for going into the war. Help the weak—always help the weak. When we are conquered it will be the misfortune of the South but the crime of the North. Let me share the misfortune rather than the crime."

"Your heart is right, doctor, but I trust you are no prophet."

And now everybody manifested a lively interest in the new company. County pride, the popular delight in military parade , personal regard for volunteers who were kinsmen, neighbors or friends, and the contagious excitement of the young soldiers, fanned the patriotic feeling into a flame of enthusiasm. Enthusiasm carries with it an assurance of victory. The general excitement became exultant, joyous. Every one hailed his neighbor as a brother. All were sons of a State which all loved with filial devotion. The citizens regarded the volunteers with a kind of generous envy, as fortunate champions of a sacred soil and a glorious cause. Virginia—the South—Liberty—Independence were words in every mouth, and they sent every man's blood bounding along his veins. Women, always prone to sympathy, to social affection and to generous and patriotic emotions, became even more enthusiastic than the men

It was necessary that the company should bo ready for active service as soon as possible. To this end, not only the officers and the volunteers but the citizens of both sexes applied themselves with alacrity and industry. The men were to be clothed, equipped and mounted. Tents and wagons were to be supplied. It was known that the government could. not instantly furnish all the military apparatus needed for the numerous army which was spontaneously springing into existence throughout the State. Moreover the citizens coveted the privilege of supplying their own companies not only with things needful but with articles of superfluity—articles which must be abandoned in the first active campaign. Colonel Fairfax presented to the company sufficient cloth of cadet grey to make all the uniforms, and canvass enough for their tents. Other wealthy citizens emulated his liberality, either to the same company or to others then in process of formation. To make up the clothing of the volunteers all the women, black and white, brought their needles into play. For these various purposes the men formed themselves into committees, and the women met in societies. As Julia Fairfax showed herself not less generous among her sex than her father among men, Roebuck became a great workshop, over which she presided. Many young ladies assembled there daily, and with the help of servants, performed the work of seamstresses or tailors. As the lively spirits of the young lighten their labors, the tongues of these maidens kept time with plying needles, and the click of sewing-machines mingled with the laughter of girls. The gallant defenders of their country could not neglect a patriotic establishment engaged in their service, and so the ladies were often favored with the counsel and assistance of the young men. It might happen there that the Power who "rules the court, the camp, the grove," sometimes lurked in the tangles of a skein or barbed the point of a needle.

The official duty of Captain Fitzhugh of course carried him to such places, and he did not fail to inspect, now and then, the work over which Julia Fairfax presided. Between her and himself there was a new bond of sympathy in the ardent patriotism which animated both. His eloquence was kindled by themes which warmed her heart. Perhaps he was proud to show her that his life was not idly wasted when he found an object worthy of earnest effort. Perhaps she felt that his awakened energy was in some degree a flattering tribute to her influence. The fiery agitation of the time, too, tended to inflame all sentiments into passions. Friendship, cherished since childhood, might be quickly kindled to a warmer sentiment when sympathy and circumstance conspired to fan the flame. But if their intercourse during a few days of burning patriotism imparted a passionate glow to the friendship between Hugh Fitzhugh and Julia Fairfax, they did not acknowledge it to themselves or to each other. Duty, paramount over selfish aims, then engaged their thoughts.

When the company was ready for the march a vast crowd assembled at the village to take leave of the volunteers. Men and women on the court green, in the street, afoot, on horseback, in carriages, everywhere, jostled one another to get a sight of the gay troop in new uniforms and on sleek, high-mettled horses, bound to the war. A neat valedictory speech was delivered by Mr. Williams on behalf of the citizens. A blessing was invoked by the Rev. Mr.

Ambler. Cheers were given by the multitude and answered by the volunteers. Hats were tossed up and grey caps waved in return. Hundreds of negroes, imitative patriots, on the outskirts of the crowd, grinned and babbled and laughed and shouted with uncontrollable enthusiasm. From all the porches, windows and carriages, and from the court green, white handkerchiefs fluttered incessantly. Under all the clamor of cheers an attentive ear might have heard the sobs of mothers. Tears bedewed the cheeks of sisters, but their handkerchiefs were used, not to dry their eyes, but to wave encouragement to their brave brothers. . There were pride, joy, anguish and devotion in that farewell. It was not surprising that the captain and his friend, Julia, each felt an unusual palpitation of the heart when they waved their final adieu ..

The entire march of the company to the scene of war was a popular ovation. The roads were lined with men, women and children, black and white, waving hats and handkerchiefs, clapping hands, cheering and offering refreshments. Whenever the company halted the people flocked around, to tender congratulation, welcome and hospitality. They contended for the privilege of entertaining every private soldier, as well as the officers, in their houses. No cottage was too poor to solicit such guests. No mansion, nor bed, nor furniture could be too luxurious for the use of those dusty horsemen. No food was too delicate, no wine too costly to be set before them. Even their servants rejoiced with African glee in the abounding hospitality which they shared. When the company marched on, the gentlemen of the county escorted them for miles over dusty or miry roads. Banners

were presented to them by processions of ladies, and
speeches addressed to them, full of grateful praise and
eloquent with martial and patriotic fervor. They fell in
with other companies marching to the field and saw
the people everywhere engaged in volunteering or
preparing volunteers for service. The country was
unanimous for war and independence.

In the meantime other companies were formed in
the county for the different arms of the service. There
was talk of forming one under the auspices of Albert
Palmer—not of cavalry but of infantry. He had been
requested by some of the young men to volunteer in
the company which was now commanded by Captain
Fitzhugh, but he evaded the request. He professed
to think that, as cavalry was a favorite arm, his assistance was not needed in that direction, and that since
many who were willing to become soldiers could not
afford to furnish horses, he could be more useful in
raising a company of infantry. He talked a great
deal on that subject. He rode over the county. He
drew up a paper to be signed by volunteers. He
procured a few signatures. He made this his osten-
sible business for several weeks. Either he was not
quite in earnest or his influence was limited. The
number of his signatures ceased to increase, though
other companies were filled up until the county had
furnished more volunteers than it contained voters.
His project, however, was a decent apology for remaining at home, while he declaimed as a zealous
Southerner and took part in proceedings designed to
promote the war. He consulted with committees.
He visited the patriotic societies of ladies. He talked
of nothing but war.

He was particularly regular in calling at Roebuck,

always expressing the deepest interest in the work of the ladies who assembled there, and seeking occasions to converse with Miss Fairfax. When the work was finished he continued to visit Roebuck with equal regularity. From day to day his attentions to Miss Fairfax became more pointed. At length the motive of them could be no longer misunderstood. He was a lover, almost declared. When Julia made this discovery she was surprised and embarrassed. She respected him as a friend, and would willingly have spared him the pain of a distinct refusal. She endeavored with delicate tact to discourage his suit without mortifying his pride. But in view of ulterior plans, he was resolved that, in this affair, there should be neither uncertainty nor delay. It became apparent that he would not be diverted from pressing his suit to a speedy and decisive issue. At length, seizing an opportunity when she could neither avoid him nor evade his addresses, he offered her, with studied grace of manner and polish of words, his heart and hand. If she had been less agitated by the distress of inflicting pain, she might have inferred from his polite self-possession during the scene that his heart was not to be broken by any decision she would pronounce. But, with modest and considerate gentleness, she signified to him that, while he had her esteem, she could not reciprocate the sentiments which he had done her the honor to express. He did not leave her until he ascertained, to his own perfect conviction, that it would be useless to renew his suit. Then, with the same urbanity of style, he expressed his disappointment and regret, and afterwards bade her adieu.

The next day he started to Richmond. Upon his

return from the capital he informed his parents that
he was a quarter-master, with the rank of captain, and
that he had made a satisfactory arrangement with a
slave-dealer in the city to sell Mr. Palmer's negroes
there at auction. He had been assigned as quarter-
master to the regiment of cavalry which included
Fitzhugh's company. Young Baxter had been appointed a commissary with the same rank, and was
assigned to the same regiment. Mr. Palmer, the
elder, expressed his satisfaction with all that had been
done by his son. He had but consummated plans
previously settled in family council. The father had
solicited an influence at the capital to procure the appointment of quarter-master; an appointment commended by safety and profit; an office which would
serve to identify Albert with the Southern movement,
and yet would not expose him too conspicuously to
Northern vengeance, in the event of adverse fortune.

When the quarter-master afterwards repaired to his
regiment, he had not forgotten the conduct of Baxter
in his father's house. Neither did he regard Captain
Fitzhugh without resentment. He had watched with
jealous eyes some of the interviews between the captain and Julia at Roebuck, and after the rejection of
his suit, he concluded that he owed his discomfiture
to the preference awarded to that rival. As the project
of marriage had been a key to his principal plans with
reference to the war and to his future prosperity, he
could not forgive the suspected author of his disappointment. But these feelings were unknown to
Baxter and Fitzhugh, and they gave him a friendly
reception.

CHAPTER XII.

MANASSA.

THIS narrative is not designed to be a chronicle of military events, and it passes now to the first battle of Manassa, only for the purpose of gathering up some incidents which affected the fortunes of persons who have appeared to the reader. That battle, it is well known, was fought on a hot day of July, in the year eighteen hundred and sixty-one, between two considerable armies, of which the Federal was twice as numerous as the Confederate. In arms and all equipments the superiority was also with the larger host. The skill of the Northern generals, as displayed on that day, was not inferior to that of their adversaries. The Federals advanced to the attack, confident of success. After a severe conflict of several hours, victory was achieved by the undisciplined valor of the Southern volunteers. Then followed such a rout, dispersion and flight of the Northern army as would have been ludicrous if so much suffering and terror could ever provoke a smile.

During the engagement but little use was made of cavalry. Captain Fitzhugh's company was for a time posted in a ravine, where they were somewhat sheltered from the direct fire of the enemy, while awaiting orders or opportunities for action. In this position, inactive and unable to see the course of the fight, while the roar of battle was deafening, Doctor Fairfax became extremely impatient. He was eager to be

6

where blows were dealt and taken. With his blood
at fever heat, he chafed at fortune, which denied him,
an active part in the grand and exciting drama. When
a report came that the brigade of his friend, Brigadier
General Bee, was pressed and in danger of being over-
whelmed by superior numbers, he could endure inaction no longer. He applied for permission to offer
his services to that gallant officer, and it was granted.
He found that the situation of Bee's brigade was extremely critical, and that every officer of the general's
staff was killed, wounded or unhorsed. The general
desired him instantly to ride off with an importunate message to be delivered to General Beauregard.

The doctor started at high speed through a tempest
of shot and shell in which it seemed impossible for a
man or horse to live a minute. He had not gone far
when he was obliged to check his horse to avoid a
number of men who were bearing Brigadier General
Bartow, mortally wounded, a short distance to the rear
of his shattered brigade. He heard that brave and
able man request those around him to lay him down
and return to assist and encourage his men. "Look,"
exclaimed the dying Bartow, "look at those Virginians under Jackson, standing like a stone wall." The
doctor's attention, as he passed on, was thus directed
to that unflinching brigade of Virginians, and he saw
the tall, angular form and handsome features of Jackson, as he sat upon his horse immovable, with nothing
but the gleam of his eyes to indicate the fiery energy
which then reposed, like latent lightning. He and his
brigade were from that day known by a name derived
from the exclamation of Bartow; but not until long
afterwards did even his own countrymen recognize in
Stonewall Jackson the first military genius on the continent.

With some difficulty, and after once riding almost into the enemy's lines, the doctor found General Beauregard, and delivering the message and receiving a reply, he returned to find General Bee; but he had been killed. Seeking his successor in command, amidst the hail of bullets and the confusion of broken, but unyielding ranks, the doctor delivered to him the communication, and at that moment his own horse was shot. Being then dismissed to his proper command, he made his way afoot to his company. He called out as he approached—"there is glorious excitement up there, boys. But the infernal Yanks have killed my horse. I must have another." "What's this?" asked one of the men, pointing at the doctor's feet. Casting down his eyes, he saw blood running from one of his legs. He drew off his boot and found that he had received a flesh wound, of which until then he had been unconscious. "Now," he grumbled as he eyed the spot, "I wonder if that Yankee expected to make veal of me by butchering my calf." Chuckling over his pun, he called for two or three handkerchiefs and bandaged his wound. He then renewed his demand for a horse. "No, no, my good friend," said the captain, "you must not mount again to-day." This prohibition was soon enforced by the loss of blood. The doctor became faint, and lay down upon the ground. He revived, but had to remain there until the battle was over.

When the day had been won, Captain Fitzhugh's company was sent, with other cavalry, in pursuit of that panic-stricken mob which had so lately been an army with banners. The pursuit was a chase. Little resistance was encountered. The most frequent impediments were abandoned wagons and other wrecks

of a ruined host. Yet a chance shot broke the left
arm of Captain Fitzhugh. He continued, neverthe-
less, to lead his men, gathering in prisoners and scat-
tering still more widely and wildly the elements of
that disastrous rout. When it was almost night, he
discovered that some preparation had been made for
resistance at a place where the road passed between
swamps and thickets, so that it was a mere defile. On
a little eminence which commanded the defile a piece
of artillery was pointed in the direction of the pursuing cavalry. A Federal captain, finding an abandoned piece there, had collected about a hundred
stragglers, and made dispositions to check pursuit.
The number of men with Captain Fitzhugh at that
time did not exceed twenty, the rest of his company
having been left in charge of captives. Halting a moment to ascertain the state of affairs in his front, he
dashed forward at the head of his little band. The
Federal officer discharged the piece with his own
hand, and the grape killed one and wounded two of
the Confederates. There was not time, if there was
ammunition at hand, to load again. The captain endeavored to hold his men firm to repel the cavalry, but
disheartened by the general rout, they broke and fled.
He stood alone, armed only with his sword, and disdaining to fly or surrender, seemed determined to sell
his life as dearly as possible. He fell, dangerously
wounded by a pistol-shot, and the cavalry rushed past
him.

Galloping on, they overtook an ambulance, in which
were two or three civilians, who had come upon the
field to be spectators of the grand Union victory
which, on the morning of that day, the entire North
had expected. Whipping and shouting, they urged

the horses to their utmost speed, and the ambulance was bounding from side to side. At its tail hung a pedestrian, and as he ran or was dragged along with his skirts flying, he begged the other fugitives to take him into the vehicle. But he lost his hold, and fell just when the Confederate captain came up, and unable to check his horse, rode over him. The terrified occupants of the ambulance, seeing cavalry so close upon them, leaped out and scampered across the fields. Their horses then stopped.

As it was growing dark, Captain Fitzhugh halted and turned back, taking with him the captured ambulance. When he returned to the man who had fallen under his horse's hoofs, that person still lay prostrate on his face, affecting to be dead. One of the Confederates, dismounting, and finding him to be alive, without a visible wound, turned him over and commanded him to get up. "O Lord, don't kill me; I am a noncombatant," he bellowed. "I can see that in the dark," replied the Confederate soldier, "but you must get up and go with us." The captive, then, discovering the officer, cried—"Captain—Colonel—General— I don't know your stripes, but whatever you are, I appeal to you as an officer. Don't let them murder me. I am only a poor newspaper devil. I am Bombyx, army correspondent of the 'New York Comet.' My name is Campbell. I just came here to pick up a few items. Oh, spare my life. If you do, I'll give you a first-rate notice in my next letter to the 'Comet.' I'll say the reb—the South has gained the day. I'll say you gained it yourself. I'll say you killed a hundred men with your own hand. Indeed I will. I'll write anything if you spare my life. The 'Comet' has the largest circulation of any paper in

New York—power-press, with the latest improvements—tremendous advertising—immense subscrip-
tion list—O, don't let me be murdered. Poor
Bombyx!"

"Is the fellow hurt?" inquired the captain.

"No—yes, I think I am—I'm lame here—a dozen
horses tramped on my leg."

"Take him up and put him into the ambulance."

When they moved on, "now," said Captain Fitzhugh, "we must look after that brave officer who fell
by the gun. I fear he is badly wounded, if not
killed." They found him indeed living, but nearly
dead. Lifting him carefully and tenderly, they laid
him in the ambulance. Afterwards they took up the
body of their comrade who had been killed, and one
of those who had been wounded, the other being able
to ride his horse. With these and a Federal soldier
whom they found lying near the road wounded, they
slowly made their way through the darkness to the
place where they had left Doctor Fairfax.

He lay there asleep. Aroused by the noise of their
approach, he sat up and cried out—"back again,
boys?—have you been to Washington City?—did you
fetch Old Abe with you?—let me see his majesty."
But when he was told what the ambulance contained,
his levity ceased, and he expressed sincere compassion
for the wounded, and sorrow for the dead. When he
learned that his captain was wounded, he was full of
anxiety. In spite of his own wound, which had become
painful, he rose to his feet and offered assistance, first
to Captain Fitzhugh, and then to the other wounded.
At so late an hour of the night, and after such a
battle, it was impossible to make immediate provision
for all the wounded. While a surgeon was sent for,

Doctor Fairfax tendered his services as far as they
might be rendered with safety to the patients, by virtue of his having once been a physician. Leaning on
a man's arm, he limped to the ambulance, attended to
the removal of the wounded, examined their wounds,
and spent the remainder of the night in ministering
to their relief. The Federal captain, as the person in
most danger, received his principal care. Last of all,
when daylight appeared, he turned his attention to
Campbell, the reporter or correspondent of the
" Comet," who had recovered from his fright, and in
full possession of his faculties, sat under a tree, leaning
against the trunk, and smoking a cigar. His leg still
gave him some pain, and he thought it was politic to
make the most of his wound. The gray light, when
the doctor approached him, revealed a person in holi-
day attire, bedizened with jewelry, but soiled with
dirt. When he displayed his wound, the doctor curtly
said, " a bruise—nothing but a bruise," and was walking away.

" I say, doctor," exclaimed Campbell, " you are not
in a hurry, are you ?"

" I believe I have nothing more to do just now."

" Oblige me then by sitting down beside me. I
know you are tired, and I wish to have a little chat
with you."

" Certainly, sir," said the doctor, sitting down upon
the ground.

" Have a cigar ? You don't smoke ? Then take a
drink. You are not very well. I have a flask here in
my pocket. You won't drink ? The brandy is excellent. I bought it in New York. I'll tell you where
you can buy the best cigars and brandy when you go
to the city. You "——

"I thank you, sir, but I don't expect to be in New York very soon."

"But information is always useful. I pick up items wherever I go. I would like to get a few from you now, doctor. I am Bombyx, the army correspondent of the 'New York Comet.' Bombyx is Latin you know for silk-worm. Capital name for a correspondent, eh? They say we spin our yarns out of our own heads—ha, ha, ha!"

"The Yankee imitation of a silk-worm—a caterpillar," said the doctor to himself, but he said aloud, "I presume you have no further occasion for my presence."

"Don't go, doctor, don't go. I want to discuss with you some points of interest to our common country."

"What countryman are you?" said the doctor.

"Am American, of course."

"But I am a Virginian."

"It's all one—Virginian and American."

"There was a question about that discussed on the battle-field yesterday."

"Now, it is the war I want to discuss with you, doctor. You rebels—but excuse me for calling you a rebel—no offence, I hope?"

"Rebel! A solecism indeed to speak of the rebellion of a State. But rebel! It is the most popular epithet in the language. Governments have always endeavored to make it infamous, but they have only made themselves odious. History is the pillory of governments. Rebellion always implies at least one virtue—courage. Three-fourths of the rebellions have been right, and seven-eighths have been applauded by mankind. If you would flatter me, call me a rebel."

"You have odd notions, doctor."

"Odd in this country! What would America have been without rebellion?"

"Well then, you rebels must acknowledge that the government of the Union is the best government the world ever saw."

"You will be equally polite, of course, and acknowledge that this is the best rebellion the world ever saw."

"But I am in earnest, doctor."

"So am I. You of the North may praise a government that serves your interest. We of the South must praise a rebellion that is designed to save our liberties."

"Speaking of liberty, doctor, I would like to discuss the subject of slavery. You know our government is pledged not to interfere with slavery, but if you Southerners had correct views on that subject I think we could soon have peace. Now I am thoroughly acquainted with the subject and would like to explain it to you."

"Have you lived among negro slaves?"

"No, I never was in a slave-holding State before yesterday. I lost my liberty the same day I entered one—ha, ha, ha!"

"Your views of slavery must be interesting."

"I believe they are. Now I can convince you in five minutes that slavery is wrong. Thus: you will admit that by nature all men are equal."

"Excuse me—not at present."

"You don't admit first principles! Then it is useless to argue with you."

"Very probably; but I prefer not to admit as a fact that which my senses contradict. I cannot see

6*

that a white man and a negro are by nature equal."

"Why, it is laid down in the Declaration of Independence."

"So much the worse for the Declaration, if it is not true."

"You blaspheme that sacred instrument."

"I worship nothing under heaven. The Declaration of Independence was a glorious event—it was a rebellion—but its glory may be due rather to the sword of Washington than to the philosophy of Jefferson."

"Why, sir, it is the great end of all the modern improvements in political science to make men equal. I have written a treatise to prove it. I wish I had brought you a copy."

"Thank you. I'll give you a hint for your next edition. If you wish to equalize two races whom nature has made unequal, you have only to degrade the higher. It is an easy process. They have done it in Mexico—a country that can do nothing else."

"You jest at everything, doctor."

"Why should we wrangle over questions which the sword is to decide?"

"Then let us talk about something else. I love to talk."

Campbell then launched forth in a long harangue which kept Doctor Fairfax listening with amusement and wonder. He talked of the battle, of his family, of the Federal generals, whom he called by their Christian names, as familiar acquaintances, of newspapers, of strategy, of boots, of ladies, of foreign nations, of everything, with a volubility that knew "no retiring ebb." His style was similar to that which he used in corresponding with the "Comet." He introduced every topic, as it were, with a great heading displayed in capitals. He magnified petty details with astounding adjectives. He spurted out every sentence as if it was designed to make a sensation, and he gesticulated interjections and marks of exclamation. He tripped through the gravest questions with a jaunty, flippant, knowing air. His statements of facts, tricked out to shine, were marvellous travesties of truth. He predicted future events like a prophet or a spiritual rapper. He made it his business, as he modestly observed, to know everything.

Dr. Fairfax had found a character quite new to him. Surely, he thought, nothing like this ever grew south of Mason and Dixon's line. What impudence! he said to himself, as the harangue went on : what flippancy! what pretention! what vulgarity of soul!—what ambitious and meretricious rhetoric! what a liar! Thus with inward comment he sat studying this novel specimen of humanity. The interest of the study inspired him with a sort of liking for his specimen. He began to covet it as a natural curiosity. This, he thought, was "a Yankee of the Yankees." He hated that tribe in the mass, but individually, he never could hate any man. Finally he interrupted the discourse.

"Come, Bombyx, my Northern light, my polar star, my epitome of all Northern intelligence, my live Yankee, come, let us look out for breakfast."

"A capital thought, doctor, ha, ha, ha!"

After feasting his communicative guest with the best scraps he could scrape together at such a time and place, Doctor Fairfax again visited the Federal officer. He learned from him that he was Captain Tremaine, and that he had been an officer in the regular army of

the United States before the war. He appeared to be
a gentleman, and his conversation increased the interest which his suffering awakened. But the doctor did
not suffer him to talk much, and as soon as it was
practicable, he had the captain, as well as the other
wounded, provided with comfortable cots and tents
and with proper attendance. · The drenching rain that
day fell on many unsheltered men, the living and the
dead, the wounded, the weary and the sick, on the
wide plain of Manassa.

CHAPTER XIII.

A DUEL.

In the evening of that rainy day they buried the soldier who had been killed, as already mentioned, by a grape-shot while engaged in the pursuit. At this early period of the war death had not lost its awe by familiarity. When a single man of a company fell in battle, the event impressed the minds of the survivors with almost as much solemnity as a death at home before the war. The body of this soldier was followed by most of his comrades in the company, with every demonstration of respect that circumstances permitted, to a small grove of stunted trees where a place of burial had been selected for some of the Confederate dead. The melancholy solemnity of the scene was deepened by the gloom of the sky and of the neighboring battle-field, yet encumbered with dead and dying. When they had fulfilled their sad duty the men in attendance were about to march away, when Abraham Marlin, the preaching cooper, stepped forward and touching his cap, requested permission to say a few words. He remarked it was a pity any human being should be buried without some religious service. He knew a chaplain could not be had when so many dying men required their attendance on them. But he thought some one might offer up an humble prayer at the grave. This suggestion was received with silent acquiescence, but all eyes looked around for the person who might perform the proposed service. Abraham, seeing that no other person was willing, felt that it was incumbent on himself to discharge the duty which he had proposed. He therefore walked to the head of the grave, took off his cap, lifted up his hands and began to pray. In common affairs which belonged to every-day life he was sensible and his language was direct and simple. But when, from religious zeal, he aspired to performances which exercise the higher faculties of educated men, he floundered into absurdities of thought and language which were almost profane in spite of his sincere piety. On this occasion he soon rambled into a kind of funeral discourse upon the life and character of the deceased, such as can scarcely be imagined without the aid of a specimen :

"We lay his mortal body in the dust—leastways it was dust before the rain. We pray that his immortal soul may go where the wicked cease from troubling and the weary are at rest, that is if it ain't popish to pray for his soul when he's dead and buried, and if it is, we ax pardon and take it back. He was a mighty good young man as we knowed him at home. He was a mighty brave soldier. He fou't in this 'ere great battle agin the great company, the mighty army that come out of the North parts which we've whipped and put to flight, only a good many of 'em was killed and couldn't fly. He was killed suddently in pursuin' of 'em when the big fight was done fou't, and it was a pity any more men was killed so late in the evenin'. He fou't in that battle when he wa'n't able to fight by good rights, becase he'd been runnin' off with chronic diree for most a month. But he wouldn't stay back. He was a willin' and a brave man, and he wood a fou't agin in the next big battle, ef any more

mighty armies come out of the North parts, providin'
the diree didn't take him off in the eend."

But after some time the pious cooper dropped this
rambling discourse and gave, in homely but sensible
language, expression to those genuine emotions which
good men feel when they stand in the presence of
death and before the Judge of quick and dead. When
in the midst of his uncouth dialect his memory supplied some of the affecting phrases which the scriptures lend to the expression of personal piety or the
sublime imagery with which they allude to the world
beyond the tomb, he seemed almost eloquent. His
pathetic earnestness melted some of the soldiers around
him to tears. They indeed did not smile at those
absurdities by which he made sacred things appear
mean and ridiculous, for besides the sadness of the
scene, they respected the preaching cooper as a sincere, faithful and brave man. His piety silenced their
censure, even when his presumption might have
shocked them.

An hour after the conclusion of this scene, Captain
Palmer, the quarter-master, sat in the door of a tent
conversing with a person who was present at the grave
about the strange proceedings of the extempore chaplain. "Abraham Marlin is a pestilent old fool," said
Palmer, in a loud tone. "Was that meant for my
ear?" asked a young man who was passing the tent
and who turned abruptly to Palmer.

"Who are you?" rejoined the latter.

"I am the son of Abraham Marlin."

"O, Mark Marlin! I've heard of you. I repeat
what I said, and this time for your ears. Abraham
Marlin is a pestilent old fool."

"It is false, and no gentleman would say such a
thing about any man to his son."

" Sir, you are a private. I am an officer."

"I knew that, or I could not have answered you with words."

· "Do you threaten me, sir?"

" As you talk about your rank, I can say no more; but I will say again, you are no gentleman."

" I'll have you punished, sir ; I'll have you punished for your insolence."

" Then you must expose yourself," said Mark Marlin as he walked away.

Palmer had fallen into this foolish altercation, because he had conceived the absurd idea that, among soldiers, he must support a reputation for soldierly bearing by blustering rudeness, and feared he might sink in the estimation of his companion if he made any concession to Mark Marlin, after proclaiming his opinion of Mark's father.

Later in the evening Palmer was in the tent of Baxter, the commissary. That functionary was present, acting as host, and his guests, besides Palmer, were Dr. Frank, a surgeon, a young lieutenant, Potter, and two or three other officers. They all sat on stools or the host's bunk. On a rough box, which served for a table, stood a bottle, two tin cups and a tallow candle stuck in a block of wood. Baxter was entertaining the others with noisy hilarity that smacked of the bottle. Dr. Frank was silent, sober and surly. He was a bachelor of fifty, with heavy, grey mustache and shaggy brows. He had served long in the Federal navy, and was reputed to be very skilful in his profession. He was as gentle as a woman with the sick, but crusty with men who presumed to enjoy good health. He was a sworn enemy of all soldiers who attempted to shirk from duty by feigning sickness. He had a habit which made his scanty conversation consist mainly of oaths.

"Drink, gentlemen," said Baxter, setting an example, " drink. I can recommend my commissary stores. This Co federate whiskey is an excellent summer drink. It would cool a fever. It is better than sherbet for this warm weather. Doctor Frank, you shall take some of my medicinal water."

' The doctor growled out a refusal with an oath.

"Don't swear, doctor, don't," said Baxter. "That reminds me, gentlemen, you have been talking of the preaching cooper. Now I'll tell you an anecdote of a preacher and Doctor Frank. The doctor, you know, swears more oaths than the Yankees prescribe to the rebels—if that's possible. Well, a few days ago, being scarce of tents, I suppose, they billetted a chaplain on our swearing friend, and the two have had to sleep under the same canvass. It is the surgeon's habit to stand at the door of his tent at an early hour every morning, to hear the applications of soldiers for certificates of ill health to excuse them from fatigue duty for the day. He thinks most of them are shirking, and he curses those fellows high and low, in order, as he says, to maintain discipline. Two or three mornings since, I was passing and saw the doctor at his levee. He had been up all night with a poor ' devil who threatened to slip through his fingers, and " his nerves, no doubt, were more irritable than usual. He believed that the entire bevy of applicants were shirkers. He looked at them with brows like a jagged thunder-cloud. He compressed his lips as if he was holding in a young earthquake. Suddenly he turned and looked in at the bunk where the chaplain lay. Then he turned to scowl on the shirkers. Again he peered in at the chaplain, and again turned to the waiting crowd. Then burst out the earthquake. 'By——,' he exclaimed, 'I will swear—I must maintain discipline—I have not cursed these fellows for a week, and now they are all shirking—what's a preacher? he's only a man—I will swear.' Well, he swore. All the oaths that he had corked up for a week, from respect to the clergy, rushed out in one | volume. He scattered that squad of shirkers faster and farther than the Yanks were routed yesterday."

The surgeon swore a little, and the others laughed, except Palmer.

"Why don't you laugh, Palmer? That was a good story," said Baxter.

But the quarter-master, perhaps, was not in a merry mood that evening, and he had a recollection of one of Baxter's practical jokes that disinclined him to applaud the commissary's wit. He replied:—

"I am not bound to laugh, am I?"

"Everybody but a churl laughs at a good joke in jovial company."

"Profanity does not amuse me."

"O, Puritan!" cried Baxter, with a sneer.

"At all events, I am not a buffoon," retorted Palmer with a scowl.

Baxter instantly rose and slapped Palmer's face with his open hand. The latter stood a moment white with rage, and then saying, "you shall hear from me, sir," he flung himself out of the tent.

"Let's take another drink," said Baxter, resuming his seat. But his visitors declined the invitation and took leave of him. They anticipated the consequences of the quarrel. They condemned the conduct of Baxter, but they did not esteem Palmer. They considered that the affair between them had proceeded too far to be stopped. Blood for a blow, was a maxim that permitted no pacification at that stage by the mediation of friends, according to their notions. Nothing was left for them but to stand aside, and let the affair take its course. When they had left him, Baxter sat looking at his bottle for some time, and then said to himself—"Now, there's poor Corporal Jones would be the better of a few drops of that liquor. I'll go to see him. I expect he'll die to-night. I'll help him to go off the hooks easy." He filled the bottle and started out with it in his hand.

It was near midnight when Palmer entered the tent of Lieutenant Potter, who was then asleep, and asked him to get up. "Mr. Potter," said he with agitation, "I want your advice."

"About what?" said Potter, turning over and yawning.

"About that affair."

"Oh—ah—yes," replied Potter, rubbing his eyes, "you mean that affair with Baxter," and he yawned again.

"Yes. What ought I to do?"

"Don't you know?"

"Really I do not."

"Then you are a fool," said Potter, and he turned over to sleep again.

"But, Mr. Potter, indeed you must advise me. I am in trouble. I have no friend here to consult with —do advise me."

"Didn't you threaten that he should hear from you?"

"Well?"

"Didn't he strike you?"

" Yes."

" Don't you intend to challenge him ?"

" It is on that point I want advice. I am conscientiously opposed to duelling."

" Did you ever tell anybody so before ?"

" Well—no—I believe not."

" You have allowed it to be understood that you acknowledge the code ?"

" Perhaps I have, thoughtlessly."

" Then you are thoughtful too late. If a gentleman is only known to be religious and consistent, he may decline a duel without disgrace. Such a man is seldom insulted and never insults. But if a man becomes conscientious only when there is a pistol in view, people draw ugly inferences."

" You think then that I must challenge him ?"

" I have not said that. I have not undertaken to advise you. We are almost strangers to each other. I can have nothing to do with a duel without resigning my commission. You must excuse me."

" To whom can I apply. I am much distressed."

" I can find you an adviser. Bullitt, from Richmond, is now in camp. He is the very man for affairs of honor. He knows all about them. He studies them. He practises them. He'd rather be invited to a duel than to a dinner. He will be glad to advise you and act for you too, as your friend. He is like a Quaker, a friend to all the world. Come along, I'll introduce you to him."

During this speech Potter got up and put on his clothes. At the end of it he started out of the tent, followed by Palmer, who felt but little encouraged by the character of the friend he was about to meet, as sketched by his guide. He was dragged onward, however, by the circumstances of his position and by his fear of losing caste among young men of spirit. Through the mud and darkness Potter marched on inexorably, and Palmer trudged after him in rueful silence. At length they arrived at a tent in which Mr. Bullitt, the man of honor, was lodging as the guest of a friend. Potter called him, and as soon as he was awake, signified to him that an officer desired some private conversation with him. With great alertness he sprang from the cot on which he slept and briskly stepped out of the tent. Potter announced his own name, for they could not distinguish each other in the dark, and then introduced Captain Palmer. He informed Mr. Bullitt that the captain was involved in a delicate affair and needed a friend. " I have taken the liberty," he added, " to recommed him to you and to assure him that you would not refuse him the favor he desires."

" On the contrary, it will afford me pleasure to act as a friend of any friend of yours, Mr. Potter," said Bullitt.

" Then, gentlemen, I may leave you together ; good night, gentlemen."

Bullett, by a few rapid and decisive questions, drew from Palmer the material circumstances, and then bounced into the tent, where he 'got a match, lighted a candle, drew forth paper, pen and ink, placed them on a board upon his knee and began to write. Palmer could then see that he was a small, withered man, with no clothes on him but a shirt and pantaloons, a red night-cap, with a huge tassel, and muddy boots, hastily pulled on so as to carry his wrinkled pantaloons with them up to his knees. He had a peaked nose, little glistening black eyes and a long, heavy mustache, which, like his hair, had been black but was somewhat grizzled. He moved with quick, decisive energy, and wrote with furious rapidity. In a few minutes he produced two documents, and requested Captain Palmer to sign them. One was a resignation of his commission as quarter-master, and the other a peremptory challenge to Baxter. Palmer read them over and signed them, not knowing what else to do. He had expected his adviser to offer him some advice, but the artificer of duels had not imagined that there could be a doubt in the mind of any one as to the proper course to be pursued.

"Now, Captain Palmer," said his friend, "I will forward your resignation to the adjutant and I will deliver the note to Captain Baxter forthwith. You can lie down and refresh yourself with sleep. I will call you when you are needed."

Palmer was not very sleepy at that moment. He looked at Bullitt while he jerked on his coat, flung aside his night-cap and covered his head with an old-fashioned cocked hat, which it was his fancy to wear. They then walked together to the quarter-master's tent, and Bullitt, having obtained the information necessary for finding Baxter, went on alone, while his principal stood wondering how soon that brisk step of his second would bring him back with an announcement that all things were ready, and Captain Palmer was to be shot at without more delay. Bullitt found the commissary's quarters, but Baxter was not there. After satisfying himself of that fact, the faithful friend, not knowing how to find the adversary except by waiting for him to return, began to pace backward and forward before his tent like a sentinel. He kept up that oscillating march with exemplary perseverance until day was breaking. He then discovered a man passing not far from him, and approaching the passenger, he inquired if that person knew where Captain Baxter might be found. "Come with me," replied the man, who happened to be Doctor Frank, on his way to visit Corporal Jones. Bullitt followed, until they arrived at the entrance of a tent, where they paused in consequence of what they saw and heard. Within the tent Baxter was standing over a cot occupied by a sick man, and as he arranged the pillow, he said—"now, Jones, I am going to leave you, old fellow. The surgeon will be here in a few minutes."

"O, captain," said the sick man, feebly, "I am so much obliged to you for staying with me all night. You have done me so much good. I had not laughed before since I was taken sick."

"You are going to be well soon. Keep up your spirits. I'll put this bottle under your head to keep your spirits up. This is the great medicine after all. It beats the doctors and the quack pills to boot. I would have been under the ground long ago if I had not been drunk half my life—or half drunk all my life. I am not sure which is the best division of time. I believe if a man was kept drunk all day and half drunk all night it would be a pretty even divide. Don't you feel better now?"

The patient laughed. The surgeon then went in, and Baxter, after making a brief report of the sick man's condition during the night, went out of the tent. Bullitt met him, touched his cocked hat, and said, "Captain Baxter, I believe? Mr. Bullitt. I am the bearer of a message for you, sir. May I see you at your quarters?"

"I am going there. But you may save time by

delivering the message at once. Is it from Captain Palmer?"

"Yes; this is the note, sir."

"What does he want?" asked Baxter, taking the note but not reading it; "does he want to fight?"

"Precisely."

"Very well; bring him along."

"How do you mean? Please refer me to your friend, captain, to settle the necessary arrangements."

"I am my own friend. We'll settle the arrangements as we walk to the ground. I have pistols in my tent—or you may bring yours."

"I do not understand this mode of proceeding. You seem to be jesting. But I'll wait until you have read the note and written your answer."

"I won't wait. I've been up all night and I must have a nap before breakfast. This affair must be dispatched at once, so that I may go to bed."

"Surely you jest, sir. This is a grave affair."

"It may be grave enough for your friend, if I can steady my hand this morning."

"But your friend—you will refer me to your friend!"

"I have no friend. I want no friend. I have no time to be looking for a friend now."

"You will not go to the field alone?"

"I hope to see you there, if not Palmer. Come along."

"But, sir, this is irregular—absolutely contrary to all rule. I protest"——

"Mr. Bullitt—I think you called yourself Bullitt?"

"That is my name, sir."

"Do you see that clump of trees, with a tall pine in the centre—there—about two miles off?"

"I see it."

"I shall be there—just beyond that clump of trees in forty minutes. If you and your principal are not there within an hour from this time—it is just five—you must take the consequences. Weapons—pistols. Distance—ten paces. Good morning, sir."

"Stop, captain," cried Bullitt, following him as he walked off, "this is most irregular. There is no precedent for it. Two against one! You on the ground alone, and the other party with a friend! It will be murder."

"Murder, when I shoot your principal? You can take care of him. Doctor Frank, I dare say, will go with us if you ask him."

"With whom shall I consult—negotiate—arrange—I'm shocked. This proceeding is out of all rule. Two against one! It will never do."

"Well," said Baxter, "since you are shocked I will compromise the matter. You shall act as the friend of both parties."

"I don't understand that at all. That's irregular too. Can I arrange terms with myself? Can I agree with myself? Can I advise one party that he should be satisfied, and the other that he should not? Must I ask myself a question from one side, and answer it myself from the other? Can I"——

"Good morning, Mr. Bullitt. In forty minutes."

"Heavens! what shall I do? Such an irregular party! Must I abandon my pricipal and go half over to the other side? Stay, Captain Baxter," he cried, running after that irregular party, "Stay. This affair must go on some way. If it must be your way, I am not responsible. I protest, but under protest, I consent to act as the common friend of both principals."

7

" All right. Be quick."

" I'll bring my pistols. I always carry a beautiful pair."

" Very well. We'll choose between yours and mine."

When Bullitt made known the arrangement to Palmer, the latter was fluttered by the precipitancy of action, and objected to the part assigned to Bullitt, as neutralizing his second. On that ground he was inclined to break off the affair. But Bullitt declared that it could not be broken off without everlasting disgrace. It must go on, even in this irregular fashion. Being thus pressed, and having neither experience nor counsellor to guide him to a loop-hole of retreat, Palmer ceased to object. When the pistols had been procured, he walked to the appointed field, escorted by his second—or half-second—and attended by Doctor Frank, with a very alarming case of instruments under his arm. When they reached the ground Baxter was there, lying asleep on the grass. After waking him, Bullitt selected the pistols, chose the ground and measured the distance. With a comical air of perplexity he tossed up with himself for the choice of position, and arranged with himself all the preliminaries in the most formal manner. He was repeatedly embarrassed by his neutral or equivocal relation to the parties. After placing them in position, and giving them their weapons, he paused and gravely addressed them.

" Gentlemen, I must now formally protest in presence of you both, as I have protested to you severally, that the mode of proceeding adopted on this occasion is entirely irregular. I have acceded to it only from necessity. I will not be responsible for the consequences, and I protest that this case shall never be drawn into precedent with my consent."

When he gave the word, the combatants fired almost simultaneously. They both remained standing after the exchange of shots. Bullitt, looking first at one, and then at the other, from his post, which was equi-distant from them, was again perplexed. He deemed it his duty to approach his principal, but which principal first? One reason came into his head for rendering his first attention to Palmer, but another reason immediately claimed that preference for Baxter. He started towards the latter, but halted and turned towards the former. After one or two more such zigzags, he threw up his hands in despair, and darted at Baxter.

"Are you hurt, Captain Baxter?" he cried.

"No," said Baxter, quietly, "neither of us is hurt. I raised the dust from his pants, but my ball struck the ground ten feet beyond him. His ball struck that weed about a yard from me. I saw it shake."

Bullitt went to Palmer, who, though not very courageous, had pride enough to carry him thus far through the scene with a fair show of firmness. Having ascertained that he was not hurt, the impartial second retired a few paces to consult with himself as to the proper step for him next to take. While he pondered, he was reloading the weapons. Suddenly he was startled by a cry from Palmer—"a constable, a constable." Repeating these words, Palmer started from his post, walking rapidly. "Stop," said Bullitt, "there is no constable about here!" But Palmer quickened his pace to a run, while the second shouted after him frantically—"stop, come back, fool, coward, poltroon, come back, I say." But faster and faster the fugitive ran, until he disappeared in a wood.

"Why, it's Hugh Fitzhugh," said Baxter, pointing at a man who was approaching them, and who had been seen first by Palmer. Some duty had brought Captain Fitzhugh near enough to the spot to hear the sound of the pistols, and thinking it was some alarm or irregularity of pickets, he hastened in the direction of the sound to learn the cause. As he came forward, Bullitt said—"Captain Baxter, I am deeply mortified at the conduct of my first principal. But, of course, I take his place now. With that view you will excuse me, I am sure, for resuming entire my original relation as his second. I trust, sir," he continued, addressing Captain Fitzhugh, "although I have not the honor of your acquaintance, you will oblige us by performing for Captain Baxter and myself the part which I had undertaken to perform for him and Captain Palmer. It is very irregular, I admit, but necessity may excuse it. Captain Baxter, does this meet your approbation?"

"What does all this mean?" inquired Fitzhugh.

"I'll tell you," responded Baxter; "this gentleman —Mr. Bullitt, Captain Fitzhugh—desires to exchange shots with me and I have no objection. You will stand by and see fair play."

"I'll do no such thing. This folly must stop here."

"Of course," said Bullitt, "such an affair must come to an untimely end when a third party steps in to interfere with it. But I protest "——

"Never mind your protest," interrupted Baxter, "let's go to breakfast."

"Now," said Fitzhugh, after he had, by inquiring of Baxter, learned some particulars of the affair, "let us agree to say nothing of Palmer's conduct. It

would injure him and do no good. He is new to
such things."

"O, he has carried the matter to camp in his heels,"
replied Baxter, "but I shall say nothing about it."

"I am not sure what I shall do about this affair,"
said Bullitt, testily; "the whole business has been so
irregular that I don't know whether I shall allow any
gentleman to allude to it in my presence without giving me satisfaction. I must look up the authorities
before I commit myself."

The three walked together towards the camp, and
after going some distance, Baxter exclaimed—"the
surgeon! we have forgotten the doctor." He had sat
in the clump of trees during the proceedings. Turning back, they saw him marching along behind them
and looking very surly. They waited for him, and as
he approached, they heard him growling and cursing.
"Humbug," he grunted, "humbug—no need of a
surgeon for this party "—with an appendix of oaths.
They spoke to him and endeavored to apologize for
leaving him, but he gave neither heed nor reply.
He marched past, muttering the same contemptuous
oaths.

Palmer did not halt until he found himself five or
six miles from the camp. Then he sat down upon a
log and held a council in his own bosom. He reflected that the failure of his matrimonial project had
cut the principal tie which bound him to the Southern
cause, and now if he returned to the army, he thought
he must encounter disgrace on account of this morning's proceedings. His commission and his character
were gone. He began to recall the obligations of
birth and to speculate upon the chances of improving
his condition by transferring himself to the North.
Upon this theme he sat musing a long time.

CHAPTER XIV.

ROEBUCK AFTER MANASSA.

FROM various causes the camp at Manassa proved
to be unfavorable to the recovery of the sick and
wounded.   In two or three days after the battle,
Doctor Fairfax became satisfied that if he remained
there his wound, already showing unpleasant symp-
toms, would be slow to heal, and he decided to return
home for a time.   Not being an enlisted soldier, he
obtained permission without difficulty.   In the meantime he had been almost constantly with Captain Tremaine.   Sympathy and respect rapidly ripened into
friendship for that gallant and unfortunate gentleman.
The doctor became so warmly interested in his recovery that he desired to take him to his own house,
where he might have the benefit of such nursing and
care as a camp could not afford.   When he invited the
captain to accompany him the wounded prisoner was
very grateful.   Through the exertions of Doctor Fairfax and Captain Fitzhugh, the consent of the proper
authorities was obtained.   The prisoner's condition
was very critical, but as the journey was to be almost
entirely by railway, it was hoped that he would be
but little injured by removal, under the judicious care
of the doctor.   Being among strangers, the wounded
man naturally found some comfort in the society of a
person from his own country and of his own political
sentiments.   He had, therefore, taken some pleasure
in the presence of Campbell, and, perhaps at the sug-

gestion of that modest gentleman, he expressed, with apparent hesitation, a desire that his Northern country-man should accompany him, if that should be found practicable and was agreeable to Doctor Fairfax. The doctor was not averse to the arrangement. His inter-est in "Bombyx," as a study, was not diminished by their intercourse, and he was willing to be amused at home by this curious specimen. Besides, he desired to oblige Captain Tremaine in every way. Camp-bell had already been informed that, as a civilian and a mere spectator of the battle, he would not be treated as a prisoner of war, but that, for military reasons, it was deemed necessary to detain him for a short time within the Confederate lines. It was finally arranged that both Tremaine and Campbell, giving suitable paroles, should accompany Doctor Fairfax. The doc-tor notified his brother that, being slightly wounded, he was about to return home with two wounded friends, and he requested that his own house might be prepared for them.

This was the first information received at Roebuck how Doctor Dick had fared in the battle. The coun-try had been informed with telegraphic brevity that the South had gained a splendid victory at Manassa, but with severe loss in killed and wounded. Then the wires conveyed the names of generals and afterwards of other officers who had fallen. Next came an esti-mate of the Confederate loss, studiously moderate, but frightful to those who had kindred in the army. Slowly a few telegrams followed from survivors to their families. But for several days nothing was known throughout the country of the fate of thou-sands of the best and bravest of the land, who had been exposed to the peril of a bloody battle. The

announcement of victory had thrilled the Southern
people with joy and exultation. Success so decisive
in the first great battle of the war was generally
accepted as decisive of the entire contest. Independence was regarded as secure. That sentiment of
security, with the subsequent inaction of the army, was
very detrimental to the Confederate cause. The first
year of the war, when the native courage and fresh
enthusiasm of the Southern troops made them irresistible on an equal field, was almost thrown away,
and the time thus lost could never be recovered. But
after the first exultant echo of triumph came the wail
of a people for the loved ones who had purchased the
victory with their blood. There was agony, borne
with patriotic fortitude, but it was agony.

The family at Roebuck were relieved of painful
anxiety when they learned that Doctor Fairfax was
returning home, only slightly wounded. Preparations
were made to receive him and his two friends, who
were supposed to be Confederate soldiers. It was decided that a bachelor's establishment was not a fit
place for wounded patriots, and that the comforts of
Roebuck and the tender care of women would be
absolutely necessary. When the train, which was expected to bring the doctor and his friends, arrived,
Colonel Fred was at the station. Captain Tremaine
was borne from the train on a cot, preceded by Doctor
Fairfax, on crutches, and followed by Campbell, limp-
ing on a cane.

"Welcome, brother Dick," exclaimed the colonel,
"welcome home; are these your friends? Welcome,
gentlemen; bring them along, Dick; here is the
carriage; here's a spring wagon with a bed on it, in
case any of you need it; let me help to carry your

friend; come along; you are all going to Roebuck; the ladies are waiting for you; not a word; three wounded gentlemen to be laid up in a bachelor's barracks! preposterous! it is all settled; come on."

"But, brother Fred," repeated the doctor, several times, while the colonel was delivering this speech with great animation; "but, brother Fred," and he plucked the colonel's sleeve, and attempted to draw him aside, for the prospect of carrying Campbell to be domiciled with the family at Roebuck horrified him; "but, brother Fred," he finally exclaimed, "they are Yankees."

"Yankees, Dick! Good God! Have you brought a brace of Yankees here? You!"

Now, the colonel was a kind-hearted man. He had been opposed to secession and war. He had not cherished that animosity against the Northern people which his brother proclaimed. But war engendered bitter hatred in the mildest tempers. Atrocities wantonly inflicted, as he believed, with the sanction of the highest Federal authorities, provoked in his bosom antipathy that was deep, stern and almost implacable. His general indignation against the North naturally tinged his feeling towards all individuals who were known to him only as abettors of the North in the war. Of all men his brother was the last whom he would have expected to find in charitable charge of such malignant enemies. The colonel had not been a soldier, and, therefore, had not felt the charities of the battle-field when the battle is over. "You!"

Doctor Dick, caught in an inconsistency, reddened and stammered. He attempted to explain. But the colonel happened to look at the face of Captain Tremaine. That prostrate and helpless gentleman, suf-

7*

fering physical agony, seemed even more distressed
by the scene which he then witnessed between the
two brothers. He understood enough of it to make
him feel that he was the occasion of embarrassment
and pain to his friend, the doctor. His eyes turned
from one brother to the other with an expression of
anguish. When the colonel looked at him, compassion took the place of anger. He bent over the captain, gently took his hand, and in the kindest voice
expressed sympathy and welcome. With his habitual
promptitude he called assistance, placed the wounded
officer on the bed, made every possible provision for •
his ease and comfort, and rode on horseback beside
the wagon, to see that the "Yankee" should receive
no injury. The doctor and Campbell followed in the
the carriage to Roebuck.

When they arrived there, about sunset, of course
Doctor Dick had an affectionate welcome. The ladies,
without investigating the nationality of the other gentlemen, received them kindly, and offered to the
wounded captain such sympathetic words and tender
offices as his condition suggested. He was carried
into a large, convenient chamber, handsomely furnished, and laid upon a bed that needed not a wound,
a journey, or contrast with a camp-cot to make it
seem luxurious. A physician of eminence was sent
for, and in the course of the evening, his skill, with
the ministrations of the family, soothed the patient's
suffering and inspired him with the hope of life and
health. At his request, a bed was placed in his chamber for his countryman, Campbell.

When those guests had been disposed of for the
night, and the wound of Doctor Fairfax had been
dressed—a wound which Mrs. Fairfax pronounced to

be alarming, and which the physician thought would require repose and care—that disabled soldier lay upon a sofa, like a warrior taking his rest, but ready, as usual, to talk.

"Now, Colonel Julia," he said, "come and kiss me, like a good girl, and then, like a colonel, you shall talk to me about war. I know you are dying to hear all I have to tell about the great battle and victory, and especially, about my own martial exploits. I believe now, my fair Desdemona, I might win your love, if I wanted it, like Othello, by bragging."

"You can never win my love, Uncle Dick."

"Why, Miss, tell me why, you saucy"——

"Because you have had it ever so long."

"Fudge! But, speaking of love, what have you done to bewitch that feather-brained fellow, Hugh Fitzhugh?"

"I am not a witch, uncle, and Captain Fitzhugh is not feather-brained, I believe," replied Julia, smiling and blushing.

"Well, he is a sad fellow; we'll not talk of him."

"But you must not disparage my friends in their absence."

"O, he's a friend of yours? Then I shall not slander him—much."

"Fie! Be serious—now do—and tell us about the battle."

The story of Manassa, as then told by the doctor to his brother and the two ladies, had for them the fascination of novelty, of tragedy and triumph. They were not yet familiar with the awful scenes of a long and sanguinary contest. To them that battle, with its victory, seemed enough of carnage and of glory for an entire war. To the ladies particularly, it appeared that the end of the war was achieved. The story filled their imaginations, like a noble history already complete. When the doctor had described the events of chief importance, he began to entertain them with anecdotes of personal adventure. One of them related to some of the personages of this narrative. .

· "There is Captain Fitzhugh, now—your friend, Colonel Julia—he has the name of being a brave man —I shall say nothing against your friend on that score—but, like the rest of us, he is a raw soldier and may blunder into scrapes—and he rides a fleet horse— that I know; the Yankees know it too, for they have seen his heels."

Having said so much, with significant looks and tones, he paused and fixed his eyes on Julia, as if expecting her to invite an explanation of his hints. But some maidenly coyness or consciousness sealed her sweet lips, and sent a blush to her beautiful cheeks. Mrs. Fairfax had no such feeling to restrain the curiosity which belongs to her sex—and to the haughtier sex.

"Go on," she said, "tell us what you have to tell about Hugh."

"Well, Hugh is a warrior, who, by the diligent study of his profession, has discovered that the whole art of war is neatly packed away in a few words of an old Greek poet, or in two lines of modern parody—

'He that fights, and runs away,
May live to fight another day.'

On one occasion, however, he would have preferred, I believe, to omit the preliminary fight suggested by the poet before running."

"Uncle Dick, you shall not"——

"What?"

"Come," said the colonel, laughing, "you shall not tease the ladies with your scandalous hints. Tell your tale like a man."

"Well, if I must, I must. But you shall not blame me, Julia, if the story does not please you. Once upon a time, then—it was a few days before the battle —Captain Fitzhugh was sent to spy out—you would say to reconnoitre, Colonel Julia—a position of the enemy. About sunrise he went some two miles in advance of his company, to a hill from which he expected to obtain a near and clear view of the position. He took with him only two men. One of them was Mark Marlin, the young man, Julia, who has taken your gentlemanly father for his model. It is not necessary to name the other man. They were all well mounted. The men, perhaps, were selected with a view to the fleetness of their horses, according to the fundamental flying principle of the captain. Hugh rode his famous black, Sultan. Mark was on the horse you gave him, brother Fred."

"Sold to him."

"Well, the other soldier had a swifter nag than either of them, as the result showed. When they arrived at the hill, it was so densely wooded that the captain deemed it necessary to descend alone to an open bench or little plateau, from which he could plainly see the whole batch of Yankees on the opposite side of a small stream. He was as clearly seen himself by the hostile pickets along the margin of the stream, and he stood within easy range of their guns. He remained there ten or fifteen minutes, while a dozen of the blue-coats were firing away at him, and how

he escaped injury I cannot imagine. Just as he returned to his two followers they had discovered a
squad of the enemy's cavalry, eight or ten in number,
making for the road by which they had come. To
return on that road was impossible. To remain was
out of the question. There was no way to get back
to the company but by scouring across open fields in
full view of the enemy, and trusting to luck and
speed. So we—so the captain led off, commanding
the two men to follow, or to make their way back as
they should find it necessary. He was able to keep
ahead of Mark, but the other grey-back distanced
them both. They were soon discovered by the Yankee squad, who immediately attempted to intercept
them. They succeeded in cutting off Marlin, and
bringing him to bay. The brave boy drew his sabre,
and endeavored to cut his way through them. The
captain, looking back, saw his follower surrounded,
and fighting furiously. Wheeling his horse, Hugh
dashed at the Yankees, and began to lay about him
with such vigor that their attention was withdrawn
from Mark to the officer, and there was momentary
confusion among them. Seeing that Marlin was ex-
tricated by the movement, his captain called out—
'fly, Mark, fly—fly, I command you.' The soldier,
with the instinct of military obedience, fled at the
word of command, although, until it was repeated
with peremptory vehemence, he hesitated to leave his
officer. The Feds did not follow him, but tried to
close in upon the captain. By the dexterous management of his horse and sword, or by marvellous fortune, he kept his life among them until he thought
Mark had a sufficient start. Then throwing his body
forward to the neck of his horse, and plunging the

spurs into Sultan's sides, he was carried at a leap between uplifted sabres clear of the Federals. They
pursued, firing their pistols. Only a few hundred
yards in advance, there was a fence over which Hugh
and Mark were carried by their horses without halting. But none of the pursuers ventured the leap.
Thus they lost time which was well employed by the
flying grey-backs. When they had crossed one or two
more fences, that fortunately crossed their line of retreat, the blue-coats were out of sight, and they were
never seen again. Hugh says that in the fray, Mark
emptied one saddle; and Mark, more liberal in his
commendation, avers that his captain cut down two
of the Yankees. It is a pity that these witnesses are
not quite impartial, and that the other grey-back, who
sneers at their testimony, had not remained near
enough to the scene of action to correct their reports.
But he had regained the company, and spread won-
drous rumors long before the captain's return."

"Who was he?" inquired Julia.

"It is none of your business, niece of mine."

"Thou art the man, I verily believe, Uncle Dick."

"Never say that, again! Don't slander your
uncle."

"Brother Dick," said Mrs. Fairfax, "who or what
is this Mr. Campbell, you have brought home with
you?"

"A genuine Yankee, my gentle sister, if there can
be a genuine counterfeit."

"Uncle Dick, you have told us that Captain Tremaine is a true man."

"One swallow don't make a summer, Miss Julia.
As for Campbell, when I first saw him, I thought he
had a good face, but upon examining it, I found it

was only a Yankee imitation of a good face--made,
like other Yankee goods, to impose upon customers at
first sight, but not to wear well.   In every feature there
was some cunning defect.   I might suspect that, like
Richard, he was cheated of feature by dissembling nature; but at cheating, a Yankee would beat nature.
When I conversed with him—O, what a rare bird! I
thought I would have some sport with him at home,
but really, sister Mary, I am sorry he was brought
here."

"Never mind; he will help to cheer Captain Tremaine."

"I hope so; poor fellow! he is a gentleman.   Ah,
me!   But fellows like Campbell will write our history."

CHAPTER XV.

BOMBYX AT ROEBUCK.

CAPTAIN TREMAINE's condition for several days remained critical. At one time it was regarded as desperate. Two or three nights Colonel Fairfax sat by
his bedside all night, and the physician was kept in
the house. But when the crisis was past his convales-
cence was rapid. Although the Federal authorities
had adopted the inhuman policy of preventing the
importation of medicines into the Confederacy, the
most necessary remedies could still be supplied to a
Federal prisoner. The patient constantly received
the kindest attention from the family and from servants who had experience in nursing the sick. Doctor
Dick spent much time in his chamber, applying the
physician's instructions with professional intelligence,
and amusing the captain with quaint conversation,
relieved of all satirical asperity by sympathy and respect for this "Yankee." His own favorite servant,
Caleb, divided his attention between his master and
the wounded captain. The good clergyman, Mr.
Ambler, visited him often, and a cordial friendship was
established between them. Tremaine won the esteem
of all who approached him by the gentleness of his
manners, his patience in suffering, his gratitude for
kindness, and, in brief, by the honorable sentiments of
an educated soldier. In a few weeks his health was
so far restored that he might be removed with safety,
and a special exchange having been arranged for him

through the interest of friends, he left Roebuck for the North. His departure was sincerely regretted by the friends' he had made there, and he expressed the warmest gratitude for all their kindness. Taking leave of him for a time, we return to his compatriot, Campbell.

Although they found the manners and sentiments of that guest by no means agreeable, yet Colonel Fairfax and his family, studious of hospitality, endeavored in every way to promote his comfort and pleasure. The colonel placed a horse at his disposal to ride at will over the plantation and through the neighborhood. The host would have deemed it unworthy of himself to watch his movements or to suspect him of any baseness while his honor as a guest and as a prisoner on parole was pledged. The doctor, whose leg confined him to the house, played chess with him or indulged him with plenty of the talk which he loved. The war was, naturally, the most frequent theme of their conversation, for the sentiment of delicacy which excluded it from the conversations between Captain Tremaine and the family, did not restrain Bombyx, especially when he was alone with Doctor Dick. At first he was much embarrassed in the society of Roebuck. His assurance was abashed by the quiet, unassuming manners of gentlemen and ladies, who, in the familiarity of domestic life, practiced the refined gentleness to which they had been born. As he dared not affect superiority after his manner, he would have fallen into servility after his nature, if he had not been made to feel that the social law of the place was one of equality at a high level and that it was equally a transgression to cringe and to hector. He suspected that there was an odious air of aristocracy about Roebuck, but he missed the haughty arrogance which, in his fancy, was associated with the aristocracy of the South. When a few days had rendered him more familiar with the usages of the place he began to despise, as a weakness, the unobtrusive gentleness which he could never comprehend.

"Check!" cried the doctor, one day, "checkmate!"

"Yes," Campbell admitted, "I believe Johny Reb has the Yank this time."

"So may it ever be," replied Doctor Dick, laughing.

"Now, doctor, let us talk seriously about that a little while. I see a great many good servants here—faithful, stout, good-humored fellows—don't you think it would be better to set them all free?"

"And turn the best of servants into the worst of freemen?"

"O, give them time—they will improve after they are free."

"The world has waited several thousand years for the negro race to originate an idea. If we are to wait for their brains to bloom we may wait until the crack of doom, or until Yankees become honest."

"Doctor, you are a bundle of prejudices."

"Very likely. Prejudices are the ribs of character."

"You know we don't intend to injure the South."

"You would not injure the watch though you would crush the works!"

"But if we should emancipate the negroes we would certainly confer a benefit on both races—let me convince you of that."

"Answer Mr. Campbell, Caleb," said the doctor, to his favorite servant, who stood with a napkin on his arm, waiting for orders. Being commanded to speak, he made a profound bow to the guest and began :

"If I am allowed to suppress my cogitation on this memorable occasion, human nature teaches me that white folks that I have never seen would not come a thousand miles just to fight for my good."

"There it is, Mr. Campbell," said the doctor, "go on and plant your oranges in icebergs."

"But you would like to be free, Caleb?"

"That's as might be according to the circumnavigation of circumstances. I do not see many white folks as free as I am, no offence to you, master, as being our prisoner. Them other free niggers, as I reprehend by my circumlocution, they are lazy beggars and thieves. They are the contemptible, black coffee-grounds of society left after the second b'iling."

"That will do Caleb; Mr. Campbell has your opinion."

"Well, doctor, however we may differ about slavery, it is astonishing that you Southerners make war against so good a government as ours."

"We make war! The South attempted peacable secession—the North attempted to prevent secession by force. The North made war."

"But no State has a right to secede."

"Then the Federal government is absolute."

"Oh, no, doctor, it is a free government."

"Under a free government the rights of all should be protected with even-handed justice. Protection should be meted to all in equal measure and with the quality of manna—he that gathered much had nothing over, and he that gathered little had no lack. The

Federal government enriches the North at the expense of the South, and when we would escape from
legalized rapacity, we are told that we are bound forever. When the forms of law to which we assented
cannot hold us, the sword is illegally drawn to subjugate our States. Is this a free government for us?
But I did not intend to be drawn into an angry discussion. It can do no good. It is better to laugh aside
subjects that irritate when we cannot be convinced."

"No, no, doctor, I am not angry. I am sure I can
convince you if you give me time. Think of the
greatness of the government you are giving up. If
we remain united we can defy the world."

"If you worship power, you should offer your incense to the Prince of Darkness. His dominion is
not confined to the United States."

"Well, doctor, if you won't discuss the matter seriously, you must not think hard of us for preserving
the life of the nation at all hazards."

"Which nation—North or South? You would take
the life of the South, in order that the North may live
at ease."

"One nation, embracing North and South, East and
West—a great, free, enlightened nation. We must
preserve its life. We regret the desolation which the
war must bring upon the South, but we owe a duty
to posterity and to mankind. We must preserve the
life of the nation. We are resolved to preserve it
with our blood."

"I thought so at Manassa—in the morning. It was
not so clear at night."

"We failed once. But we shall succeed in the end.
A just cause must succeed."

"You have a surer ground for confidence, perhaps,
than the justice of your cause. I wish you had not."

"What is that, pray?"

"The fact that the just cause is seldom successful in war. The Reverend Mr. Ambler thinks this is because Providence would admonish good men to avoid war by teaching them that if a righteous cause cannot be upheld by reason, it cannot be enforced with the sword. I only see that, as a rule, the big dog whips the little one, and that dogs are usually insolent and unjust in proportion to their size."

"Do you not believe that Providence awards victory in accordance with justice?"

"Kyd, the pirate, had victories. England conquered India. We have exterminated the American Indians. Victors have dined on minced missionary. Brutus died for liberty, and Cesar had the empire. Napoleon was the genius of victory—was he a man after God's own heart? Did Providence change sides at Waterloo? We must not turn Pagans."

"At all events, you will see the amazing energy of our government displayed in suppressing the rebellion."

"A government, in ceasing to be free, may display terrific energy, like a steam-boiler in exploding."

"But our government does not cease to be free."

"Has not the habeas corpus been suspended by a Presidential edict—the chief justice flouted by a military officer—newspapers suppressed—legislatures broken up—citizens imprisoned—laws defied? Your government cannot subjugate the South without first enslaving the North."

"We shall return to the bulwarks of liberty after suppressing the rebellion."

"*Nulla vestigia retrorsum.*"

"Let us have another game of chess, doctor."

Mr. Campbell was not satisfied that the luminous opinion delivered by Caleb correctly represented public sentiment in the African branch of Southern society. His professional curiosity pricked him to pry into the thoughts and feelings of the slaves. He deemed it his duty also to enlighten them on the great question of their own destiny, if he found them benighted like Caleb. His philanthropy was as meddlesome and egotistical as his curiosity. Being troubled with no scruples of honesty or honor, and having set up a Deity in his own image, he persuaded himself that he would be doing God service in sowing dissension between his host and his servants by exciting delusive aspirations in the minds of the credulous negroes. Before he had been long at Roebuck he conceived the ambitious and atrocious design of serving the Northern cause by fomenting a servile insurrection. Under the influence of those motives he sought opportunities to converse with the slaves at Roebuck and on other estates. As he rode about at his pleasure, he found such opportunities without difficulty. Being conscious, however, of an illicit and odious purpose, he avoided observation, and gave to his intercourse with the servants a clandestine character. He supposed it was quite unknown to the persons whose hospitality he enjoyed. His interviews with some of the negroes who have become known to the reader may be briefly described.

He found old Valentine sunning himself one morning before his cabin, and after some questions about his health, age and recollections, inquired if the old man knew that the negroes would all soon be set free.

"Den God help us, poor niggers," ejaculated

Valentine. "What will become of us if we lose our masters? Who will take keer of old fellers like me?"

"But your children and grandchildren—think of their good."

"Dey's mighty well off, master. We's all niggers, and we wants white folks to take keer of us. We ain't got no sense to take care of ourselves. God help us if dey sets us free."

Mr. Campbell passed on, attributing these craven and servile sentiments to senility which he could not enlighten. Again, he was riding past a shop in which a likely young fellow was at work.

"How are you, my man;" he said, "what is your name?"

"Bob, sir; dey calls me carpenter Bob, for short."

"What pay do you get, Robert, for the work you are doing?"

"Pay, master? I belongs to Colonel Fred."

"Does he pay you nothing for your work?"

"What for would he pay me when I belongs to him?"

"He ought to pay you, I think."

"What make?"

"Because no man ought to labor for nothing."

"I don't work for nothin'. I gits as much as I wants off'n dis big plantation. I don't pay master nothin' for tendin' to it."

"If you were free you could go North, and get good wages as a mechanic."

"Would I have a big plantation, like dis one, to live on?"

"Perhaps not; but you don't own this one."

"It sarves me mighty well. I ain't agwine to leave it, sartin sure, sir."

When Campbell fell in with Joe, he thought that head-man more intelligent than Bob, until he touched his favorite theme. Joe denounced the idea of separating himself from his master as basely disloyal.

"Why," he said, "my folks has belonged to de Fairfaxes since de very first man. We's all Fairfaxes. We's always been Fairfaxes. We's always agwine to be Fairfaxes. What would Master Fred do widout Joe? I toated him and played wid him when he was a boy. I was wid him when he was at de University. I went a courtin' wid him. I's bin his 'pendence all his life. My children's bin wid his children. We's jis like brothers, only he's white and I's black; and he's master and I's sarvant, dat's all de difference 'twixt Master Fred and old Joe."

"Well, Joe, I was only trying you. I see you are faithful. You need not say anything about this conversation."

"No, master, only to Master Fred. We tells one another everything."

Campbell encountered Juba dodging about, and found that this broad-shouldered, bullet-headed, belligerent brother, by dint of meditation in the woods, had solved the question of the negro's destiny in a different fashion. He listened to a long harangue of Campbell in silence, fixing his eyes upon a fence-post with that look of profound imbecility and unobservant attention which none but a negro can give, and then, without shifting the conspicuous whites of his eyes, he propounded his conclusion:

"It seems to me as ef dis was a white man's fight over de nigger. All de nigger is got to do wid it is to lay in de bush till de white folks is done fou't it out. Den, which whips, de nigger he comes out'n de

8

bush and takes his shoer.' 'Ef de Rebels whips, den we
gits our corn and bacon, jis so. Ef de Yankees whips,
den dey gives de land to de niggers, and de nigger
what stays here, he gits de first slice. I stays here."

Campbell found by his African explorations, that
either from affection or apathy or stupidity or timidity, or from obscure motives which they could not
explain, the negroes generally were at that time inclined to remain with their owners, or, at least, were
not inclined to make any adventurous effort to change
their condition. In a few cases, however, the teaching of the philanthropist took root in the minds of the
slaves and bore fruit after the kind, not precisely of
the doctrine but of the negro. When Campbell had
been for some time delving in this mine of black dia-
monds, his work was suddenly interrupted. Colonel
Fairfax had, of course, become aware of his frequent
interviews with his own slaves and others, but attributed them to the natural curiosity of a stranger or
the professional curiosity of Bombyx. He did not
suspect him of abusing the privileges of hospitality for
unworthy purposes. He casually remarked to his
guest—" I see, Mr. Campbell, you have been amusing
yourself with talking to the servants on the plantation."

" Never, colonel—you must not believe the tales of
the negroes."

" What!" exclaimed the colonel, with surprise,
" do I understand you to deny that you have conversed with the negroes."

" Never, except with the servants who came to our
chamber."

" Mr. Campbell, I was not complaining of your conduct. I said nothing about tales of the negroes. But
you surprise me."

"Do you suspect me of falsehood, Colonel Fairfax?"

"I suspect nothing, Mr. Campbell. I know." The colonel's manner expressed his scorn of falsehood.

"Since I find myself an object of suspicion under your roof, sir, I had better relieve your house of my presence."

"You will use your own pleasure, sir."

Mr. Campbell, without unnecessary delay, took up his quarters at the Swan tavern. The change had become desirable to him, for it relieved him of some obstacles to the prosecution of his main design. He had been wishing to escape from the restraints of Roebuck, when the accidental altercation with Colonel Fairfax, and that gentleman's indignation at his falsehood, opened the door.

CHAPTER XVI.

A FEW days after Campbell established himself at the Swan tavern a rumor began to be whispered through the neighborhood that the negroes were plotting an insurrection. It was vague and without a known origin. It gathered circumstances as it flew, and suspicion supplied the defects of testimony. Until then the slaves, where the invasion had not penetrated, were quiet, submissive, and remarkably attentive to their duties. Few attempted to escape, and none to rebel. The war, and the general arming of the dominant race impressed them with awe. But experience had not yet proved what effect upon their inflammable passions might be produced by the progress of a vast conflict, waged, as they understood, by the North for their deliverance. While it was believed that servile insurrection was one of the agencies by which the North expected to subjugate the South, a rumor of commotion among the slaves might readily cause anxiety. It was soon reported that there had been midnight meetings of negroes—that there had been secret intercourse between Campbell, Palmer and blind Pete—that Pete was more active than ever in his clandestine dealings with slaves by night. Suspicion fell upon Campbell because he was a "Yankee;" it was promoted by a circumstantial story of his dismissal from Roebuck because he had tampered with servants; it was confirmed by exaggerated accounts

told by some of the negroes of his conversations with
them. Palmer's nativity, reserved habits and equivocal conduct had lost him the confidence of his neighbors, and his position was further compromised by a
report that his son had deserted and gone over to the
enemy. These various rumors and suspicions produced uneasiness, which rapidly swelled into popular
agitation.

In fact, the ingenuity of Mr. Palmer was constantly
exercised by his plans for making the war subservient
to his interest and revenge, and by the embarrassments which must beset a secret adherent of the
North, who, in a Southern community, ostensibly
though faintly supported the Southern cause. When
blind Pete visited him, as well in pursuance of his
own invitation as of the stipulation exacted by Baxter
at a rope's end, a negotiation took place in which the
trained intelligence of the retired merchant outwitted
the purblind cunning of the vulgar knave. Pete was
led to reveal, not only the whole transaction of the
sugar-tongs, but the apprehension which he felt that
the Northern stranger would be less indulgent than
the good-natured Southerners, who so often winked
at his pilfering in compassion for his blindness. By
playing upon this fear and by a liberal bribe, Palmer
enlisted Pete in his secret service. He thus established
an espionage upon the families of his neighbors and an
agency which might be turned to account in the prosecution of schemes yet unhatched. Through this
channel he was informed of Campbell's position at
Roebuck and was enabled to estimate his character.
He wished to open communication with him, but was
too cautious to attempt it until the guest had removed
from Roebuck to the tavern. Soon after that event

he commissioned Pete to convey a private intimation
to Campbell that Mr. Palmer desired to consult him
confidentially, and would be pleased to receive a visit
from him at his own house by night. The invitation
was accepted, and thus at a late hour one night those
two natives of the North were sitting in Mr. Palmer's
parlor, with the doors locked and the window-shut-
ters closed.

"I have now intrusted you," Mr. Palmer was saying, "with a candid exposition of my real sentiments
respecting the rebellion, and of the urgent reasons for
disguising them at present. May I rely upon your
friendship to make this explanation in the proper
quarters when you return to the North? I hope my
conduct and motives will be kindly appreciated there.
If the forces of the Union should hereafter reach this
part of Virginia, as of course they will, it may be desirable that the commander shall be informed of my
views, but you will perceive that, for the benefit of
our cause, it may even then be prudent for him to retain the knowledge in his own breast."

"I understand you, I believe," responded Campbell,
drily.

"Then there is a report current that my son Albert,
who was a quarter-master in the State service for a
short time, has resigned his office, and visited the
Union lines. You may meet him at the North, and,
I believe, you will find that he is as loyal as I am.
Possibly he will desire to enter the Federal service.
If you can promote his plans in any way, you will
oblige me by doing so, and will render service, no
doubt, to the cause."

"I understand you."

"Then may I count upon your friendly offices?"

"That question, Mr. Palmer, must be answered with solemn reference to my paramount duty as a loyal citizen of the United States. When you solicit the favor of our benign government it appears to me that you may reasonably be required to give some tangible proof of your loyalty. This is a most wicked rebellion, and neutrality is a great offence."

"What can I do here and now for the Union?"

"Much. You have a glorious field for usefulness in your situation. The confidence reposed in you by your rebel neighbors, under the belief that you sympathize with them, will enable you to operate effectively, secretly and safely. You have a glorious opportunity."

"I do not understand you."

"There is in the South a population of four millions who should be loyal supporters of the Union cause. They require only to be stimulated and guided. Why are they not summoned to the aid of those arms which are to strike from their limbs the manacles of bondage? They are within the rebel camp. They sleep in the citadel. They could grasp the keys. They can disband Southern armies, by destroying Southern homes. If they have not guns, there is the knife and the torch. Many of them are around you. With them you can serve the Union."

"Would you resort to servile insurrection—to universal massacre—to the assassination of families—to the violation of women—to the murder of innocent children—to"——

"Enough, Mr. Palmer. In a word, all means are lawful to suppress this unprovoked, this wicked, this atrocious rebellion against the best government the world ever saw. It is a rebellion of slave-holders. It

is fit that we cry havoc, and let slip the slaves. If
they are savage, let those who have made them savage
by oppression pay the penalty."

"Mr. Campbell, you chill my blood with horror."

"Then, sir, your loyalty is hypocrisy."

"Why, the Federal government has solemnly declared that the war is not waged to interfere with the
institution of slavery."

"Politic words! Words! The government ad-
vances before the swelling breeze of popular feeling.
Hostility to slavery is the master passion of the
Northern heart. This was the prime cause of the war.
By inexorable logic the abolition of slavery must be a
consequence of the war. The government must intend the necessary result of its own action. They are
blind who do not foresee the end. The North sees
it and therefore sustains the war. Press and pulpit,
by turns masters or slaves of opinion, are furiously
hostile to slavery and slave-holders. A servile insurrection would be hailed there with more enthusiasm
than ever was the name of John Brown. Be not deluded by politic professions of the government. Chiefs
of administration are known to believe that the name
of John Brown has become historical as a martyr in
the cause of human nature. Whoever most resem-
bles him is most faithful to the instincts of this war."

"Old John Brown! It cannot be true that a
Christian government approves his desperate character and diabolical design."

"All good Christians at the North revere him as a
martyr."

"But he was hung," said Palmer, not pleased with
the precedent.

"What, then? He is canonized. If you would be

a saint, be a man. Defy the slave power. Stir up
the slaves. Recognize your mission."

"You are mistaken in your estimate of the negroes.
We who have lived long among them know them
better. They are inert and cowardly. The love of
liberty is not in them, as in the white race, an aspiring and unconquerable passion, but a languid love of
ease. They failed John Brown."

"But then they were not encouraged by a powerful government and an invincible army."

"Perhaps the recent event at Manassa may not encourage them."

"Mr. Palmer, are you loyal or disloyal to the
Union?"

"Loyal, Mr. Campbell, loyal to the core. I have
humbly ventured to suggest difficulties which occurred to my mind. But if there is really anything
that I can do for the Union cause, I am ready to do
it."

"On no other condition will I consent to represent
you as a loyal citizen, or to interest myself in the fortunes of your son."

Pressed by such considerations, Palmer finally consented to lend himself to a scheme which he believed
to be dangerous to himself, impracticable and atrocious. He compromised with his conscience and his
prudence by resolving that he would do no more than
might be absolutely necessary to satisfy Campbell,
and by assuring himself that the project could have
no important result. He promised to ascertain the
temper of the negroes, and report to Campbell. That
gentleman, returning to his room in the tavern, rumi-
nated coming events which would immortalize his
name, and furnish material for several telling letters

8*

to the "Comet." Already his brain began to flame
with the composition of amazing paragraphs, and daz-
zling rows of capitals danced before his mind's eye,
like rustling banners of triumph.

Mr. Palmer sought an early opportunity to signify
to blind Pete, with cautious circumlocution, that he
desired to learn whether any of the slaves were
ambitious to become free, and what exertions they
were inclined to make, or what risks they were prepared to run for that object. He wished to leave that
blind rogue in doubt whether the inquiry was intended
in the interest of the North or of the South—of slave-
holders or of abolitionists. But Pete was astute
enough to resolve that doubt by laying together
various circumstances which had come to his knowledge. He insinuated his conviction of the truth, and
declared that the service in which Mr. Palmer proposed to employ him would be attended with extreme
danger to himself. By insisting upon his real or
affected fear, he extorted a larger bribe than he had
ever before ventured to demand. As Mr. Palmer was
also called upon to supply the necessities of Mr. Campbell, his purse was now subject to a double drain in
consequence of his loyalty. Moreover he was kept in
an agony of apprehension. He had little confidence
in the negroes, and less in Pete. He dreaded every
moment that his perilous plot might explode to his
own ruin.

He had sold all his slaves except two men and the
wife and children of one of them. This one was a
dull, stupid fellow, named Gabe, who was retained
because his master was obliged to keep at least one
man-servant, and thought this doltish creature would
not run away. The other man, whose name was

Mike, was a shrewd, restless, unmanageable negro.
He had been "in the bush" for several months.
During his absence his family had been sold and sent.
Southward. He resented this transaction, as well as
the sharp discipline to which he had submitted before
he took to the woods. He expected, if he should be
caught, to be sold also and sent to the Cotton States.
To avoid this fate, Mike conceived a plan of escaping
into the Federal lines with such of the neighboring
negroes as he could induce to join him. With their
aid he desired, before leaving the country, to procure
money, and, perhaps, to gratify his resentment. He
was hatching this project while his master was med-
dling with a more atrocious plot. Mike was tampering with blind Pete to further his own scheme,
while Pete was tampering with him in pursuance of
his engagement with Mr. Palmer. Mike sought an
interview with Campbell, and affecting to adopt his
views, obtained such information and assistance as he
thought necessary to his own plan. He was quite too
shrewd to believe in the success of a servile insurrection. He and two or three other negroes who were
conspiring with him or with Pete or with Campbell—
they scarcely knew with whom or for what—obtained
some fire-arms through Pete's illicit traffic. They
had an old musket, two shot-guns, with broken locks,
and a pistol. Mike supposed that these weapons
might be useful in perpetrating a robbery or in taking
vengeance on an obnoxious master, or in defending
the fugitives on their route of escape.

·The black chiefs of the conspiracy held a council.
They sat in an old tobacco-barn, near the edge of a
- wood, remote from any habitation. The time was
midnight, and the moon had just risen. The barn

had long been disused and had fallen into decay. It was built of round logs with the bark on them. The roof was of clap-boards. The bark was hanging in black flakes from the logs, and the roof was all gone, except a few of the rafters which sprawled like spiders' legs in the moonlight overhead. The door had been carried away, and the frame in which it had stood, being rotten, ceased to uphold the ends of the logs, and these, swaying downward, left a wide, ragged hole in the side of the barn. The assemblage within, mottled with patches of moonlight and of shadow, numbered four persons. They were squatted upon the ground. Mike presided on a flat stone. The other three were two slaves of Mr. Eckles, named Jake and Cato, and a slave of Mrs. Fitzhugh, called Hannibal. Jake and Cato had been, like Mike, for some time in the bush. Cato was a timid, crouching fellow, but Jake was a stout, fierce, savage-looking negro, with the marks of severe treatment on his person. Hannibal had been corrupted by the laxity of discipline at Willowbank, under the administration of a woman, and roaming about in idleness, he had fallen in with the other sable conspirators.

"Now, boys," said President Mike, " we's a gwine to hold a council to see what we's a gwine to do. What you all gwine to do now?"

"I's a gwine to stop in de bush," responded Cato, "'case it's de nighest to git somethin' to eat from de t'other niggers."

"I want to run off to de Yankees," said Hannibal, "'case it's de furdest off to cotch us."

"What's we done got dem guns for?" inquired Cato, "dat's what I want to know. I's afeard of guns. Dat's what."

"You're a fool," growled Jake, "guns is to shoot."

"Dem guns won't shoot nobody," pronounced the president.

"Dey must shoot somebody," said Jake.

"Who?" cried all the others.

"Old Eckles."

"O Lord," exclaimed Cato, with alarm, "ef dar's shootin', I's off."

"I'd shoot everybody," rejoined Jake, "let's raise all de niggers."

"How many kin you raise?" asked the president.

"Lots."

"Has you axed 'em?"

"Yes, I done ax 'em."

"How many of 'em promised to raise?"

"Two; me and another feller."

"What did de rest of 'em say?"

"I was afeard to ax 'em, afeard dey'll blab. But Yankee Campbell says there's lots of 'em ready."

"Yankee Campbell is a liar," declared the president.

"Dat's jis what he is," chimed in Cato and Hannibal.

"Hush! Somebody's a comin'," whispered Cato.

"You's a coward," said Mike, "go to de door and watch." When this order was obeyed by the trembling Cato, the president continued: "Now, Jake, you's a fool. You's all fools. I's got all de sense. You see..de moonshine comin' down through dem rafters. Dat's de way de sense shines down through my head. I's de Moses to lead you all out'n de house of bondage. Mind me. To-morrow night I'll lead you away to de land of promise. But first we must git some money and things. We's a gwine to Willowbank. De ole woman dar has got piles of money and silver things. You know dat, Hannibal."

"Yes; but she keeps 'em locked up in a chis in her own room, and she sleeps up stairs wid 'em since de war."

"Well," said Mike, "we'll git into her room and break open the chis."

".But you mustn't hurt missus," cried Hannibal.

"No; she shan't be hurt."

"We'll rob de chis, but you mustn't hurt missus."

"Now mind me, Jake, you bring Cato and meet me at de Poplar Spring to-morrow, jis when it gits dark. Hannibal, you go to Willowbank, and git inside to open de door. We'll be dar at 'leven o'clock. Now, mind me, I'm Moses."

"A ghose—a ghose"—shouted Cato, and took to his heels. Jake and Hannibal ran out of the barn, and being also frightened at a ghost or a man, followed the sentinel. Mike, who had given them their orders, and thus accomplished all that he designed, did not attempt to detain them, though he stood his ground. Presently blind Pete advanced from the wood, and a long consultation took place between him and Mike, of which it is necessary to record only that Pete agreed to be at a certain grove near the mansion of Willowbank, with his cart, on the next evening, in consideration that he should receive a certain share of the spoils; that he was to take with him three pistols and some saddles, which the negroes were to use in mounting themselves on stolen horses; that he was to be accompanied by two men, who had agreed with Mike to run away, and that the spoil was to be carried to a convenient spot for division, and the plate reduced to a suitable form for transportation by the fugitives.

CHAPTER XVII.

INSURRECTION.

THE next morning—it was Sunday—when Colonel Fairfax walked out upon the lawn in front of his house, he saw a large number of his slaves collected in clusters about the grounds, and discovered at once that there was agitation among them. Presently Joe advanced as their spokesman, and informed his master that the servants were in great alarm on account of rumors which they understood were afloat. The rumors were that the negroes were plotting insurrection, and that some of the white men had organized themselves as a committee of vigilance, to suppress the conspiracy. They feared the violence of these men, acting, as they believed, under a groundless panic. The Colonel was aware that such panics were usually attended with danger to the negroes. The greatest excitement was apt to inflame the minds of those who owned few or no slaves. Owners of many slaves, living among them, could easily bring all rumors of servile commotion to the test of actual observation, and, besides, they felt bound by interest and duty to protect their servants against the effects of incautious suspicion. Others who had not the same opportunity of knowledge, nor the same responsibility, allowed their imaginations to be stuffed with unsifted reports and horrid alarms. Colonel Fairfax had already heard some of the rumors which were in circulation, and after listening to Joe, he said—

"Well, Joe, what do you think about this insurrection?"

"Lord, master, da won't be no resurrection of niggers, sure?"

"I wish to talk with some of the other boys about it."

"Dey will be mighty glad, master."

The colonel went among them, and conversed with many of them, separately and together. Being thoroughly acquainted with their habits, he was able to glean from them all they knew or believed, and to determine what was true. Indeed his servants, having confidence in his justice, seldom attempted to deceive him, unless it might be by that sort of exaggeration which a negro regards as but a decent dress of naked truth. He became convinced that there was no danger of an insurrection. He promised his servants the protection which they desired, and admonished them to keep closely to their work in day-time, and to their cabins at night.

At the church, that day, he heard of popular excitement and of preparations which threatened violence to the negroes. He exerted all his influence with the people whom he met, to allay the excitement, and to discourage rash action. When he returned home, his anxiety on the subject was so great that, after dinner, he rode out in search of the persons who were reported to be engaged in the lawless organization for the suppression of insurrection. He had not gone far from home, when he met half a dozen men on horseback, armed with fowling-pieces and pistols. He knew them to be ignorant persons of inflammable tempers, and they were manifestly under great excitement. One of them, who seemed to be a ring-

leader was our acquaintance, Bob Faris, who had not
yet executed his purpose to enter the army and fight
for the principles of free government. On meeting
Colonel Fairfax they addressed him civilly, though
abruptly. They asked what steps he had taken to
prevent his negroes from joining in the projected insurrection. He told them that he did not believe
there was any such plot, and that, having no fear of
his servants, he had done nothing but advise them to
remain quiet at home, until the agitation should sub-
side. They angrily rebuked his negligence, announced themselves as a volunteer patrol for the regu-
lation of negroes and abolitionists, informed him that
they had conclusive proofs of a wide-spread conspiracy, with Yankee leaders, and finally declared
they were going to examine his slaves, and arrest all
of them whom they might find to be accomplices.
He remonstrated, and reasoned with them upon the
impropriety of their conduct, the folly of their fears,
and the mischiefs they were about to cause. He advised them to abandon their lawless organization, and
appeal to the magistrates in due form. Their minds
were too highly inflamed to listen to reason, and in
the face of such imminent and horrible danger as
they fancied, they would not await the slow operation
of law. He then offered to pledge himself for the
good behavior of his servants, and besought the
patrol not to molest his family and dependents with
their inquisition. They professed respect for him
and his family, but insisted that he was deluding himself with misplaced reliance on the fidelity of his
slaves, and they felt bound to proceed. "Then, gentlemen," he said, firmly, "let me warn you that you
will encounter resistance. I will protect my servants.

I have arms." He turned his horse's head homeward, and left them. Before he was out of hearing, Bob Faris called him back, and informed him that they had consulted together and concluded, out of respect for him, not to visit his plantation that evening. They swore, however, that Palmer, the —— old abolitionist, should not escape. They rode off toward that part of the county in which Palmer resided.

Colonel Fairfax, thus apprised that there was danger of violence to that gentleman, sat a few minutes considering how it might be averted. It was nearly dark. He was reluctant to go so far from his own house as to Palmer's while the neighborhood was disturbed. But he could think of no other way to prevent a disgraceful if not fatal scene. As any delay might defeat his purpose, he set off at once, riding rapidly, and taking a by-path which saved some distance and enabled him to pass the patrol without being seen. In little more than an hour he arrived at Mr. Palmer's house. That gentleman received him with surprise and embarrassment. He was not aware of the danger in which he stood at that moment, but he was conscious of participation in a scheme which might prove perilous to his visitor. The latter proceeded at once to make known the circumstances which induced his visit, and expressed the opinion that the regulators would be at the door in a few minutes. He added a hope that he might be able to dissuade them from violence, but advised Mr. Palmer to retire from the house for a short time, offering to remain with the family and save them from insult. But Palmer, whose domestic affections were strong, and who did not lack courage to defend his household, refused to leave his family. He told his wife

and daughters of the danger, and directed them to remain quiet in their chambers, whatever might happen.
The colonel avowed his readiness to assist in defending the house and person of Mr. Palmer. The latter
brought out his arms—two revolving pistols and a
double-barrelled fowling piece loaded with buckshot.
All the weapons were kept loaded, in anticipation of
trouble, which was constantly apprehended by the
owner of them. The hasty preparations for defence
were scarcely completed when the tramp of horses
was heard.

The horsemen quickly dismounted and posted themselves in preconcerted order about the house, to prevent the escape of Palmer. Faris then drew near
the front door and knocked at it for admittance. Mr.
Palmer opened a window and would have spoken,
but the colonel drew him back and requested permission to try his influence with the patrol. Looking
out of the window, he said—

"Faris, what do you want?"

"Heavens!" exclaimed Faris, "Colonel Fred's here
too."

"Yes, I am here before you, and I am still determined to prevent you from disgracing yourselves by
lawless violence. Now tell me what you intend to do?"

"We want the old abolitionist, and we will have
him, colonel."

"What has he done?"

"He's at the bottom of the insurrection."

"How do you know that?"

"A nigger confessed it all."

"I suppose the negro was in the hands of your
patrol?"

"Of course he was."

"You flogged him to make him confess?"

"Of course we did."

"On the extorted confession of a negro you proceed to this outrage, then!"

"We know his story's true."

"How can you know it? If you are so sure of it, go to a magistrate and get a legal warrant. . Shame on such lawlessness!"

"Colonel, it's no use talking. We are bound to have him out."

"Then you must take me first. Beware! You are in more danger than Mr. Palmer."

At this moment screams of women were heard in the house. During the parley one of the besiegers, tempted by an unfastened sash, entered a back window. Hurrying forward in the dark, he opened the door of Mrs. Palmer's chamber and rushed in. The ladies screamed, and Mrs. Palmer ran to the parlor in which the gentlemen were, followed by the intruder. As soon as he appeared, Mr. Palmer fired a pistol at him, but missed him. The intruder attempted to seize that gentleman, at the same time brandishing a knife. As he turned towards Mr. Palmer, Colonel Fairfax grasped him round the body, lifted him from the floor, carried him to the front window, which had been opened, and hurled him out. He fell heavily to the ground, and lay there, stunned by the fall.

All this passed so rapidly that Faris stood still at the spot from which he had held the parley, and was waiting for some explanation of the noise within the house, when he saw his comrade hurled from the window. He imagined that the man had been killed by the pistol-shot. He was afraid to approach the window. He withdrew to a more remote part of the grounds. After waiting a short time in vain for his fallen comrade to rise and follow him, he began to consider that the house was prepared for defence, that the defence was resolute and might be desperate, that it was conducted by a citizen of unblemished reputation and great influence, and that in the end the penalties of law might be enforced. He therefore whistled the signal of retreat and drew off his forces. Soon afterwards the man who had been thrown from the window crawled away and followed his comrades.

At first it could not be known how far they had gone nor how soon they might return. It was some time before the alarm of the ladies subsided. To assure them of safety and to resist another attack, if another should be made, Colonel Fairfax remained until a late hour of the night. When all danger appeared to be over, the colonel, now anxious for the security of his own home, was about to depart. The ladies were profuse in expressions of gratitude to him. Mrs. Palmer paid out a neat little speech, redolent of fine sentiments and garnished with scraps of Latin. Even Mr. Palmer so far overcame the restraints of habitual reserve and conscious turpitude as to thank the colonel quite warmly. He accompanied him out of the door and detained him a minute or two on the portico to repeat his grateful words. While he was thus employed, a pistol was fired in the shadow of one of the pillars of the portico. A moment afterwards a negro man rushed from the pillar and aimed a blow with a pistol at Mr. Palmer's head. Colonel Fairfax, throwing up his arm, intercepted the blow. The negro, foiled in both his murderous attempts, ran past and soon disappeared. Upon examination, it was found that a bullet had passed through the collar of Mr. Palmer's coat, but he was unhurt.

"It was Mike," he remarked, but he offered no conjecture as to the probable motive of the assault, nor did he propose pursuit. This incident renewed the agitation and alarm of the ladies, and detained the colonel still longer. At length he started homeward.

During his absence from Roebuck events had happened which it is necessary now to recount. On Sunday afternoon his daughter, Julia, went two or three miles from home to visit a poor woman who was sick. Finding the woman quite ill she remained with her until it was growing dark. Then, mounting her horse—her favorite "Arab"—she started homeward alone. Her road was little more than a bridle-path, and led through the skirt of a wood by the spring which was called the Poplar Spring, and which, it may be remembered, Mike had appointed as the place where Jake and Cato were to meet him about the same hour that Julia was riding home. The spring rose just beside the path and flowed across it. When Julia was passing it her horse dropped his head to drink, and she permitted him to stop. While he was drinking three negro men stepped into the path. One of them seized the bridle; the other two posted themselves at each side of the horse. Each of them carried a club. They said nothing. She was surprised, but she was not accustomed to fear negroes. Even their formidable appearance and movement did not deprive her of courage. Instantly drawing her rein, she struck Arab sharply with her riding-switch, intending to break away from the fellow who held the bridle. The horse sprang forward, but the negro held fast, and threw him back on his haunches.

. "You better be quiet," he then said. She leaned forward and struck him across the face with her switch, saying, "Begone! how dare you?" He winced, but still held the bridle.

"Better be quiet, I tell you agin, Miss Fairfax; you shan't be hurt; close up dar, boys; don't let her git away."

"Who are you?"

"I's Palmer's Mike. I don't keer who knows me, but I won't tell you who dese other fellers is."

"What are you going to do with me?"

"Jis take you to a safe place."

. "For what purpose?"

Mike made no reply. He set the party in motion, turning from the road into the pathless wood, himself holding the bridle and the other two men walking close by the sides of the horse. They went on silently for some time. Their progress was slow among the trees and thickets. Their course led them into the deepest part of the forest. Julia, ignorant of their design and of her destination, a prisoner of three black ruffians, could not wholly resist the depressing influence of these alarming circumstances. In the gloom of night and of the wilderness her imagination was filled with frightful visions of coming danger. She watched in vain for some opportunity of escape. Several times she attempted to converse with her captors and to learn her probable fate. But they maintained a sullen and ominous silence. Still her natural courage was not quite subdued. By a vigorous effort she kept her faculties in readiness for an emergency or an opportunity, in spite of the quick beating of her heart. In the dense wood sometimes the low branches of the trees almost swept her from her saddle. This annoyance at last suggested to her a method of escape.

A long, large limb, growing square out from the body of a beech tree, at a height level with her chin as she sat upright, was about to strike her face in the darkness. She happened to discover it in time to throw her arms over it. In that way she lifted herself out of the saddle and let her horse walk from beneath her. She remained thus suspended in the air until the negroes had passed on so far that she thought they could not hear the noise of her movement, and then she swung herself along to the body of the tree, and then, climbing above the limb, she sat upon it. She intended to remain there until her captors, who would, doubtless, miss her very soon, should have failed in a search for her and left the wood free for her escape. In a few minutes they discovered that she was not upon the horse. Mike railed at his followers for their negligence, and they were wholly unable to conjecture how or where she had eluded their vigilance. They all turned back and commenced a search for her in every direction through the forest. She could hear them shouting to each other and sometimes consulting together. Mike appeared to apprehend serious consequences from her escape, and gave vent to his chagrin in curses. When they had been searching a long time and seemed almost in despair of success, Mike, still leading her horse, passed under the branch on which she was perched. The sagacious and affectionate Arab raised his head and uttered the low whinnying sound which is the natural note of recognition and of pleasure with his kind. The attention of Mike was instantly directed towards the tree, for he was familiar with the habits of horses and knew the superior intelligence of Arab. He began to pry among the branches, and in a short time he discovered his captive. She was compelled to descend and resume her place in the saddle. Thenceforth the vigilance of the guard was redoubled, and avoiding the darkest parts of the forest, they moved along paths which were known to the negroes. Now and then they paused and whispering consultations took place among them, which Miss Fairfax was not permitted to hear. Some of these conversations, however, appeared to be on the point of running into violent disputes between Mike and Jake, and she thought her own name was repeated in tones of remonstrance or of anger. How long a time or how far she had been journeying in captivity she could not determine, when Jake, who walked on her left, approached very close to the horse, and laid his hand upon her arm. "Stand back, villain!" she cried, and the cry arresting Mike, he turned back towards her just as his ruffianly comrade seized Miss Fairfax by the waist. She screamed and struggled, but she was as child in the grasp of the stout negro. Mike sprang at him, wrenched his hands from Julia, and flung him upon the earth. His follower rose and rushed with fury at Mike, but the latter struck him on the head with his club and felled him. Jake lay outstretched, as if he was dead, and Mike, not knowing whether he was dead or alive, left him and resumed the march. He took care, however, to supply the place of the missing guard by his own watchfulness, so that the captive could not escape.

Julia was unable to recognize any of the places through which she was carried, until, at length, they

9

came upon a road and she saw Marlin's cabin, which they were about to pass. The sight of it revived her hope of escape. When they came nearly opposite to the cabin she suddenly struck her horse with all her force, and at the same time called the name of Mrs. Marlin. Arab bounded with such violence that he overthrew Mike, but the determined fellow held fast by the bridle and was dragged along the ground. She repeated her blows until the spirited horse was plunging frantically, but still Mike held on. She repeated her cries also until Mrs. Marlin ran out of the cabin. Awakened and startled by the voice of alarm, she hurried towards her door and stumbled over a stool. The accident, and her quick apprehension of danger, prompted her to pick up the stool and carry it with her as a weapon of defence. Hastening into the road, she recognized the voice and the horse of Julia, and saw Cato running about her. Advancing to the rescue of her friend, she gave Cato a vigorous blow with the weapon she carried in her hand, and that timid rascal rolled over in the dirt. He lay very quiet, affecting to be quite disabled. Mike, seeing the turn which affairs had taken, let go the bridle, scrambled to his feet and ran away.

Mrs. Marlin then assisted Julia to alight. She was much fatigued, and with the revulsion of feeling that overcame her when she saw that she was free, she became faint. The good woman led her into the cabin, and she sat down to rest and recover her spirits while Mrs. Marlin busied herself in getting a light, bringing restoratives and preparing a bed. Eliza also, aroused from the dreamless slumber of girlhood, chattered her sympathy and flew about, eager to do something for Julia's comfort. In a short time, however, the young lady declared herself able to ride, and thanking her kind friends, she determined to return home immediately. She knew that her father and mother would be in great distress and alarm on account of her absence, and she was anxious to relieve them as soon as possible. Mrs. Marlin would have persuaded her to take some repose, and offered to ride to Roebuck herself. When she could not prevail in this, she insisted on walking beside the horse, as an escort for Julia. But Miss Fairfax would not suffer her to undertake such a journey afoot, and expressed her belief that she would be in no further danger during that night. She had quite recovered her courage, and resolved to ride home alone. But when she left the cabin for that purpose, her horse was not to be found. Both he and Cato had disappeared.

What then was to be done? The distance to Roebuck was not less than six miles. Julia, whose strength was almost exhausted by the events of the night, was wholly unable to walk so far. Yet she could not bear to leave her parents without intelligence of her safety. After much discussion she was about to accede to the proposal of Mrs. Marlin to walk to Roebuck, when Eliza offered to go to Willowbank and procure a horse for Miss Fairfax. It would be a walk of about two miles, and it might be attended with some danger, as the occurrences of the night had proved. But the warm-hearted girl desired to serve her friend, and the idea of danger rather stimulated than daunted her. When the project had taken possession of her lively little brain she did not rest until she had brought her mother and Miss Fairfax to consent to it, and then she tripped away through the darkness.

Before there was time for her to have sent a horse
from Willowbank, a neigh was heard by the women
in the cabin, and Julia, who was lying down, lifted
her head and said, "that's Arab." They went out
and found that her horse had returned and was standing at the gate. Without further delay Julia mounted
him and turned his head homeward. Mrs. Marlin
walked half a mile with her, and then, as no sign of
danger appeared, and she was retarding the impatient
horse-woman, she was persuaded to return. The road
to Roebuck was rather obscure and rough, being but
little travelled. At night it was dreary. Julia rode
on, however, safely and pretty briskly, until she was
about two miles from the cabin. Then she was slowly
ascending a hill, and on turning round a jutting
point, she saw a black man walking towards her
and already close to her horse's head. She did not
know the truculent Jake, but he recognized her, and
immediately seizing her bridle, raised his club. His
threatening movement startled her, but she did not
lose her presence of mind. Seeing that by no effort
could she escape, she determined to try the effect of
talking to the fellow.

"What do you want?" she asked.

"I want you," he answered, and instantly clutched
her arm in his great, rough hand. He dragged her
downward with such sudden violence that she fell
heavily to the ground. Jake stooped over her and
then paused. He heard the clatter of a horse's hoofs
on the road. He stood listening and looking until he
ascertained that a horseman, rapidly approaching, was
near at hand, and then he plunged from the road
down the hill-side into a wood. He left Miss Fairfax
lying almost insensible. When the horseman arrived

he leaped from his saddle and knelt by her side. He lifted her head and said, in a tone of tender anxiety— "Julia, are you hurt?"

Receiving no reply, he placed his arm about her, drawing her head to his breast and said, "Julia, dear Julia, tell me—are you hurt?"

She feebly answered, "no, not much." Presently reviving somewhat, she added, "no, thank Heaven, I am not hurt. I was frightened. My nerves are shaken, but I feel no pain." After another pause she continued, "I can rise now."

But he whispered, "rest a moment—you are not yet strong enough."

Then looking up, she asked, "whom shall I thank for this deliverance?" and as the moon, gleaming through the tree-tops, began to give some light, she exclaimed—"it is Captain Fitzhugh."

"Yes, it is I," he replied.

"O, how thankful I am," she murmured.

With his assistance she rose and stood a little while, not without his support. Then, as she recovered her strength, she blushed and withdrew from his arm, saying she was able to ride. After assisting her to her saddle, Captain Fitzhugh—no longer captain, however, for the major of his regiment had died of wounds received at Manassa and he had succeeded to that rank—mounted his horse and rode beside her towards Roebuck.

CHAPTER XVIII.

LOVE AT ROEBUCK.

MIKE's principal plan embraced only a speedy flight from the country after providing a good supply of money or of portable plate and of horses. He thirsted for a particular revenge, but he did not desire to commit unnecessary acts of violence which might provoke pursuit or subject him to severe retribution in the event of his capture. When the evening arrived for the execution of his project, he was not yet provided with a horse such as he thought desirable for a rapid flight, and he feared that those which were to be brought to him might not be very swift. When Miss Fairfax appeared at the Poplar Spring, riding an animal which was reputed to be one of the fleetest in the county, he was suddenly tempted to obtain possession of the horse. But he reflected that if he permitted Miss Fairfax to go on to Roebuck after taking her horse, the alarm which she would give might lead to the defeat of his entire scheme. It occurred to him, therefore, that it would be safer to carry her with him and detain her in some secure place until he was ready to set off on his long journey. Besides, in attempting to justify a rash act to himself, he conceived a vague notion that she might be valuable as a hostage in certain contingencies. His conduct and his reasoning were alike absurd, and served to prove how incompetent a negro is—even one comparatively shrewd—to devise or execute any complicated scheme. Without explaining to his followers, Jake and Cato, the object of his proceeding, he gave them the orders which, as we have seen, they executed until Jake, obeying his own passions, attempted an act of violence, inconsistent with Mike's plan.

When Mike fled from Marlin's cabin he hastened to Willowbank. The'hour which he had appointed for meeting blind Pete in the grove was already past. The two men upon whom Mike had relied, with the assistance of Hannibal in the house, to execute the robbery under his lead, were left behind. On arriving before the mansion he deliberated whether he should undertake the enterprise with no other aid than that of his confederate, Hannibal. He anticipated no resistance which they could not easily overcome. But he feared that if any force should become necessary, Hannibal might fail to support him, or possibly might oppose him. He therefore concluded to call in the two men who were to accompany blind Pete. With that view he proceeded to the grove and found Pete with the two negroes. They had been greatly perplexed by Mike's delay, and were about to abandon the enterprise and return to their several haunts. He offered them some plausible explanation of his detention and of the absence of Jake and Cato. He told them of the treasure which was to be obtained in the house, and enlisted them in the robbery. While he was engaged in making this new arrangement, Cato had mounted Arab at Marlin's cabin and followed him; but when he came to Willowbank he could not find his leader, and knowing nothing of the rendezvous at the grove, he turned back, and after riding some distance, let the horse loose and took to the woods. Arab, finding himself at liberty, went on to the cabin.

Mike, followed by the two negro men whom he had just enlisted in the scheme of burglary, approached the front door of the house, expecting it to be opened by Hannibal. The whole house was dark and quiet. He made a concerted sign at the door, but it was not opened. He whispered the name of Hannibal through the key-hole, but heard no response. He went along the porch, and at every window endeavored to attract the notice of his confederate. Still Hannibal gave no answer. Mike had almost concluded that he had failed to fulfil his engagement when one of his men, listening at the door, heard a loud snore within. Hannibal had stationed himself there at the appointed hour, but during the delay which occurred he fell asleep. Becoming convinced that he was there, Mike was at a loss how to wake him without arrousing all the inmates. After scratching his woolly pate for some time, he hit upon a plan. He found the old door fitted its frame so ill that there was space for the insertion of a small stick beneath it. He procured a rod, sharpened it, and began to puncture the person of the somnolent Hannibal. Partially awaking, that sentinel uttered, "ugh, ugh," and sunk back into profound sleep. But by perseverance in punching and whispering, Mike finally roused him up, and he opened the door. While he stood rubbing his eyes the three men who entered passed by him, groped their way to the foot of the stairs and began to ascend. At that moment they were startled by a light which appeared at the head of the stairs.

Mrs. Fitzhugh being a nervous invalid, never slept profoundly. She had heard almost the first sound made by the negroes on the porch. When it was repeated she called her servant, Belle, a faithful negress, who

slept in the same room, and sent her to ascertain the
cause of the noise. She returned and reported her
belief that robbers were trying to break into the house.
Her mistress made her light a candle at a taper which
was kept burning dimly in the chamber. Mrs. Fitzhugh rose and took down an old sword which hung
in the room and which had belonged to her deceased
husband. She directed Belle to arm herself with the
old lady's cane, and then the two women sallied out
of the chamber to the head of the stairs. The servant
set the candle on a stand in the hall and they peered
downward to discover what was passing at the front
door. It was then that Mike and his accomplices
started up the steps.

When they came into the light, Mrs. Fitzhugh,
seeing that they were negroes, sternly ordered them
to go back, and haughtily rebuked their insolence in
thus intruding into the house of a lady. They kept
on until they stood upon the landing of the stairs, a
few steps below the two women, and facing them.
Mike then paused. It was part of his plan to avoid
fatal violence, if possible. He saw that the women
were prepared to make resistance, and he knew the
proud and resolute spirit of Mrs. Fitzhugh. She
stood before him in her night-dress, pale, emaciated
and feeble, but holding a sword and breathing scornful defiance. He did not doubt his ability to overcome her resistance, but he hesitated to commence a
conflict in which blood might be shed. Perhaps, too,
the habitual ascendancy of the white race somewhat
cowed his spirit. But, after standing a short time,
the temptation of plunder or the reckless feeling that
he had gone too far to recede prevailed. He rushed
forward. The two men who had stood cowering be-

9*

hind him while he hesitated did not immediately follow him. As he approached the head of the stairs
alone, Belle, who stood above him, struck a blow with
the cane, which sent him swaying and staggering
back to the landing. He soon recovered his balance,
and enraged by the stroke, he called upon the other
men to follow, and was about to ascend again. But
Hannibal, now fully awake, and hearing the noise of
conflict, cried from below—"you shan't hurt missus.
You promised you wouldn't hurt missus." The
worthless fellow, willing to rob his mistress if he
might share the spoil, had too much gratitude for the
indulgence which had ruined him, or was too faithful
to permit any personal injury to be inflicted upon
her. He ran up the stairs with long strides, and
seizing one of the men by the throat, began to drag
him down. - Just then another person unexpectedly
entered the scene. A white man ran up the steps,
and hurrying past the others, caught Mike, when he
had almost reached the floor above, and hurled him
back headlong to the landing. Snatching the sword
from Mrs. Fitzhugh, he faced about and descended
towards the negroes. They did not wait for him, but
leaped, rolled or tumbled down the stairs pell-mell,
and escaped, "My dear Hugh! My brave son!
Thank God!" exclaimed Mrs. Fitzhugh.

There was not time after this affair for many ex-
planations between her and her son, when Eliza Marlin arrived on the errand she had undertaken for Miss
Fairfax. When her story had been briefly told, Mrs.
Fitzhugh asked her son if he was too much fatigued
to go to the relief of Julia. He was eager to act
upon the suggestion, and since his mother was willing,
and he thought there was no danger of a renewal of

the attack at Willowbank during his absence, he started off, and though his horse was jaded, he rode rapidly. He directed a servant to follow him to Marlin's cabin with a horse for Julia. At the cabin he heard what the reader knows of her departure, and hastened to overtake her.

When Mike's attempt at robbery was defeated, he ran to the grove in which he had left blind Pete, and mounted a horse which one of the negroes had stolen and brought there. He rode away, leaving his accomplices without any explanation of his purpose or any instruction for their own conduct. Frightened and furious, he thought only of perpetrating an act of vengeance and then flying from the country. He went to the house of Mr. Palmer, with no definite plan, but with a general purpose of revenge. To his surprise, he found a front window open and light streaming through it. Peeping in, he saw Colonel Fairfax, seated with Mr. Palmer, and he then stationed himself by a pillar, to wait for the colonel's departure and for his own opportunity. He had been there but a short time when the opportunity offered itself, and he attempted to take the life of his master. Failing in that attempt, he concluded that nothing remained for him but speedy flight. But the Federal lines were distant, and he distrusted his own ability to make his way to them. He had before thought of inducing Campbell to act as a pilot for the fugitive party—he now resolved to apply to him. Going to the village, he sought the rear of the Swan tavern, and by a method which he had already used for a clandestine interview with Campbell, obtained admittance into his chamber. Rousing him from sleep, he told that ambitious plotter of insurrection that Cap-

tain Fitzhugh, with his whole company, had returned
to the county, that they had that night attacked a
large party of armed negroes and defeated them, and
werethen approaching the village to arrest Campbell.
That gentleman, dreadfully alarmed, anticipated Mike's
suggestion of flight, and thankfully accepted the negro's offer to go with him.

"But I have no horse," said Campbell, in an agitated tone.

"Da's a good hoss in de stable of dis tavern," said
Mike.

"But he is not mine."

"Den steal him."

This sharp solution of the difficulty was perforce
accepted, though Mike's unceremonious designation
of the process of appropriation was more consonant
with the negro's morality than with the white man's
pride. Pride and honor, with human and divine
laws, yield to military necessity. In the grey of the
morning, Campbell and his sable comrade, mounted
on stolen horses, caught a last glimpse of the distant
village.

When Colonel Fairfax, after foiling Mike's last
attempt upon Mr. Palmer's life, returned to Roebuck, he was astonished at meeting with his wife in
the avenue. She was walking there, in deep distress.
His first thought was that his absence from home had
excited such fears for his safety that she had started
out in search of him. Then he thought—but before
he could shape out another conjecture, Mrs. Fairfax
had cried—"Julia—have you seen our own dear
Julia? We have lost her." Wringing her hands,
she gave way to grief and apprehension. Her husband, alarmed by her cries and tears, could not imme-

diately obtain from her an intelligible explanation.
At length he learned that Julia had not returned
home, and that during the night search had been
made for her in every direction and by every person
on the plantation, without finding her or discovering
any clue to the mystery of her disappearance. The
last that could be heard of her was that, after visiting
the sick neighbor, she had started to go home alone
about dark. The servants were still searching the
fields, the woods and the roads. Doctor Dick, though
riding was yet painful to him, was scouring the country in pursuit of his favorite niece. Several wounded
Confederate soldiers who were entertained at Roebuck, as in a hospital, had left their beds and, on
crutches, were looking about in impossible places for
the missing matron of their infirmary. Everybody
loved Julia.

When her father had reflected a moment on what
was told him, he inquired whether any one had gone
to Marlin's cabin. He was told that some of the servants had been sent on the road which led in that direction, but it was not known that any one had
thought of going the whole distance to Marlin's.
Without any distinct reason for supposing that she
might be heard of there, her father could not discover
that anything had been left undone which was less
unpromising than inquiry at that place. Impatient
to do something that might enable him to trace his
daughter, and agitated by fears which even her mother
did not entertain because she knew less than he did of
the disturbances in the neighborhood, he set out towards Marlin's. His wife, whom he soothed with
hopes which he could not feel, consented to return
to the house and await the result of his inquiries.

He had not rode more than a mile when he met his daughter with Major Fitzhugh. Recognizing her at some distance he exclaimed—"my child! thank God! my child!" He leaped from his horse and ran to embrace her. He saw by the moonlight that she was extremely pale. When she leaned down to kiss him, and he felt the tremor of her hand, tears welled up in his eyes. The emotions which succeeded his extreme anxiety for her safety could find no other utterance.

"Where have you been all this night, my daughter?" he asked as soon as he could command his voice.

"I will tell you all, papa, when we get home. I am fatigued but unhurt."

"You seem to be very feeble, daughter. Can you ride home?"

"Yes, papa, but I must ride slowly. Poor mamma! I fear she is in distress. Captain Fitzhugh, will you have the kindness to ride on and relieve her mind? Papa will take care of me. You neglect to speak to your friend, Captain Fitzhugh, papa! He has placed us under the greatest obligation to him for my safety to-night."

"Pardon me, Hugh. You are welcome to the county. I will find words to thank you when we arrive at the house."

After a hasty return of the colonel's greeting, Fitzhugh rode on, while the father and daughter followed slowly. When Julia arrived at home, she was carried to her chamber and laid upon her bed, completely exhausted. She could not leave her room for several days.

In spite of hospitable entreaties, Fitzhugh left Roe-

buck as soon as she arrived. He was not willing to
be longer absent from his mother. He, too, needed
repose. His wound, which at first was not very troublesome, had, in the heat and unwholesome camp of
Manassa, threatened serious consequences. The sur-
geons insisted that he should go home, and when he
found that the army was to remain inactive, he
yielded to their advice. Wishing to give his horses
the benefit of a furlough, he traveled on horseback.
He found himself within a few miles of home when
night overtook him—the night of the events just
related—and he pushed on. When he alighted before the mansion of Willowbank, he saw a light
moving in the house, and, approaching the door, he
found it open. What followed is known. For a
week after this night he could not move from the
house, and it was a month before he could return to
the army.

, The history of Major Fitzhugh and Julia Fairfax
during that month would be the most delightful of
narratives, if a story of true love, when its course
runs smooth, could impart to a reader the happiness
of the lovers. But the sweetest passage in the life
of every man and every woman who has loved truly
and happily is sweetest only to two beings. Such
love, which is the wine of life in the experience, turns
to lees in the description. The reader who has ever
read by "the purple light" knows that when, on that
memorable night, Hugh Fitzhugh knelt beside Julia,
with his arm about her waist, and called her "dear
Julia," the affection which had been budding on the
friendship of their youth bloomed into the perfect
flower of love. By what more explicit words the
compact of lovers was afterwards sealed they might

not remember; but they were plighted. The approval of their families and the favor of circumstances left no impediment in the way of their wishes.

During the last three weeks that Major Fitzhugh remained at home he was a daily visitor at Roebuck. Colonel Fairfax had regarded his talents and his generous, frank and honorable temper with almost paternal interest, even when he feared that the bright promise of his youth might be blighted by the mildew of indolence or the canker of pleasure. But now, when the strength and dignity of his character were developed by the vocation of a patriotic soldier, and he displayed also the grace which a true man derives from wise love, the colonel proudly recognized in him the qualities which he would most desire in his daughter's husband. Mrs. Fairfax, with a mother's gentle pride and a woman's natural delight in a happy match, built castles in the air for her daughter, and made her own substantial home more smiling and radiant than those fabrics of her fancy. Julia, lovely, loving and beloved, was more beautiful than ever, and happier than the happiest dreams of her childhood. Her voice, like the melody of birds, often warbled her happiness in song. Hugh Fitzhugh fondly believed that until then music so melodious had never been heard. Perhaps it was most pleasant to his ear when it would have been least agreeable to a less passionate listener, for of all her songs his favorite was,

THE SOUTHERN CAVALIER.

The lance of chivalry is broke, its iron mail is rust,
But knightly truth and courage live when knights have
    turned to dust:
There never rode a truer knight in battle or career
Than this grey-coated gentleman, the Southern Cavalier.

For nobler cause no champion did ever wield his brand
Than ours—the cause of liberty and of our native land;
Nor ever did more loyal knight uplift his knightly spear
Than this grey-coated gentleman, the Southern Cavalier.

The brave who for their country die like setting stars go
    down,
To rise again from eve to eve, immortal in renown :
None braver stands a mark for death, without reproach or
    fear,
Than this grey-coated gentleman, the Southern Cavalier.

The gallant soldier after war remains his country's guest,
With praise of men and woman's love and peace within his
    breast,
And Heaven, that loves a righteous cause, hath smiles his
    life to cheer
For this grey-coated gentleman, the Southern Cavalier.

CHAPTER XIX.

TREMAINE.

In the spring of the year eighteen hundred and sixty-two, both Fitzhugh and Tremaine had been promoted to the rank of colonel in the cavalry of their respective services. In the previous autumn Captain Fitzhugh, with his company, was sent to the Valley, and served under Jackson in guarding the junction, in the winter expedition to Bath and Romney, and in the brilliant spring campaign, beginning with Kernstown and ending with Port Republic, which first made the name of Jackson renowned.

Probably no other campaign made by so small a force in so short a time ever produced more important effects than the rapid succession of remarkable victories then won by Jackson over several armies. The immediate influence of this brilliant and unexpected success upon the minds of the Southern people was as extraordinary as it was timely. Never at any other time during the war until the final catastrophe was at hand, was the South so despondent as in the spring of eighteen hundred and sixty-two. About that time the overweening confidence inspired by the Confederate successes of the previous year was turned to dismay by several disasters. Most of the volunteers who composed the army of the South had enlisted for a year only and their term of service was about to expire. It was apprehended that not many would renew their engagement, and that a new army

could not be formed before the disbanding of the old,
if at all. It was deemed necessary to pass the law of
conscription, which compelled all white male residents
between the ages of eighteen and thirty-five (with a
few exemptions) to serve in the army three years or to
furnish substitutes. It required those who had volunteered for a year to remain in service two years
longer. Many feared that this severe measure would
provoke resistance, but it was obeyed with almost
uncomplaining patriotism. The law, however, was a
violent and impracticable measure, and was afterwards
among the prominent causes of the downfall of the
Confederacy. The general alarm which led to its
enactment was suddenly relieved by the achievements
of "Stonewall" Jackson in the Valley, if it is proper
thus to ascribe to him alone victories which were due
to the marvellous endurance and unconquerable valor
of the little army which he led, not less than to the
genius of their leader. It will be readily understood
that the activity of that army, the extent of country
which it protected, the number of its battles, with the
skirmishes and other incidents of such a campaign,
afforded to every man opportunities for the display
of the best qualities of a soldier. The large amount
of intelligence then in the ranks, the general spirit of
patriotism and the individual independence nourished
in Southern society fitted almost every man to play an
effective part.

This volume cannot be adorned with a history of
that noble army. We cannot even take space to record the particular exploits of our friends. It must
suffice to mention briefly that Hugh Fitzhugh became
a lieutenant-colonel during the winter, that when the
whole army was reorganized in the spring, under the

law of conscription, he was elected colonel, and tha.
he was acknowledged to have fairly won his promo-
tions by his gallant and skilful conduct. At the new
election Mark Marlin was chosen a lieutenant, with
the unanimous approbation of the young gentlemen
and other members of his company. With his commission he acquired the social rank of a gentleman,
according to the theory of his youthful ambition, and
his deportment was faithful to his model.

About the same time such changes took place in
the military lines that Roebuck became accessible to
the Federal troops. The county remained for a time
debatable ground, and was visited occasionally by
cavalry from both sides. At length, however, a
Federal detachment was stationed in the village,
under the command of Colonel Tremaine. It was sufficient, with the support of a larger force at no great
distance, to hold the county, but not to prevent occa-
sional and rapid incursions of Confederate horse.
The Federal cavalry in Virginia was still inferior, and
poverty had not yet unhorsed the Confederates. At
the time of the events about to be narrated, Colonel
Fitzhugh, with his regiment, was stationed some
twenty miles from the village, and a considerable distance in advance of any large Southern army. The
force under Colonel Tremaine was composed of his
own regiment of cavalry, and a regiment of infantry.
The latter was commanded by Lieutenant-Colonel
Wesel, a German, who was in daily expectation of
being promoted to the office of colonel of his regiment, then vacant. He had been a butcher in a
Northern city. He was a blatant politician of the
prevailing order, and had been active in drawing his
countrymen into the regiment. He was, therefore,

patronized by some influential persons. He and his men had been taught to look upon "rebels" as atrocious criminals, out of the pale of humanity, and upon their property as lawful prey. Some companies of the cavalry, though composed of native Americans, had similar notions, and their officers were not unwilling to fill their pockets, or furnish their houses, or decorate their wives by the pillage of their Southern brethren. Among the officers attached to this force was Albert Palmer.

We left that gentleman, just after the battle of Manassa, and on the morning of his duel with Baxter, deliberating upon the expediency of transferring himself to the North. Having resolved that question in favor of his native land, he proceeded on foot towards Washington, taking care to avoid the parties of Confederates who were then to be expected on his route. The next morning about dawn he approached a Federal picket on the Southern side of the Potomac. He approached cautiously, and, as it was thought, suspiciously, dressed in Confederate uniform, and the picket took alarm and retired. The panic of Manassa had not yet subsided. A report soon spread as far as the city of Washington that a large rebel army was at the southern bank of the river and produced great commotion for several hours. In the meantime Palmer, by skilful manœuvres, contrived to get within hail of a Federal party, and made known his friendly purpose. A deserter from the rebel army, at such a moment, was received with distinguished consideration. Of course, he professed to have been a staunch friend of the Union from the beginning, and told marvellous stories of the persecutions which he had suffered until, affecting to favor the rebel cause, he had accepted employment in the Southern army, with a view to desert at the earliest safe opportunity. Thus he won favor, and his efforts to ingratiate himself with those who had the disposal of offices were seconded by Campbell after his flight to the North. Thus he returned to the county of his residence an officer in the army which he had gone forth to oppose. He came back with some particular resentments to gratify, and to some remains of the original prejudices of a stranger by birth he might add the vindictive zeal of a renegade in regard to the people of Virginia.

Soon after Colonel Tremaine established his headquarters at the Swan tavern, he was visited by Colonel Fairfax. The meeting between them, though not wholly free from constraint, was friendly on both sides. Colonel Tremaine took occasion to repeat the expression of his gratitude for hospitality and kindness which, he said, had probably saved his life. Colonel Fairfax, premising that his former guest would not expect him to express pleasure at the establishment of a Federal force in the county, added that, since that misfortune could not be averted, he was sincerely gratified to find Colonel Tremaine in command. He proceeded to state the special object of his visit.

"I desire to know (if you think proper to inform me) what course you intend to pursue with reference to our unarmed citizens who remain at home. You have heard me express my political opinions. The fortunes of war do not change our convictions of right. My sentiments are the same as those which generally prevail in the county. But we acknowledge the duties which spring from adverse events, and intend to perform them as, I doubt not, your duties will be performed with equal fidelity."

"Since you allude to my duties," replied Colonel Tremaine, smiling, "I would be pleased to know what duties you think I owe to your citizens in the present situation of affairs here?"

"Pardon me, colonel, I am not here to lecture you. I intended only to express courteously my confidence in you."

"But, really, I desire to know your opinion. I have confidence in your fairness and your judgment. It may be necessary for me to understand the sentiments of the people in order to determine how they should be treated. I believe that whatever you tell me will be true, and whatever you promise will be performed. I wish you to speak-freely in behalf of your people."

"We know, Colonel, that your first duty is to promote the success of your government in the war. To that end we expect you to do whatever a just and humane man may do. We expect, while you remain in possession, to submit in good faith to a power which we cannot resist and desire not to irritate: I take it for granted, that you will refrain from harassing citizens who refrain from hostile conduct. I should think, if you permit me to say so, that it will be your duty to protect them, as far as you can, in their homes, property and innocent avocations. Your force supersedes all other authority in the county, and it would seem that, where submission is a duty, protection is a right."

"I believe we shall not quarrel, Colonel Fairfax, if your citizens act in the spirit which you attribute to them. I cannot make explicit stipulations with you. I must reserve the free exercise of discretionary authority. For the present tell your people to trust me and I will trust them. I shall issue such regulations as I deem necessary to be observed on their part. Some of them will be strict and may appear unreasonable. I cannot publish the reasons for them. But, if you make allowance for the harsh necessities of war, I believe you will consider me both just and humane. I shall expect obedience to my regulations at all events. If any of my men insult or pillage or oppress the citizens, let those who are wronged apply to me for redress."

After some further conversation, in which an invitation was given and accepted to visit Roebuck, Colonel Fairfax retired. The next day Mr. Palmer called on Colonel Tremaine. Notwithstanding his son had so openly appeared in the Federal service, that cautious gentleman still hesitated to offend his neighbors by a precipitate display of Union sentiments. He did not call on the commander of the Federal force in the village until he heard that so conspicuous a rebel as Colonel Fairfax had visited him. Even in conversing with Colonel Tremaine he rather insinuated at first than avowed his adhesion to the cause represented by that officer. But by degrees he led the conversation to political topics and to the affairs of the county, and broached some opinions for the guidance of the colonel. He represented the citizens of the county as, almost without exception, uncompromising rebels. He complained, especially, that the wealthy gentlemen devoted their riches to the support of the rebellion. Glancing at Colonel Fairfax, he said that one of the most prominent of that class had, during the past year, devoted the whole of his large revenue and valuable crops to the support of the Confederate cause or to the families of soldiers, and had induced the county court to make such liberal contributions that those families lived in greater abundance than they had known before the war. He thought that such powerful stimulants of rebellion ought to be suppressed by depriving the wealthy rebels of their property. He suggested that their estates might be administered under military rule for the benefit of the government. As Colonel Tremaine listened in silence to the long and winding discourse in which he cautiously developed these ideas, he even ventured to intimate that he was willing to administer those estates. At length he paused, and the colonel observed:

"I suppose the gentlemen to whom you allude have been generously supporting a cause which they honestly approve."

"I do not perceive, however, that their honesty makes their conduct defensible."

"Would you expect honest men to support a cause which they believe to be wrong?"

Mr. Palmer winced at the question, for he suspected that it was a hint at some meagre contributions which he had made to the Confederate cause. But, after a moment's hesitation, he replied:

"We have to deal with effects rather than motives."

"It is a fact, however, worthy of observation, that nearly all the honest men of the South appear to be against us in this struggle. In proportion as they scorn sordid interests, in comparison with high principle, appears to be their zeal for the Southern cause. They evince, too, in supporting rebellion, generous sentiments—sentiments which we would certainly applaud if we could approve their cause."

"Do you, then, justify the rebels?"

"Far from it. For many reasons the public welfare, in my judgment, requires the rebellion to be suppressed. For that purpose I have used my sword and risked my life. But our government is not now dealing with a rabble of rioters or a mob of desperate and wicked insurgents. Already for a whole year it has been carrying on a vast war against great communities, constituting powerful States and embracing most of the worth and wisdom of the South. These communities have acted in the exercise of a right which they have been educated to believe is inherent in their States. They act through their ancient State governments and through a new government formally organized. They carry on regular war with large armies. If we treat this as a case of simple rebellion we shall fall into a fatal fallacy. It is war—civil war. All history proves that in such wars it is equally unwise and unjust for one party to treat the other as criminals. Civil wars usually divide a nation and spring from political questions about which honest citizens honestly differ. They are so doubtful that a large portion of the nation is found on the one side and on the other. Frailty, passion or error of one party or of both, brings them to blows. Each believes its conduct to be patriotic. Without criminal purpose how can there be crime? It is a case of war which courts cannot adjudicate and for which laws cannot pro vide. There is no arbiter between the parties to a war but the sword. The sword is senseless and decides no question of right. It determines only the preponderance of force. It is absurd then for either party to accuse the other of crime."

"At all events, colonel, you must admit the propriety of taking from the rebels the means of supporting the rebellion."

"Let me answer you in the language attributed by the most renowned author in our language to his favorite hero. We give express charge that, in our marches through the country, there be nothing compelled from the villages, nothing taken but paid for, none of the French upbraided or abused in disdainful language; for when lenity and cruelty play for a kingdom the gentler gamester is the soonest winner."

"According to your ideas, nobody should be punished for this rebellion after it is suppressed."

"War should end in peace, not punishment. Punishment then is the revenge of victors upon the vanquished, of the powerful upon the defenceless. As we shorten war by making submission safe we shall confirm peace by making it honorable. A civil war, being between brethren, should, if possible, end like the quarrel of Brutus and Cassius on the stage, in a rivalry of loving penitance. But, since we cannot expect such a romantic revulsion of the passions of war, we may at least remember that, if submission is the duty of the conquered, magnanimity is the virtue of conquerors. The offence is the offence of a community; war and defeat are the punishments of a community. Among millions of people engaged in resistance, human judgment cannot discriminate and assign to each his peculiar share of blame. We must deal with the community."

"It is easy to discriminate between the leaders and the rest."

"If that were true, why should we take vengeance on the best, the chosen men of a people, and let those who have chosen them go free?"

"I cannot imagine, colonel, how you propose to assert the supremacy of the government and dispose of the rebels."

"Suppress armed resistance by the most vigorous measures—establish again the laws of peaceful society —and trust the defeated party as a party of honest, but mistaken citizens. I am confident that when its military power is broken, the South will submit, and once submitting, will frankly fulfil the duties of its new position. I believe that the South will always be true to its ancient instincts of frankness and manly honor."

"I am glad that, at least, you speak of the submission of the South."

"Yes; submission to lawful authority, not to dishonor. That I could never require. I wish to see the people of the South remain my countrymen, and I desire no dishonored men for my countrymen."

"What guaranties can you have that rebellion will not be renewed, unless you inflict punishment and strip these people of power?"

"Unless the might of armies, the awe of defeat, the experience of war, and a restoration of fraternal feeling shall bind the people to the government, the blood of their martyrs will not cement the Union, nor will the desperation of poverty and disgrace make men quiet citizens. We may compel them to submit by force; if we would have them loyal at heart, we must win their hearts."

"Ah, colonel, you do not know their bitterness. But you must have heard Doctor Dick Fairfax at Roebuck."

"Yes; when I heard his invectives against the North—though they seemed to be spoken half in a spirit of waspish jest—I listened always with pain and sometimes with indignation. I suppose his virulence is an exaggerated specimen of the antipathy engen-

dered in the minds of the Southern people by our unhappy controversies. When I heard him I thought
of those Northern fanatics and demagogues, who, by
the injustice of their conduct and language respecting
the South, had excited such enmity in a heart which
I found otherwise amiable and generous. If we, as
the stronger section, provoke resentments and then
punish them, we are doubly unjust. But, Mr. Palmer,
we have wandered into a discussion of questions
which we have not to decide. It would have been
enough to say that I do not intend to deprive the
citizens of their property unless it may be taken from
necessity, and in accordance with the rules and usages
of civilized warfare."

"I must confess, sir, that you appear to be luke-
warm in the great cause."

"When you have shed your blood for the Union
you may reproach me. Good morning, sir."

"You are very attentive to the rights of rebels."

"All men have the rights of humanity. Do you
require me to teach you that I have the rights of a
gentleman? Once more, I bid you good morning,
sir."

Mr. Palmer did not wait for another repetition of
the hint, but retired.

Under the mild and firm administration of Colonel
Tremaine, the county was quiet. Disorders were repressed. The citizens soon felt almost the same security as in time of peace. Those who had fled returned. The people instead of invoking the Confederates to attack the Federal force at the village for
their relief, deprecated the approach of Confederate
troops. They wanted repose. Some of them, weary
of war, began to repent their separation from a gov-

crnment which showed itself benignant in the conduct of its officer. Perhaps, if a similar policy had
been pursued everywhere during the war, the predic-
tion of Doctor Fairfax that the South would not
maintain the struggle more than two years, might
have been fulfilled.

But the conduct of Colonel Tremaine was censured
by Lieutenant-Colonel Wesel, and some others of the
command. They chafed under the restraints of discipline. Their passions demanded licence. Mr. Palmer
also, and his son, were disappointed and offended.
An intrigue was hatched for the removal of Colonel
Tremaine from the command. He was accused of
inertness, of cruelty to his men, of indulgence to
rebels. It was insinuated that he felt a criminal gratitude for the kindness which he had received as a
wounded prisoner. It was observed that he dined
with a noted rebel, and listened on Sunday to a sermon delivered by an old preacher, who was known to
sympathize with his fellow-citizens in their trials. It
was alleged that he would neither force nor entice
servants away from their masters. In fine, it was
concluded that he sympathized with the rebellion.
At length this intrigue was successful. Colonel Tremaine was ordered to Washington to answer for his
conduct, and Wesel, promoted to the rank of colonel,
was left in command, with ample authority to scourge
the spirit of secession from the county. Then commenced a new administration of a different order.

CHAPTER XX.

GABRIEL.

THE savage and futile policy of reducing the South to submission by destroying provisions and implements of husbandry, and by converting the land into a barren waste, had not yet been formally avowed by high authority. It was executed in particular places with more or less ferocity, according to the temper of each commander. Those who were prone to that mode of warfare derived sufficient encouragement from the orders excluding medicines from the South, and other acts of the government, denying to the Southern people those rights of humanity which are conceded to enemies by the usages of civilized warfare. Such atrocities received no countenance from Colonel Tremaine, but they suited the temperament of his successor.

During the first two years of the war, discipline in the vast armies of the North was less perfect than it afterwards became. Small bodies, detached from the main armies, soon became very disorderly and lawless, unless controlled by a firm and judicious officer. In a short time, the force under Colonel Wesel became little better than a licentious rabble. At first the baser sort of men, sweepings of streets, brawlers and bruisers at home, became drunken, thievish and riotous. Their impunity, and the contagion of vice, corrupted others. Many men, not thoroughly vicious, require the curb of military discipline when they are exempt from the gentle but constant restraints of civil society. Towards the citizens the demeanor of the colonel was so brutal that his worst men were encouraged to indulge their worst passions. Thus, under his orders, or through the licentious effects of his administration, the county was given up to pillage and oppression. All horses were captured as legitimate prizes. Cows, sheep and swine, were killed in wantonness. Mills and barns were burned. Fences were destroyed. Dwellings were entered and ransacked by night or day; private papers found in them, were torn and scattered; clothing of women and children was rent to ribbons, or carried off; jewelry was rudely wrenched from the persons of ladies, and families were put in terror of death or a fate worse than death. Farming implements, food and forage were systematically destroyed or removed. Men were insulted, and upon the slightest show of resentment shot down. The slaves were persuaded, and, in some cases, compelled to leave their homes. The men were drawn to the camp as servants, or suffered to roam about and live by pillage. The women, easily corrupted, were kept by the soldiers in sties about the village, or wandered they knew not whither. Many of the servants deserted Roebuck, charmed with the idea of freedom. Negroes, parasites by nature, cling to the strongest power that stands near them. How ever absurd the notions which they associate with liberty, exemption from compulsory labor has a special charm for the indolent and thoughtless creatures. Credulous and servile, they were easily deluded and led away by men who belonged to the race they were accustomed to revere, and who came with professions of exclusive friendship for them. They could not re-

ject a boon offered by a subtle tempter, promising that
it should make them to be as gods, notwithstanding
the decree of nature forbidding this fruit of freedom
to their race on pain of death.

Mr. Palmer, it may be remembered, had reserved
from sale a negro man, named Gabe, who was expected to be kept at home by a stupid contentment
with his lot or a stolid incapacity to compass another.
When some of his Northern patrons, rambling from
the village, plied him with temptation, his woolly
head was profoundly perplexed. The novel thought
of running away from his master, after it once obtained a lodgment in his brain, stuck fast, but he did
not know what to do with it. He went moping and
stumbling about in woful contemplation, until at
length he arrived at a conclusion which he expressed
to himself in the formula—"I's a thinkin' I better be
a gwine." Greatly relieved by the resolution of his
doubts, he kept muttering his formula, as if he feared
that unless he kept the words in his mouth the idea
would fly out of his head. For several days he sat,
or walked, or worked, with constant repetition of the
sentence—"I's a thinkin' I better be a gwine." Some
knowledge of his frame of mind reached his master
and mistress, and they began to fear they would lose
their only man-servant through the officious kindness
of their Northern friends.

One evening this subject, among others, engaged
the attention of a family council held in the parlor—
present, Mr. Palmer, Mrs. Palmer and their son,
Albert. It was agreed that, under existing circumstances, Gabe could not be detained by force, and
that it would be dangerous to attempt to spirit him
away to a slave-market. It seemed almost certain

10*

that he would prove a total loss. This prospect made them for the moment regard the proceedings of a benign government as rather oppressive. At last a desperate expedient occurred to Mr. Palmer the elder. He rang the bell and summoned Gabe to the parlor.

"Gabe," said he, with solemnity, "I am afraid you are thinking about running away to the Yankees."

"I's a thinkin' I better be a gwine, master," responded Gabe, in his well-conned formula, without insolence of manner, but with stolid apathy.

"Gabriel," resumed his master, with impressive condescension, "you ought not to go. You are a poor, ignorant nigger, and you do not know what is for your good. I have only your own welfare at heart. You have now a good home. If you run away you will have none. These Yankees are fooling you. They care nothing about you. They merely want to injure the South by taking away its labor. I take care of your family. You and they fare better than poor white folks at the North. You are going to leave friends and protectors for strangers. Nobody will feel any interest in your welfare. Everybody will strive to take bread out of your mouth to feed themselves. You cannot compete with white laborers among white employers. In fact, you know you won't work without a master. You will let your children perish. You will be a beggar, an outcast, a vagabond. Take my word for it, if you trust these Yankees you will rue it as long as you live. Now will you run away, Gabriel?"

"I's a thinkin' I better be a gwine," answered Gabe, as before.

"Gabriel, you will commit a grievous sin. You would not go against the Bible, would you? I will expound your duty to you out of the Holy Scriptures."

Taking up the Book and drawing his spectacles down upon his nose, Mr. Palmer proceeded to read and expound some selected passages, while Gabe stood before him, twisting a button and perusing the carpet.

"Hear now," he continued, "what is commanded in the twenty-fifth chapter of Leviticus—'Both thy bondmen and thy bondmaids'—that means our slaves, Gabriel—'which thou shalt have, shall be of the heathen that are round about you; of them shall ye buy bondmen and bondmaids. Moreover of the children of the strangers that do sojourn among you, of them shall ye buy and of their families that are with you which they begat in your land: and they shall be your possession. And ye shall take them as an inheritance for your children after you, to inherit them for a possession; they shall be your bondmen forever.' Now, Gabriel, your forefathers were heathen, you know, and so the white people were commanded to buy them for slaves, and to hold them and their children as a possession forever. My forefathers in New England bought many of them, and made great gains by them, which proved that their trade was blessed. When slavery became unprofitable in New England, whereby it appeared that the institution was no longer blessed there, they sold their slaves to the Southern people, with advantage to all parties. So my ancestors again had golden experience that godliness is great gain, and they have continued to be a godly and a gainful people to this very day. The passage I have read requires the slaves to be an inheritance for the children of the masters. I did not receive you by inheritance, but New England men

can, by the Divine blessing, obtain the inheritance of
the children of Virginia as Jacob got the birthright
of Esau by substituting kid for venison. Thus it is
proved out of Scripture, Gabe, that you must stay
with me. What confirms this interpretation is that
the institution of slavery in the South has been
blessed with wonderful usefulness to mankind. While
the slaves multiply and thrive, they have added more
to the wealth, comfort and civilization of the world,
by tillage, than any other equal number of laborers
ever did in the same length of time. You know they
never would have done all this work if they had been
free, and you know that white men could not have
done it. So it is the will of God, Gabriel, that you
shall not run away to the Yankees. Do you understand ?"

"I's a thinkin' I better be a gwine."

"Now, my good and faithful servant, let me read
to you what Saint Paul says—'Exhort servants to be
obedient unto their own masters and to please them
well in all things ; not answering again ; not purloin-
ing but showing all good fidelity'—that means you
must stay with me, Gabriel—and again, ' Let as many
as are under the yoke count their own masters worthy
of all honor. * * * And they that have believing
masters'—like me, Gabriel—'let them not despise
them because they are brethren but rather do them
service'—mark that, Gabriel, do them service. Now
will you fly in the face of Scripture ?"

"I's a thinkin' I better be a gwine."

"Poor Gabriel, I fear your understanding is dark
and your heart hardened. Perhaps we may obtain
light to direct your steps, or to stop them, by prayer.
Let us pray."

He knelt down, as did also his wife and son. Gabe, who had been taught, not to pray, but to stand, in the presence of his betters, and who did not understand that he had been ordered to kneel, remained in his erect posture. He twisted his button and perused the carpet, shifting his weight from one foot to the other, while his lips moved, not in prayer, but in repetition of his fugitive formula. His master prayed very earnestly, in a manner which he thought must impress the mind and melt the heart of his servant. Then he paused, and casting his eyes on Gabe, discovered that he was still standing.

"How is your mind now, Gabriel?" he inquired.

"I's a thinkin' I better be a gwine."

"Kneel down, Gabriel."

Gabe obeyed. He crossed his arms over the bottom of a chair and laid his forehead upon them. The prayer was resumed with increasing fervor. It became so eloquent, unctuous and importunate that Mrs. Palmer was moved to sigh, and then to groan, and finally to respond audibly Amen and Amen. Again pausing, Mr. Palmer turned to his bondman, bought with his money, and said—"how do you feel now, Gabriel?"

"I's a thinkin' I better be a gwine," muttered Gabe.

"Good God!" exclaimed his master, bouncing to his feet, "have we a government that will not protect our property?"

Mrs. Palmer and Albert also rose, but Gabe remained kneeling, with his face upon his arms, and his arms upon the chair. His mistress, gazing at him a moment with rising scorn, then strode with rectangular solemnity to his side, and stretching out her arm over his head, thus addressed him:

"*Et tu, Brute*—ungrateful nigger—*nigroque simil-*

lima cycno—after all we have done for you—we might
have sold you with the rest—we might now have the
money in our pockets—you will run away, will you—
what black ingratitude—who would believe it—*credat
Judæus Apella*—I'll never trust a nigger again—go
then—run, starve, beg, steal, die, rot—go this night
—don't sleep again under this roof—and mind, don't
steal anything when you go—take off that suit and
put on your old clothes—obey me or I'll have you
whipped—I hope you'll rue this hour in want and woe
to the end of your days—begone, you black rascal,
begone."

But Gabe did not rise. He was fast asleep. As
soon as his head rested on a chair slumber began to
creep over him. When his master addressed him he
was partially aroused, and muttered his well-conned
response between asleep and awake. Under the
monotonous declamation of Mrs. Palmer he lost all
consciousness. After the close of her address his only
reply was a sonorous snore. Albert, discovering the
truth of the case, and being himself cool enough to
feel the ridicule of the situation, quietly approached
Gabe, and laying a hand on his shoulder, woke him.
Gabe leaped up and looked about him with amazement.

"Begone!" said his old master.

"I's a thinkin' I better be a gwine."

Gabe hustled out of the parlor with less servile ceremony than he had been accustomed to display in
retiring from the presence.

The family council, resuming its session, discussed
various topics, and among them the Fairfaxes of Roebuck came under consideration. The course and conclusion of the consultation respecting that family need
not now be stated. So far as results followed from it,

of interest to the reader, they will appear in the
sequel. While the name of Fairfax was yet upon
their lips the signal of blind Pete was heard, and he
was admitted. He came to report that Colonel Fitzhugh was spending the night at Roebuck. Albert
Palmer, eager to avail himself of the information,
mounted his horse, and after giving an order to Pete,
rode to the village.

Pete's clandestine information was so far correct
that Hugh Fitzhugh visited Roebuck that night, but
left there before Albert Palmer could have arrived at
the village. Going with his regiment upon an expedition, he passed near Roebuck in the night. While
the regiment halted for a brief rest he rode off with a
small escort to visit Colonel Fairfax, and ascertain
from him whether the rumors were true which
he had heard of the outrages committed upon the
people of the county. After conversing with the
colonel upon that subject, he indulged himself with a
brief delay, to talk with Julia upon a subject of more
tender interest to them than to the public. Then,
while he lingered yet a little longer, conversation
turned upon the desolation of Virginia and the suffering of her people. A large portion of the State was
already ravaged and devastated. The flower of her
youth and manhood had been cut down by thousands.
From the first to the last hour of the war the blood of
the State flowed in torrents, and in all her borders it
seemed that nothing could stand erect under the in-
cessant storm of war but her unconquerable spirit.
Those who then fondly protracted a hurried conversation, to deplore the afflictions of their beloved Commonwealth, could not foresee that they would never
meet again under the roof of Roebuck. They knew

not the ruin that was yet hidden in the darkness of
that very night. Happy ignorance of the future!
They had fortitude to bear the ills which they had
known, but who could endure a knowledge of the
time to come? Fitzhugh took leave of Colonel Fairfax and Mrs. Fairfax with words of cheerful anticipation, and in accents that became sad, in spite of his
efforts to cheer their hearts, he was about to bid farewell to Julia. He paused and said, "My dearest
Julia, I must carry with me the memory of your sweet
voice in song. Sing one song for me before I leave
you." At such a moment her voice could not be
quite free from the tremulous effect of her emotion, but
she, too, was exerting herself to lighten the sadness
of hearts she loved, and not permitting her tones to
betray her heart too plainly, she sung a song—

VIRGINIA.

Virginia bleeds and weeps for woe
  But feels no touch of shame;
Beneath eclipse her glories glow
  With undiminished flame.
A virgin queen with laurel crown,
  A sovereign of the free,
She vows to trample tyrants down
  And bleeds for liberty.

Not always thus shall droop her head,
  She will rejoice again:
No blood so pure for freedom shed
  Was ever shed in vain.
An altar every battle-field
  On which her sons have died—
Its smoke, like incense, has appealed
  Where right is ne'er denied.

CHAPTER XXI.

BUSHWHACKING AT ROEBUCK.

AMONG the Federal officers at the village was Captain Dakin, who led a company of marauding cavalry. He was active, daring, cruel and treacherous. He was a favorite instrument of Colonel Wesel in executing all plans of bold adventure or ruthless revenge. By virtue of a round, red face, a jolly laugh, and a fondness for the bottle, he was called a good fellow. The licence which he allowed to his men made him popular among them. He had been a preacher. After wearing out religion as a theme of popular eloquence, he took to preaching politics from the pulpit. The political agitation of the day was the controversy between the North and South, and that, curiously enough, turned mainly upon Southern slavery, which excited no dissension where it existed, but offended the North, where it was unknown. The pretext for introducing it into the sacred desk, and beating the "drum ecclesiastic" for recruits in the political warfare of the North against the South, was that slavery was a sin. From the exclusive attention given to it, the reverend gentleman's hearers might have concluded that it was the only sin extant, and, consequently, that those who were free from it were saints. It was so atrocious a crime, that the preacher in denouncing slave-holders, danced in the pulpit with sacred fury. The sentiments which foamed from his lips were unearthly. A mortal who has not been in Heaven, dares not affirm with confidence that they were Heavenly. But it may be presumed that there is a world above or below us in which they might take their origin. As all his hearers were free from the guilt which he denounced, his denunciations may appear to have been superfluous; but they had the happy effect of cultivating in the hearts of his congregation a comfortable sense of their own perfection in comparison with those distant sinners, together with a holy hatred of those reprobates. Besides, they swelled a certain volume of votes. Ambitious to extend the sphere of his usefulness, or preferring the applause of a multitude to the still decorum of a church, this clergyman turned street-preacher. From porticos of public buildings, or from board-piles in vacant lots, he harangued the mob on Sunday afternoons as they were harangued by the other demagogues from similar platforms on week days. At last, weary of teaching others to disdain the commandment against coveting a neighbor's servants, he abandoned the pulpit, and regaled himself with a breach of the commandment against coveting a neighbor's wife. A member of his congregation had a very pretty wife. Her beauty was to blame in the affair. Besides, a sweet sin that nestles in our own bosoms looks less ugly than another man's sin afar off. One may be embraced, while the other is anathema. When the war broke out, however, he left the arms of his charmer, to take up arms for his country.

Albert Palmer, arriving at the village, hastened to communicate to Colonel Wesel the information which he had received from blind Pete. The colonel embraced with alacrity an opportunity to capture the

Confederate officer. Fitzhugh's cavalry had been en-
terprising and troublesome. They had cut off several
parties of Wesel's men, besides harassing him with
alarms in his camp. Aided and stimulated by the
people, who were exasperated by oppression, they had
made it necessary of late for the Federals to restrict
the range of their operations within narrow limits.
The capture of the Confederate colonel, therefore, was
very desirable. It would gratify, also, for Albert
Palmer a private pique, and, perhaps, open the way
for the renewal of a matrimonial project, which, for
certain reasons, he desired to revive. Love had failed,
but arms might prevail. The possession of the heiress
of Roebuck would be convenient in any event of
the war, and he still distrusted the success of the
Federals.

Captain Dakin was aroused from slumber, and intrusted with the duty of capturing Colonel Fitzhugh,
and he was directed also to arrest Colonel Fairfax,
and carry him before the tribunal of the Federal commander, upon a charge of harboring the rebel officer.
He was to take with him but a small party, because
success might depend on secresy as well as promptitude of action. The ready captain soon had his men
in the saddle. In moving about, he stumbled over
Juba, who was asleep on the porch of the Swan
tavern. As it was no longer necessary for him to
take to the bush for the enjoyment of leisure, he
lounged about the village, day and night, waiting for
his slice of land. It occurred to the captain that this
fellow might be useful as a guide about the grounds
of Roebuck, and waking him with a kick, he ordered
him to mount a horse, and accompany the party.
Albert Palmer also went along. When they were

within a mile of the mansion of Roebuck, Captain Dakin informed Juba of his destination and design, requiring the involuntary guide to lead a squad to the rear of the house, and to point out every path, gate and outlet by which Fitzhugh might escape. To quicken his intelligence, he was told that, if the rebel officer was not captured, he should be hung.

Arriving near the mansion, Captain Dakin quietly posted his men so as to shut up every loop-hole of retreat, and then rode up to the front of the house. Awaking the inmates by beating on a door, he called for Colonel Fairfax. That gentleman soon appeared at an upper window, and inquired who was there.

" Captain Dakin desires to see Colonel Fitzhugh."

" He is not here."

" I know better. I have direct information. You can't deceive me."

" There is no attempt to deceive you, I assure you he is not in the house."

" You want to parley while he escapes. I understand your game. It won't do. Your house is surrounded with my troops."

" Captain Dakin, upon my honor he is not here."

" You lie, you —— old rebel. Send Fitzhugh to me, or I will set fire to your house in five minutes. It ought to have been burnt long ago."

" It is impossible for me to send a man who is not near me."

" Then the house shall burn."

" Surely, you are not in earnest ?"

" You will see."

Captain Dakin called two of his men, and ordered them to bring fire from a negro cabin, and apply it to the house in front and rear. Colonel Fairfax remon-

strated, and invited him to search the house. The
captain replied that he was not to be taken in by that
trick. He was then requested to give the ladies time
to put on their clothes, and leave the house before it
was fired. He answered, with an oath, that they and
Colonel Fairfax should remain in the house, and be
burnt with it, unless he delivered up Colonel Fitzhugh. "Give him up," he added, "or his sweet-
heart shall answer for it." This brutal threat was
heard by Julia, who stood at a window of her chamber listening to the dialogue. Mrs. Fairfax stood
near her husband. He requested her to go to Julia's
room, and directed that they should both prepare to
fly from the house. He then went for a gun which
he kept concealed, because the inhabitants were generally disarmed by the Federals. Returning to the
window, he saw the two soldiers approaching with
fire. He called out to Captain Dakin, and said—"if
you attempt to burn the house with my family in it,
I will certainly shoot the man who applies the torch,"
The captain ordered the men to fire the house. One
of them, coming to the front, applied the fire, and
stooped down to kindle it. Colonel Fairfax discharged a load of buck-shot from one barrel of the
gun, and one or two shots entered the soldier's leg.
He ran away, making a great outcry of pain. The
colonel passed over to a back window, and saw the
other soldier putting fire to the house. He discharged
the other barrel, and the man then ran, alarmed, but
not hurt. Colonel Fairfax re-loaded his gun, and resumed his place at the front. In the meantime, a
negro man, who slept in the house, was awakened by
the report of fire-arms, and ran to the assistance of his
master. He came to the window just as some of the

soldiers fired a volley at it, and he was slightly
wounded. His master, having no weapon for him,
sent him to the assistance of the ladies, with a request
that they would go down stairs, where he would presently join them, and endeavor to escape. The man
found them dressed; but Mrs. Fairfax, overcome with
alarm, had sunk upon the floor, and Julia knelt beside
her, urging her to fly. When the servant came, she
left her mother with him, and going to her father, insisted that he should convey Mrs. Fairfax from the
house, while she would remain at the window, and
engage the attention of the soldiers. He directed her
to return, and, with the assistance of the servant,
carry her mother down stairs, saying that he would
detain the soldiers at the front, until the ladies were
ready to pass out from a back door, which he designated, and then he would follow. In obedience to his
directions, they descended to the door. While this
was taking place within, Captain Dakin found means
to fire the house, and very soon the flames began to
ascend on every side. The colonel, without further
delay, followed the ladies, and found them waiting for
him at the door.

Taking his wife, almost inanimate, in his arms, he
went out, followed by Julia and the servant. They
walked rapidly away from the house, and for a short
distance were concealed by shrubbery. But they
were soon discovered and were pursued with cries of
"here they go—shoot them—kill the —— secesh."
Several pistols were fired at them. A ball took effect
in the colonel's thigh and he fell to the ground. His
wife became quite insensible. Julia stood a moment
bewildered. She saw some of the soldiers seize her
father and others her mother, dragging them away.

She felt the grasp of two men who drew her along; and before she could recover from the stupefaction of terror, they placed her on a horse before the rider. He held her firmly and dashed off at a rapid pace, which soon recalled her faculties. She struggled to free herself, but the horseman, tightening his grasp about her waist, said—" be not alarmed, Miss Fairfax; you are safe; I will carry you away from those ruffians." She recognized the voice of Albert Palmer.

"My father," she cried, "my mother—I must not leave them. O, Captain Palmer, release me."

"That would be madness, Miss Fairfax. You would run into danger and could do no good. I will take you to a place of safety and then look after them."

"I must go back. Release me, sir."

"No, my sweet bird, that is impossible."

He struck his spurs into his horse, and in spite of her entreaties, remonstrances and struggles, he bore her away through the darkness.

While the fire was raging, Captain Dakin was moving about in great excitement, cursing and giving orders to secure the rebels and keep strict watch for Fitzhugh. He was expected every moment to issue from the burning building. When the house was so far consumed that Captain Dakin was sure the rebel officer could not be in it, he called for the negro who had acted as guide, swearing that he had played false. Poor Juba was found and brought before him. "Hang him," was the peremptory order. In vain the negro protested his innocence and implored mercy. His cries, his groans, his tears were disregarded. While the flames yet raged, he swung from a tree before the house—a corpse. Sparks fell on the cabin

of old Uncle Valentine, and it was soon in a blaze.
He was carried from it by some of the negroes, dreadfully burned, and in a few minutes he died. It is
believed that Joe perished in the burning mansion.
He ran towards it when he saw it in flames, and hearing that his master was inside, he rushed in to rescue
him.   He was seen running to and fro in the upper
part of the house when the fire was licking the highest windows.   He was never seen afterwards.

Mrs. Fairfax, after being dragged a short distance
by the soldiers, was left by them lying upon the
ground, her age and sex, perhaps, obtaining for her
the compassion of neglect.   Some of her servants carried her to a negro cabin, where the faithful creatures
ministered to her with assiduous care until morning,
when she was conveyed to the house of a friend in the
neighborhood.   Colonel Fairfax, after being drawn
along the earth in great agony from the spot where
he was wounded to a place more remote from the
flames, was guarded as if he had been able to fight or
fly.   He lay in pain and in view of his burning home;
but more intolerable than his wound was his anxiety
for the safety of his wife and daughter.   He was kept
in ignorance of their fate, and when the rising sun
shone upon the smoking ruins of his mansion, he was
thrown into a cart and carried to the village.   He was
there placed in a house which was used as a hospital.
The surgeon in charge treated him with professional
skill and with extreme kindness.   He left nothing
undone that was within his power for the relief and
comfort of the wounded and bereaved gentleman.
During the day a considerable number of Federal
officers called upon him to express their sympathy
and respect.   Of these, some had enjoyed his hospi-

tality, and esteemed him from personal acquaintance.
To others he was a stranger, but they knew his character and acted in the spirit of generous courtesy
which becomes the profession of arms.

When Colonel Wesel heard his subordinate's report of the proceedings or operations of the night, he
commended the captain's conduct, and was enraged at
the audacious attack made by Colonel Fairfax on the
Federal troops. He looked upon it as the cap-sheaf
of crime in the county. He denounced Colonel Fairfax not only as a " secesh," a rebel and an aristocrat,
but as a " bushwhacker "—an epithet commonly
applied to those persons, who, not being in the military service, waylaid enemies and shot them from
bushes, trees, rocks, houses or other places of concealment. The insolent offences of the secesh citizens, he
declared, had been increasing of late. Women had
worn Confederate colors in their garments and had
declined the acquaintance of Federals. Men had refused to remain at home and till the ground. Negroes
had been chastised. Rebel soldiers had been harbored
by their families and others. Loyal citizens had been
insulted. The venerable clergyman of the village had
refused to pray for the President of the United States
These, and other enormities, were recited in an order
issued by Colonel Wesel, and it was added that lawless barbarity had at last culminated in an attempt
made by a bad old man to assassinate a Federal officer
and several men, at midnight, by clandestinely shooting
at them from the concealment of darkness and of a
private dwelling. The colonel announced his determination to suppress all these diabolical practices, and
especially that of bushwhacking. He threatened
that other dwellings should be destroyed, and that, if

such offences were repeated, the county should be made a barren waste.

He proceeded to make an example of the church and the pastor. He appropriated the ancient edifice to the uses of a stable for the cavalry. He caused the Reverend Mr. Ambler to be arrested and brought before him. After interrogating and bullying the old gentleman, and lecturing him on theology; he condemned the meek and venerable minister to work upon the street of the village daily, during the pleasure of the colonel. The sentence was instantly carried into execution, and, beside a negro, the village pastor, guarded like a felon, bowed his white head over a spade. He bore his cross with Christian resignation, but he called to mind the words of the Preacher—"If thou seest the oppression of the poor and violent perverting of judgment and justice in a province, marvel not at the matter: for He that is higher than the highest regardeth; and there be higher than they."

CHAPTER XXII.

VENGEANCE.

In the afternoon of the same day, Captain Dakin was sent out upon an errand of devastation. At Roebuck he burned barns, fences, stacks and everything else that was valuable and combustible, except a few cabins inhabited by negroes—a faithful remnant of the blithe black population that once enjoyed the wealth of that estate. He then led his troopers to Willowbank, and proceeded to execute vengeance upon Hugh Fitzhugh and his mother, by destroying their ancient mansion. He sent one of the servants to notify his mistress that he was about to burn the house, and that she would be allowed ten minutes to remove her indispensable clothing. She was confined to bed by sickness. She sent her faithful servant, Belle, to inform the Federal officer of her condition, and to request him not to disturb her at that time. He replied that he was up to the tricks of the "she-rebels;" that her illness was feigned, to save her house, but that it should not avail. He ordered Belle to tell the old woman up stairs that the house would be fired in precisely ten minutes by the watch.

When the lady was informed of this savage threat, and was convinced by Belle's representations that the captain intended to execute it, her eyes flashed and her bosom swelled with indignant defiance. The energy of her spirit overcame the languor of disease. "Go," said she to Belle, "tell the brutal wretch that

I will remain here. Let him burn the house and me too." Belle descended again and informed the captain that her mistress could not be removed without risk of her life, and would not consent to leave the house. She implored him not to burn the house with her mistress in it. He repeated his former threat, with many oaths. When the servant returned to the chamber she found that Mrs. Fitzhugh had composed herself in bed with rigid resolution, and was evidently preparing her mind for the death which she expected. She said to her servant—" Stay here until they fire the house ; then save yourself. I hope this sacrifice will arouse the indignation of men and the justice of Heaven to arrest the atrocious system of warfare that is desolating my country. Tell my dear Hugh that I die blessing him. God save Virginia. Now farewell, my good girl. I must prepare for death."

Belle uttered loud lamentations, and, on her knees, entreated her mistress to leave the house. She even attempted to carry her away forcibly, but the authority and resistance of the energetic old lady prevented her. When the fire began to rise she ran to and fro wildly, and then, after a final effort to remove Mrs. Fitzhugh with affectionate violence, she fled from the flames. When Captain Dakin saw her run out, leaving her mistress in the burning building, he began to think that the old lady really could not be removed by her servant, and that she would be consumed by the fire. Shocked at that probable event, he ordered some of his men to enter the house and carry her out. They rushed into her chamber, caught her up, without regarding her remonstrances, and bore her into the yard only a moment before it would have been too late to descend the stairs. They laid her on the grass, and there she witnessed the final destruction of her house. When the flames had sunk into smouldering ashes she inquired for the officer in command. Captain Dakin presented himself to her.

"Captain," she said, looking at him sternly, "you have destroyed my home, thrusting me from it when I am too feeble to rise; but my misfortunes are as nothing in the general calamity. I bear them patiently, as sacrifices for my country. It is not of them I wish to speak to you. But I have heard of the outrages you have perpetrated upon others—upon rich and poor—upon men, women and children. Now, while you look on the last embers you have made, your latest victim, a feeble old woman, warns you to desist from your ferocious warfare on the innocent and defenceless. As sure as there is a God who pities the widow and the fatherless, you and your people will rue these crimes. Divine justice will not always sleep"——

"Divine justice!" interrupted the reverend captain, with an oath and a satirical laugh, "that's played out long since at the North. No more of that sort of talk, old woman."

"Have you dethroned God?"

"Take this woman away," he said to some of her servants who had assembled around her. They carried her away tenderly. Some of them had lately been corrupted by evil association, but the sight of their old mistress in distress moved their passionate hearts to eager demonstrations of affection. She thanked them, and when she was refreshed with rest she called some of her women around her and thus addressed them:

"I thank you, my poor girls, for your service. I am grateful to all my servants. I do not reproach those who have left me. I pity you all. You do not foresee the evils that are coming upon your race. I can no longer protect you. Our house, that gave you and me shelter, is destroyed. Our family is broken up. We shall be no more together. But I shall never forget the love and fidelity of my servants during so many years. God grant that you may never regret our separation. I cannot give you counsel hereafter, and let me tell you, once for all, that if you would be happy you must be humble, industrious and good. Bless you, my girls; may you be happy!"

After Captain Dakin had fulfilled his mission of destruction at Willowbank, he led his troopers away to other work of a similar kind. Passing near the cabin of Marlin, the preaching cooper, he remembered a report that Eliza Marlin had committed the offence of carrying medicines to the rebels. He could not recollect the particulars of the accusation, but it arose out of the circumstance that, when her father had an attack of fever, she visited him in camp, and carried some drugs for the use of him and others. Halting before the cabin, he called Eliza and charged her with the offence. She admitted it, stating all the circumstances. He declared that she should be punished on the spot. By his command some of the men seized her, and tying her thumbs with cords, drew them up until her arms were stretched above her head and she stood upon her toes, and then they attached the cords to a joist. Others tied her mother to a chair, so that she could not release her daughter. Thus the two women were left. Eliza had struggled while they were binding her, until she found resistance useless, and then, disdaining to beg for mercy, she submitted in silence. When her face reddened and her eyes flashed with indignation, she seemed beautiful to the rude and pitiless troopers. Her defenceless situation and the degradation to which she had been subjected by their captain encouraged them to entertain a licentious and outrageous design against her. On the march, when it had become dark, four or five of them separated themselves from the command and returned to the cabin. Releasing Eliza, they began to insult her with the rough familiarity of affected fondness, and then ensued a scene of violence which cannot be described.

When the men were departing they released Mrs. Marlin, and with mock compassion bade her take good care of her pretty daughter. That wretched girl was left nearly dead, and praying for death as a refuge from shame. Her mother's brain reeled, and she was almost incapable of rendering any assistance to the form that writhed upon the floor. "O, mother, mother," was the despairing cry of the girl in her deadly anguish. "O, God, O, God!" was the cry of the mother. Throwing herself beside her daughter, and embracing her with frenzied passion, she sobbed and wept until the motionless stillness of the girl startled her with a new fear. "O God, my daughter is dead!" she exclaimed. The dim light of a poor candle could scarcely reveal her low breathing, her eyes were half-closed, and she appeared to her distracted mother the image of death. Still clinging to hope, Mrs. Marlin hastened to apply the simple restoratives at hand, and gradually recalled so much animation that her daughter could faintly converse. In that condition she lingered some hours of the night.

Having laid her on a bed, her mother sat beside her. With her strong will she drove back the madness which she felt to be creeping over her brain, in order that she might ward off death, which, she feared, was stealing into the heart of her daughter. Alone, through the dark and dreary watches of a terrible night, she sustained that awful conflict. The dying girl sometimes, in delirium, uttered words that cleft the soul of the lonely watcher at her bedside. Sometimes, in rational moments, she whispered such despair, such pity for her mother, such affection for her absent father and brother, that the miserable mother wavered between madness and death. At length Eliza started up, and staring with all the dreadful feelings of that night concentrated in her eyes, she cried, "it is over," and fell back upon her pillow. Then a more placid expression settled upon her face, and she died.

The mother at first refused to believe that all was over. She fancied that a light breath still came from those lifeless lips. She laid her hand over the pulseless heart and stood fondly waiting to feel the motion of life. While thus she stood a change came over her own features. Still feeling in vain for the pulsation of her daughter's heart, her pallid features became rigid and then relaxed to an unmeaning simper. "I can't find it—I can't find it"—she repeated, moving her hands about over the body of her child. Presently she walked to the door—then out upon the road, and she stood there a few minutes in silence. Suddenly she burst into a loud laugh, and cried—"I know where it is. Abraham's got it. I'll go for Abraham." She walked rapidly away through the darkness. By chance, or from some recollection that her husband had passed that way the night before, she followed his regiment. She kept on its track during the remainder of the night, in the morning and throughout the day. On she went, without food or drink or rest. Now and then she stopped and looked bewildered, as if she had forgotten her errand. Then she would start, saying, "I'll go for Abraham—he's got it." Thus onward she strode, drawn by the insane fancy that her husband could restore that mysterious spring of life which had ceased to vibrate in the bosom of her daughter, though she had lost all rational recollection of that which she had lost and for which she searched. "Abraham's got it—I'll go for Abraham;" this fragment of thought survived the wreck of her intellect, and was drifting her towards her husband.

At evening she came upon the regiment where it had halted. Moving about among the men, she took no notice of any one until she saw her husband. Running to him, she seized his hand and attempted to lead him along, while she said, "Come, Abraham—I knowed you had it. Bring it home. Eliza's waiting for it. She is lying on the bed. She looks so pretty." She laughed aloud, and then began to talk rapidly and incoherently, making no allusion to her daughter or to her husband's return home. Having fulfilled the purpose which had kept her wandering mind partially fixed during the day, she lost all control of her wild imagination. In vain her distressed husband endeavored to learn from her the object of her journey and the rational explanation of the words with which she had greeted him. When her son, hearing of her arrival, went to meet her, she fell upon his neck, exclaiming, "my brave boy." Then her talk rambled again into unintelligible mazes. Her husband and son were afflicted beyond expression. They feared,

11*

too, that some dreadful event must have occurred to shatter her intellect, and both her first allusion to Eliza, and the absence of the daughter from the mother in her present condition, suggested the most terrible apprehensions for the beloved girl.

When Colonel Fitzhugh became acquainted with these circumstances he expressed the deepest sorrow for the afflictions of this poor family, and considered what might be done for their relief. Among other measures which he suggested or adopted, he relieved both Abraham and Mark from military duty, advising the husband to take charge of his wife, and the son to go home immediately and look after the safety of his sister. They followed his advice, and Mark was soon riding rapidly towards the cabin in which Eliza had been left by her mother.

CHAPTER XXIII.

BAXTER.

SOME time after nightfall, while Captain Dakin was absent from the village, upon his foray against Willowbank, and other defenceless dwellings of women and children, Colonel Wesel was seated in a great arm-chair, in a room of the Swan tavern. His rotund figure swelled with importance, his face was red, and his eyes were moist with the dew distilled by drink. Altogether, he looked mellow, though duly formidable, as he said pompously—"bring in the prisoner." The order was obeyed, and a young man, followed by a guard, swaggered into the room, and, without waiting for an invitation, took a seat. He looked first at Colonel Wesel, and then at Albert Palmer, who was sitting at the colonel's right hand, as a counsellor. He gazed at them both with an insolent stare, and then, leaning back in his chair, threw his feet upon a table. He was clad in the uniform of a private of Confederate cavalry. He was not known to the colonel, but Palmer at once recognized his old antagonist, Baxter. That eccentric commissary resigned his commission at the time of his duel with Palmer, and returning home, he remained there in inglorious ease, until the next spring, when the law of conscription was enacted by the Confederate Congress. Being then obliged to enter the service, he became a private in the company formerly commanded by Hugh Fitzhugh. When the regiment passed near Roebuck,

just before the burning of that mansion, Baxter took
the liberty of withdrawing from the ranks and visiting the village. He intended to spend an hour there,
and return to the regiment. But he fell in with a
boon companion and good liquor. His habitual
weakness detained him several hours, and, at last, he
lay down to sleep himself sober. He slept until evening, and then, in attempting to pass out of the village, he was captured. When he found himself in
the presence of Wesel and Palmer, his first thought
was that the one was a fool, and the other a coward.
He conceived the idea of escaping from durance by
some stratagem, and with that view, he determined to
protract the proceedings, which would keep him about
the tavern, and to try the effect of bullying his
judges. He gave free rein to his insolence, affecting
to be drunk, although he was as sober as a man ought
ever to be, according to his theory.

"So," said Colonel Wesel, sternly, "you be'st our
prisoner."

"I suspected as much," answered Baxter.

"And moreover, besides, you be'st a spy."

"That's a lie."

"Mein Gott! That is impudence."

"You are a fool, and you speak broken Dutch."

"Vat you say? You impudent slavery institution.
Donner! That institution is impudent. Vat you say?
Eh-h-h?"

"Colonel, you are right in objecting to the institution, but you do not urge the right objection."

"Vat is das, you secesh puppy."

"The only valid objection to our peculiar institution is that the niggers sing at their work, and sing
slow tunes. They work to hymns, and dance to jigs.
It won't pay."

"Vell, I vill hang you. You bees a spy. Now let us go 'on wid the examination. I vill hang you, but I vill examine you first. You shall not say, when you are dead, that I does not the fair thing."

"I think we might pass over the examination, since the sentence has been already pronounced. That would save time."

"No; I vill examine you, to hang you according to law."

"Then I will lie down on this bench, and take a nap, while you are engaged in the examination. When you are ready to hang me, please wake me up. I want to see it done."

"You dinks I von't hang you; but I vill, by ——."

"No, you won't."

"What for I won't hang you? Eh-h-h!"

"Don't put your face so near me, when you speak to me. Your breath smells of onions and Sweitzer cheese."

"I vill stop your breath vid a rope, hundsfut, Johnny Reb."

"Now, don't. I prefer to be shot. Can't you spare me a bullet? A bullet is the decent dose for a gentleman. There is Palmer—he can tell you so. By the way, did he ever tell you about the exchange of bullets between him and me when he was in the rebel service?"

"You slander mine friend. He is not a rebel nor never vas not."

"Not rebel enough to hurt him. He deserted the first chance he got."

"Don't mind what a drunken fellow says," interposed Palmer.

"But, colonel, I must tell you about our duel. It is a capital story. This was the way of it."

"He will talk here all night, if you let him," again interrupted Palmer, uneasily, "you had better send him to the guard-house."

"But, colonel, it is a good story. Send for a bottle, and I will tell you all about it while we drink."

"You saucy sesesh! You shall not drink my liquor, nor tell me no story. Let us go on vid the examination."

"Now, colonel, I know you are dry. So am I. You won't refuse a poor devil a drink, when he is going to be hung."

"Das is true. Das is fair. Palmer, please get the bottle."

"That, now, is handsome for a Dutchman," said Baxter, taking up the bottle, which Palmer produced from a closet, "now, I will tell the story."

"You are an infamous liar," exclaimed Palmer, livid with rage.

"You shall be a toddy," said Baxter, as he hurled the bottle at Palmer's head; "whiskey to milk-and-water;" but the bottle missed the head, and was shattered against the wall; "a dead loss," added Baxter.

Wesel stormed furiously, and threatened the prisoner with a thousand deaths, in German and English. Baxter sat quiet, until the storm had somewhat subsided, and he then said, "Colonel, as we have nothing to drink, we had better resume the examination."

"Vell, I vill hang you."

"You dare not."

"Vot for I dares not?"

"Because Colonel Fitzhugh will hang you before to-morrow-night, if you do."

"Fitzstue! Where is he? I vas looking for that rebel. I burnt him up in that——old rebel roost."

"He is with his regiment, and near enough to you to hang you to-morrow."

"Vas he in this village vid you ven you didn't get out? Tell me truth, or I vill hang you again, two, three times."

"He may be in the village now."

"Ambuscade, eh? That—— rebel cavalry is everywhere. I can't sleep. I can't eat mine dinner, I can't take mine little dram—you broke mine bottle, you —— butternut—till some fellow comes running in to tell the rebel cavalry is upon us. It is the black-horse and the white-horse, it is Ashby's and Stuart's, and it is Fitzstue's all the times. Where is he? Send out some of them cowardly cavalry of mine. They runs back ven they sees a bush. Send the prisoner to the guard house."

"I won't go to the guard-house."

"You won't. Why won't you, then? Eh-h-h!"

"Because I am a gentleman. I'll give you my parole."

"You are a rebel—that's vot you bees."

"A rebel owing allegiance, I suppose, to Dutchmen hired to conquer American States!"

"I bin colonel of a loyal regiment. I bin gentleman."

"A Dutch colonel of a Yankee regiment! What a conjunction! Krout and clam-chowder! Hessian and Yankee! Hush—listen—there is Fitzhugh's cavalry now!"

A clatter of hoofs was heard on the street. Colonel

Wesel started up and ran to the door, followed by all
the others who were in the room. He called to arms.
He peered into the dark to ascertain the cause of the
alarm. Captain Dakin with his troops rode up. In
the confusion and darkness Baxter had slipped away.
By his intimate knowledge of all places about the village he was able in a few minutes to reach a place of
concealment, where he remained until a late hour of
the night favored his escape.

After passing out of the village, and walking a mile
or two, he heard the rattling of a cart on the road.
Stopping behind a tree until it came up, he found it
was blind Pete's. That knave still continued his nocturnal rambles, and practised his villainies now without even the trouble of giving bail. Baxter hailed
him, and taking a seat in the cart beside him, told him
to drive on. As they rode along, he drew from Pete
a variety of information about the Federal force and
other matters, sometimes by wheedling and sometimes by brow-beating. It was not difficult to do, for
Pete parted readily with whatever knowledge he possessed. He would yield it up at any time to bribes
or threats, and often threw it away recklessly, from a
propensity to gossip. From him Baxter derived
some information respecting Colonel Fairfax and his
family, which, with additions not known to the blind
gossip, it is proper to convey to the reader.

When Pete, on the night before, left Mr. Palmer's,
he went with his cart towards Roebuck, by order of
Albert. That young gentleman could not have anticipated the fire, but he appears to have conceived the
capture of Fitzhugh and the arrest of Colonel Fairfax,
and may have thought that the execution of such a
plan of violence would offer an opportunity for using

Pete's cart in some such enterprise as he afterwards
effected. On his way thither the carter met Palmer,
carrying Miss Fairfax on his horse. With Pete's
assistance he forced her into the cart and took a seat
beside her. He then directed Pete to drive to his
father's. The young lady frequently implored Palmer
with pathetic entreaty to release her or to carry her
to her parents. Sometimes, as the cart moved on, she
tried to get upon her knees before him. She appealed
to his manhood, to his pity. Sometimes, after she
found him unrelenting, she gave way to helpless and
hopeless indignation, more pitiable than her tears. He
spoke but little. At first he affected to soothe her
with professions of regard and promises of safety.
Then, becoming impatient, he rebuked her sternly
and relapsed into silence. When they arrived at his
father's house she was taken to the front door, which
was opened by Mr. Palmer, in answer to Pete's signal,
and then the blind agent was dismissed.

The next morning the elder Palmer called on Colonel Wesel at the village. He and his son were con-
fidential advisers of that officer in all affairs of the
county. He was trusted as the head of the "loyal"
element in the county, as he had a right to be—being
the head of his own family. After congratulating
Colonel Wesel upon the vigor and success of his
administration, especially as shown in the last night's
operations, he proceeded to dilate upon the importance
of the capture which had been made in the person of
Colonel Fairfax. Besides denouncing the offences
specially charged against him, such as harboring a
rebel officer and bushwhacking, he represented that
the colonel was the main stay of the secession interest
in the county. He suggested that the removal of one

so influential from the State would tend to quell the
spirit of resistance, and produce quiet and submission.
He suspected that if such a prisoner remained at the
village desperate efforts would be made to rescue him,
and Colonel Wesel might be attacked by an. over-
powering force.   He advised that the distinguished
rebel should be sent to Washington, with a suitable
representation of his offences and of his importance,
in order that he might be detained there as a prisoner
of State.   Colonel Wesel, elated with his good fortune, and apprehensive of a rescue, embraced the advice
with alacrity.   That very evening Colonel Fairfax
was started to Washington.   He had to make the first
stage of the journey in an open wagon and over rough
roads.   He suffered intolerable pain.   But he was
hurried off without mercy, escorted by a strong guard.
He requested permission to see his wife and daughter
before starting, but it was refused.   He was not informed of his destination, and that was kept a secret
from others, lest a knowledge of the route to be pursued should facilitate a rescue.   He was not even
permitted to know what had become of his wife and
daughter.

Mrs. Fairfax remained at the house to which she
had been carried, as already mentioned, on the morning after the fire at Roebuck.   Mrs. Fitzhugh was
carried to the same place, after the destruction of her
house.   To that high-spirited lady the exertion required by her misfortune proved an antidote to melancholy.   As she had suffered only in the loss of property,
and not, like Mrs Fairfax, in the loss of those who
were dearest to her, she became more cheerful than
she had usually been during the war.   She devoted
herself to the consolation of her more afflicted friend.

Mrs. Fairfax, of a gentle, tender, delicate nature, accustomed to be cherished by her husband and daughter, and hitherto sheltered by fortune from the storms of life, pined under her calamities. The shocks which she endured in that dreadful night, when her house was burned, and her husband and daughter were snatched from her to be carried, she knew not whither, almost bereft her of existence. She had not the stubborn qualities which might have enabled her to rally her strength and spirits. No consolation could lift her from despondency. Sorrow withered her strength and her health vanished. Her form wasted away. She lay night and day, scarcely uttering a word but the names of her husband and daughter. Life waned in her until it became the shadow of death.

CHAPTER XXIV.

ALBERT PALMER'S LOVE.

WHEN Mr. Palmer, on the night of the fire at Roebuck, had opened his door, he was informed by his son that Miss Fairfax was there, desiring refuge and repose, in consequence of the destruction of her father's house. "No, no," she cried, "I am brought here against my will, and I implore you to let me go home." But Albert Palmer thrust her in, and drew her to the parlor, where he placed her on a sofa. He then requested his father to get a light and to summon his mother to the care of their guest.

When Mr. Palmer returned, with his wife and a light, Julia sat on the sofa, with her hands clasped on her lap and her head drooping. She wore no bonnet, and her brown hair, dishevelled, flowed down over her shoulders and bosom. She was pale as death. Her lips were slightly parted. She breathed quickly. Her breast heaved with agitation. Her dress, hastily put on while she was attending to her alarmed mother, was in disorder. Her feet were bare. Even Albert Palmer was startled when he beheld that figure of beautiful desolation. His parents stood in mute wonder. Julia, lifting her eyes, discovered that one of her own sex had entered the room, and springing from the sofa, threw herself at the feet of Mrs. Palmer, clasping her knees and turning up her face, with tears raining from her eyes, while she appealed in broken accents to a woman's compassion for a woman.

"O, save me," she cried; "let me go to my father and mother. I have been cruelly torn from them. Their house is destroyed. My father is wounded. My mother is in distress. They may be dying. I know not what is to become of them this dreadful night. Let me go to them.' You have a woman's heart. O, have pity on a broken-hearted girl. Release me, O, release me."

"Rise, Miss Fairfax," said Albert Palmer, taking her by the hand; "you know not what you say. You are distracted with grief. Mother, there has been a terrible scene to-night. Miss Fairfax needs repose. We must, for her own good, do some gentle violence to her wishes. Please conduct her to a chamber and persuade her to take some rest."

"Hypocrite and tyrant!" exclaimed Julia, rising to her feet, "you are my enemy—my father's foe—a traitor to my country. You are leagued with invaders and oppressors. To you we owe the calamities of this night. You hold me a prisoner. You have torn me from my parents. O, my father! O, my poor mother!" Again she sunk upon the floor, dissolved in tears, and sobbing as if her heart would break.

In a few moments she rose again and ran towards the door, saying, "I will go to them." But Albert Palmer intercepted her, seized her, and, carrying her to a chamber, told his mother to follow him. When they had entered the room he left the two ladies there, locked the door, and put the key in his pocket. He returned to his father, and after relating to him the events of the night, explained to him his plan with reference to Miss Fairfax. She was, he said, without a home. Her father was a prisoner, under grave accusations. He might be long detained or sent out of the State. His property might be taken from him. But if Julia should become Mrs. Palmer it would probably be restored, if not to Colonel Fairfax, at least to his daughter, through the influence of her new relatives. The hope of thus relieving her parents and of procuring the liberation of her father through the same influence, he believed, would induce her to accept his hand. The greater the distress and danger of her father might become, the more she would be inclined to accede to measures necessary for his relief. Perhaps it would be expedient to have Colonel Fairfax sent to Washington, so that the hopes and fears of his daughter, deprived of communication with him, and uncertain as to his fate, might render her more pliant. Of course, Mr. Palmer and his son would ultimately procure his release, as well as the possession of his property, and his daughter would be provided with a husband and a home. This scheme appeared to the elder Palmer so wise and benevolent, that he cheerfully consented, at his son's request, to keep Miss Fairfax in his house and to visit Colonel Wesel the next day, as we have seen he did.

Mrs. Palmer was ignorant of this plan when she found herself shut up in a chamber with Miss Fairfax, and she had nothing to guide her conduct but confidence in her son and obedience to his wishes. She could not frame a suitable speech, but she put her arms about Julia and gently urged her to a bed, beseeching her, in a motherly way, to sleep. The unhappy young lady lay down without resistance, and remained for several hours, not sleeping, but weeping, with her eyes closed and her arms folded over her bosom, without speech or motion. She was alone, friendless, hopeless. She was exhausted in mind and

body, by the fatigues, the sufferings and the terrors
of that night. At length, when the day was breaking, nature yielded to slumber, and she endured,
rather than enjoyed, for an hour, a dreamy, restless
sleep. She awoke with a more vivid sense of affliction.

In the morning, Mrs. Palmer was released from
confinement by her son, who intimated his plan to
her, and while his father was calling on Colonel
Wesel, sent her with his compliments to Miss Fairfax, and requested permission to wait upon the young
lady in her chamber. She desired him to excuse her,
and even protested against his visit. But he declared that it was necessary for him to see her, and
his message to that effect was immediately followed
by himself. He drew up a chair to sit beside her, but
she rose, and remained standing. He made no allusion to her movement, but in cool and civil tones proceeded to address her.

"Miss Fairfax, misled by appearances, you have
placed an erroneous construction upon my conduct.
I came to offer you an explanation." He paused, but
receiving no reply, he resumed. "You have thought
me unkind to you, but really my motives have been
more than kind. In all that I have done, I have
aimed at your welfare and happiness. Perhaps the
ardor of my affection for you has impelled me too far.
I could not avert the misfortune which has befallen
your family. I could not rescue your parents from the
military. I saved yourself in the only way that was
possible. I brought you to my father's house for
shelter. Now, I offer you a home for life. My
heart has long been yours. I now offer you my
hand."

While he delivered this speech with sedate manner
and level voice, Julia stood with averted face, apparently unmoved. When he ceased to speak, she
turned her eyes full upon him, and still restraining
her emotion, she said, "Mr. Palmer, your motives are
known to yourself. If you would prove to me that
they are kind, set me free."

"I have proved more—my love. I offer you the
strongest proof of love."

"Surely, you would not hold me a captive, and
take advantage of my captivity to press a suit which
has once been respectfully declined."

"Love, my dear lady, is blind to circumstances,
and deaf to refusal. Let me believe that time has
rendered you more favorable to my wishes. Let me
hope that you will give me a right to protect you in
all dangers and difficulties. Until you decide upon
my proposal, I cannot consider any other subject."

"If that is a covert threat, I must speak without reserve, and tell you that there is an insurmountable
barrier to your proposal. Let the subject be dismissed forever."

"I cannot imagine a barrier really insurmountable,
Miss Fairfax. May I ask what it is?"

"I—yes—my hand is promised to another."

"Indeed!" he said, commencing his reply in the
measured accents which had hitherto mocked his victim, but the avowal of an engagement with a rival
whom he hated already, because he believed him to
be a successful rival, roused his anger, and as he went
on, he spoke with manifest asperity; "such engage-
ments are not usually deemed irrevocable by young
ladies. Times have changed. When I shall convince
you that the person to whom you have incautiously
promised your hand is unworthy"——

"Unworthy, sir! Can a gentleman disparage a rival? Can a man traduce the absent? Can a being with a heart insult a captive lady by maligning her affianced? Hugh Fitzhugh is that which you prove yourself not to be—a man and a gentleman."

"I admire your spirit, Miss Fairfax, but you have not quite fathomed the question. There are other affections and obligations sometimes to be considered, even before a girl's fancy for a lover. Your love and duty to your father"——·

"My dear, my noble father! What can you tell me of him?"

"That, in disposing of your hand, you may do well to consider his safety."

"I do not understand. What threat lurks in your words and sneer?"

"Be seated, Miss Fairfax. Let us discuss this matter rationally. You will not sit? Well, as you please. You are aware that he is wounded, and a prisoner."

"O, Heavenly Father, protect him."

"He will be sent to Washington."

"To Washington?"

"And detained there as a prisoner of state."

"A prisoner of state! Then he is lost. May Heaven have mercy on him, for man will have none."

"He can be saved."

·"How? Tell me how. I will bless you, as our good angel."

"It depends upon yourself alone."

"Thank God! Then he will be saved. Bid me toil, suffer, die to save him, and he shall be saved."

"There is no need of toil, or suffering, or death.

12

Through the influence of my father and myself, I
doubt not, he can be released. If, in bestowing your
hand "——

"O, horror."

"You give me a right to solicit a favor to your
family as a favor to myself; the loyalty of my family,
and my services may be accounted as an atonement
for the guilt of your father, and we may procure his
release. I have received some tokens of consideration in high quarters. My father is trusted by the
authorities. But it would be - useless, it might be
deemed offensive if we were to intercede for an obnoxious person having no claims upon us. Family
ties would entitle us to ask that he be restored to us.
It depends upon yourself alone to release your father
from captivity."

While he was speaking, Julia's head sunk down
upon her breast, and tears streamed from her eyes.
At last she fell upon her knees before him, and implored him to be merciful.

"You say you have power to save him. O, save
my father, and spare his wretched child. Do not—
do not annex a cruel condition to an act of mercy.
Respect my truth. Spare my grief. O, save my
father."

"Rise, Miss Fairfax. This abasement is unnecessary. Your father's safety rests with yourself. You
understand the condition."

"Then you are inexorable ?"

"I am."

"O, my father! Would that his wisdom could
now direct me. Will you not let me consult him ?"

"No."

"Wounded—a prisoner—sent away to perish in a

cell. If my death could save him! If anything but
falsehood and dishonor—— Sir, I am alone. You
will not let me consult my father. I must recall, then,
the lessons he has taught me. I will be true, and
leave the consequences to Heaven. I cannot violate
my engagement without perfidy. I cannot become
your wife without falsehood. I will preserve my truth."

"Then you reject me again, Miss?"

"I can give no other answer."

"Reflection may change your mind. Good morning, Miss Fairfax."

He left the room. Julia threw herself upon the
bed and gave way to a conflict of emotions. Sometimes she reproached herself, and was ready to recall
Palmer and submit to his terms, rather than leave her
father in captivity and in danger of a more terrible
fate. But his image rising before her mind, rebuked
her meditated falsehood. She thought of him as,
while she sat upon his knee, he had often taught her
the lessons of truth and fortitude and faith. His simple dignity and loving authority again impressed her
heart as they had impressed it in her childhood. She
felt assured that he would approve her decision. He
would sacrifice himself for truth and for her happiness—ah, yes, that thought of her own happiness
again awakened self-reproach. Her happiness was
involved in the question of her father's safety. Her
love for Hugh Fitzhugh, thrilling her whole frame at
that moment, might it not be selfish? Ought she to
sacrifice her father to her own happiness? She was
racked with doubt. Her soul, exhausting itself in
agitation and perplexity, wavered and groped for the
path of duty. Believing that she had done right, and
yet doubting, she sunk at last to sleep, through phy-

sical and mental weariness. She slept several hours.
When she awoke, Mrs. Palmer sat at her bedside.
That fluent lady, having a speech ready, began at once :

"These are sad times, Miss Fairfax. But *tempora
mutantur*, you know. You have lost one home but
you are offered another—the darkest hour is just before the dawn —We must bow to the decrees of Providence —When we submit a cause to the arbitrament
of arms we must abide the event.—We have determined what is best for you, and you should be thankful.—Albert's plan is the best for all parties —His
father thinks so, and he is very wise —Albert is one
of the kindest men alive —You will think so when
you know him better—I have always said he was.—
He is firm—very firm—*justique tenorem flectere non
odium cogit non gratia suadet*, as the poet says—he
never gives up a project.—So, my dear Miss Fairfax,
you had better consent "——

"Mrs. Palmer, you seem to be an accomplice in
your son's scheme, which I begin to comprehend.
My course is taken. If you are appointed to be my
jailer, I will thank you to spare me your lecture. If
you are permitted to leave me alone, I beg you to
grant me that relief."

"Albert thinks that in your present frame of mind
solitude would not be good for you.—*Solitudinem
faciunt et pacem appellant.*—That is not right—it is
not good for man to be alone, nor woman either, as
the Bible says "——

"Then let me have silence, I pray you."

In the evening of that day, and during the next
day, the importunate suitor repeated his visits, and
endeavored, by every art at his command, to overcome the reluctance of his captive to become his

bride. When her faculties had recovered from the
first shock of calamity, she was able to detect the
drift of his plot, and to weigh his threats and his
persuasions with a clear judgment. She doubted no
more as to her duty. He found her purpose immovable. His persecution sometimes wrung tears from
her eyes, and sometimes provoked her to repel him
with indignant scorn. He was neither melted by her
sorrow nor shaken by her scorn. His cruelty was
cool, but he was not insensible to the impression of
beauty that varied with her varying passion. Love
for one whom he tortured was impossible; but the
torture revealed charms in the victim that kindled
desire in a pitiless breast.

CHAPTER XXV.

MARK MARLIN.

ABOUT sunset on the second day of her imprisonment, the chamber in which Miss Fairfax was detained, was again entered by Albert Palmer. She arose and stood as she always did while he was in the room, thus silently protesting against his intrusion. He advanced, addressing her in words of ordinary salutation, with an air of deferential courtesy. Receiving no response, he proceeded to speak in a strain of sentiment, which became warmer as he went on, and, finally, less delicate. With some ardor of expression on his lips and in his eyes, he moved towards her, with an arm extended, as if he would lay his hand upon her. Stepping backward she waved him off, and said, quietly, but decisively, "no nearer, sir." He paused, clasped his hands together, and spoke in an obsequious tone:

"Ah, my dear Julia, do not continue to trample on my love."

"Mr. Palmer," she replied, "I beg that this insulting mockery shall cease."

"Then you doom your father to a dungeon?" he asked, with a sneer.

"My duty to my father, sir, is not a subject for discussion between you and me. Use it not to barb your taunts. I am now proof against them. I know you now and I despise you, I detest you, I defy you."

He turned to the chamber door and locked it. He

then returned towards Julia, his eyes glaring with ignoble passions. "By Heaven," he cried, "you shall consent to marriage or prate no more of honor." She retired before him, but springing forward, he attempted to seize her. She eluded his grasp by stepping up on the bed. Retreating to the opposite side of it, which was against a wall, she stood there in a posture of defiance, pointing a pistol at Palmer. Her movements, as well as his, were so rapid that his face almost touched the weapon before he was aware that she held it. Seeing it then, he started back with a gesture of fear, and stood in a shrinking attitude, gazing at the pistol. While they thus confronted each other, they heard a light rap on the door, and understood that Mrs. Palmer desired admittance. He slowly retreated to the door and opened it. As he retired, Julia descended from the bed. She had restored the little weapon to her pocket when Mrs. Palmer entered, and her son, scowling at Julia, went out.

The small pistol which Julia had held in her hand, rather a toy than a weapon, was one which her father had procured for her after she had been endangered by negroes, as related in the preceding pages. He gave her some lessons in the use of it, so that she might be able to defend herself in sudden peril, such as the recent events and the condition of the country led him to apprehend. She seldom carried it, however, and it was by chance that, when she was preparing to flee from the mansion of Roebuck, she put on a gown, in the pocket of which the pistol had been left. In the excitements of that night she did not observe it, but she discovered it the next day. She remembered it when Palmer attempted to seize her, and instantly availed herself of it, as we have seen, for her defence.

When she was again left with Mrs. Palmer she walked to and fro, agitated with an indignant sense of insult and outrage. She uttered no word of complaint to the mother and agent of her persecutor. Her spirit was bruised, but it was roused. Still alone, in the power of her enemies, she defied them. She would not bow before a foe who left her no choice but between defiance and dishonor.

Night came on, but, at Julia's request, the room was not lighted. She sat down by a window and looked out at the sky. Mrs. Palmer, seated in a rocking chair at the opposite side of the chamber, began to yawn, and finally fell asleep. The night was clear and still. While Julia gazed at the bright stars, her excitement gradually abated. When her veins yet throbbed with passion, the quiet heavens seemed to her imagination to regard with cruel indifference the woes and crimes of earth. But as the tide of violent emotion subsided, higher and serener sentiments responded more faithfully to the sublime sense of that eternal quiet. " It is not indifference to wrong," she said to herself, " that we should read in those sleepless eyes of Heaven, but their far-seeing watch regards the end as well as the beginning of these dark scenes in which we grope and suffer. Their serene silence is the homage of nature to the unerring Providence which guides all events on earth as in Heaven. Darkling, but not dismayed, I will endeavor to walk by the light that comes from above, and trust the consequences to Him who ordains right and redresses evil."

While her mind was composing itself by such reflections, she was startled by the sight of a man's head near the window. Wondering, but rather hoping than fearing, she leaned her face against the pane and looked out into the dark. She discovered that the man was upon a ladder, and as he drew near to the window, he made a sign of silence to her. She did not recognize him, but believing that all her enemies were within the house, she readily concluded that he was a friend. Listening for the deep breathing of Mrs. Palmer, and being thus assured that she still slept, Julia opened the sash quietly and heard her name whispered. "What do you want?" she whispered, in reply. "Follow me;" and the man descended the ladder. Dreading no danger equal to that which she left behind, she followed without hesitation. When they were upon the ground, the man, who was then seen to wear the Confederate uniform, led her in silence to a clump of trees at some distance from the house. There they found another person, mounted, and holding the bridles of two horses. There was a woman's saddle on one of them, and, as Julia soon discovered, this was her favorite, Arab. First assisting her to mount, her conductor got upon his horse and the three rode away through the fields. They moved cautiously, and not a word was spoken until, after riding a mile or more, they entered a wood.

"Now, Miss Fairfax," said the man who released her, and whom she recognized as Lieutenant Mark Marlin, while she knew his companion to be Baxter, "we are safe for the present. It is for you to say where we shall go."

"To my father, if I can," she replied.

"We hear that he has been sent out of the county."

"Alas, it is true, then. Let me go to my mother."

"We will conduct you to her. She is now about ten miles from here. We must ride pretty briskly if

you please, because, after leaving you, we must travel
as far as we can before morning, for our own safety and
and to rejoin our regiment."

As they rode rapidly and cautiously over rough by-
ways to avoid pursuit, they could hold but little conversation. Julia, however, learned from Marlin what
he knew about her mother, and that Baxter had obtained from blind Pete the information on which they
had acted in facilitating her escape. Thus they knew
in what chamber Miss Fairfax was detained, where
her horse could be found, where a ladder was kept,
and other particulars, the knowledge of which made this
enterprise tolerably safe and easy to the two Confederates. Her horse had been taken from Roebuck by
the Federal soldiers, but, by order of Colonel Wesel,
was delivered to Mr. Palmer, at that gentleman's request. He stated to the colonel that the young lady
had taken refuge in his house, and insinuated that she
did not agree with her father in political sentiment
and that she might possibly become connected with
his own family. These representations served not
only to secure the possession of her horse, but to
silence inquiry, if it should otherwise become known
to the colonel that Miss Fairfax was at Mr. Palmer's.
Baxter, after his escape from the village, concealed
himself in the neighborhood until the next morning,
and then starting to overtake his regiment, he fell in
with Mark Marlin, who had come home to take care
of his sister. Notwithstanding his own affliction and
the sad duties which the death of his sister imposed
upon him, the lieutenant, as soon as he heard of Miss
Fairfax's situation, resolved to rescue her. He immediately set about the attempt, with Baxter's assistance, and we have seen the result.

Arriving before the house in which. Mrs. Fairfax was then a guest, Marlin informed Julia that he and his companion must leave her, and requested that their presence in the county might not be mentioned, until they would have time to travel beyond the reach of the enemy.

"How can I ever thank you as you deserve, gentlemen?" said Julia.

"I am still your debtor, Miss Fairfax; but, if you please, we will leave these things to be spoken of some other time;" replied Marlin, to whom Baxter left the conversation with Miss Fairfax; for his own audacity was cowed, and his saucy tongue was mute in presence of a lady whom he was obliged to respect.

"I know," she said, "that I must not detain you, and I fear that already your delay, for my sake, has exposed you to danger. Never can I cease to be grateful to you. In happier times, for us all, I hope, I may be able to prove my gratitude."

"Have you any message for the regiment—the boys, Miss Fairfax."

"Tell the brave men that the hearts of their country women are always with them. May God bless them. Tell Colonel Fitzhugh that—that I—I have not for gotten him."

"You remember, then, as gallant a soldier as ever drew a sword. Farewell, Miss Fairfax."

"Farewell, Mr. Marlin; farewell, Mr. Baxter. I shall never forget"——

Baxter briefly echoed her farewell, while she shook hands with them both, and they hurried away before she concluded the sentence. Julia, alone, approached the house in which she expected to meet her mother.

At that late hour all was silent, but alarms were then so frequent, that every family was alert. As soon as she knocked at the door an upper window was cautiously opened, and a voice inquired who was there. She gave the necessary explanation, and was admitted. Her mother, who slept but little, recognized her voice, and immediately called her into her own chamber. The meeting between them could not be without joy, nor yet could it be without sorrow. To be thus united, after such a separation, was rapture. To remind each other of the absence, suffering and danger of another, so dear to both, was anguish. In smiles and tears, in embraces and regrets, in conversation about the one on whom their anxious thoughts were centred, they spent the hours, until the sun was high in the heavens. It was not until the flush of excitement faded from her mother's face, and the pitiless light of day fell upon it, that Julia was fully aware of the ravages that terror and affliction had made there. When she looked upon that form so frail, those cheeks so wan, the pallid lips and the sunken eyes, apprehension for her mother's health divided her heart with anxiety for her father's safety.

Julia's sensibility was both delicate and warm. But no excess of feeling ever prevailed long over the clear judgment and steady sense of duty which habitually regulated her conduct. Under a delicate surface of feminine beauty, grace and tenderness, her character contained a strength of principle which made even the play of her emotions, like the vibrations of a watch-spring, contribute to the practical uses of life. Her sympathy with sickness and distress did not vanish in sighs. It prompted her to give relief with quiet and thoughtful energy, whilst

only the extreme gentleness of her ministrations
showed how much of another's suffering she felt as
her own. Thus, during the next few days, she devoted herself to the care of her afflicted mother.
Knowing her tastes and habits, anticipating her wants
with quick intelligence, providing for her physical
comfort with untiring diligence, her daughter also endeavored to soothe her mind. If anything could have
had that effect, it would have been the presence of
Julia. Withdrawing her thoughts from her own
troubles in order that she might win her mother from
despondency, she became almost cheerful. Her
noiseless step seemed rather light from hope than
stealthy from fear. When to the loveliness of her
person, and the sweetness of her countenance, was added the tender earnestness of filial affection, she looked,
while she hovered over her mother's pillow, as if her
love alone might dispel all gloom from the brow on
which her soft, white hand was fondly laid. She exerted all the charms of her voice and conversation to
banish the spectre of despair that haunted her mother
by day and by night. Yet, she found that, as the
reader already knows, the delicate lady continued to
pine and waste away. Indeed, Julia became convinced that the life of the wife depended upon the
restoration of the husband to liberty. Father and
mother—the lives of both, she believed, were in peril,
and might depend on the same contingency.

When she had arrived at this conclusion, her
thoughts naturally reverted to the proposal of Palmer,
which, as he declared, might have led to the release
of her father. But, even now, she could not repent
that she had rejected it. She remembered it with
increased disgust, when it appeared to her as a profli-

gate proposal to traffic with two lives so dear to her, so worthy of honor, and so afflicted. But it was not in her nature to look on misery without an effort to relieve it, and, least of all, the misery of her own parents. Her mind addressed itself with customary directness and force to the question how she might procure the restoration of her father to his family. After much reflection, she came to a resolution, which she first disclosed to Mrs. Fitzhugh.

That lady treated Julia as a daughter and shared all her cares and counsels. She, too, believed that the days of Mrs. Fairfax would be few unless her husband were released, and that his life might be endangered by his imprisonment under the actual circumstances. Of course, she participated in his daughter's desire to obtain his liberation. But there seemed to be no means within the power of the two women to effect that object. They were assured that the Federal officer commanding in the county was hostile to Colonel Fairfax, and that the Palmers were accomplices in the oppression practised upon him, if they were not the instigators. It was not deemed possible to induce those men to relax the rigor of persecution except upon a condition known only to Julia, and regarded by her with horror. The two ladies discussed the subject several times without a satisfactory result. At last, when it was again renewed, Julia said to Mrs. Fitzhugh—"I believe I can obtain my father's release."

"How is it possible, my dear Julia?"

"I will go to Washington and petition the Federal authorities."

"You are a brave girl, Julia, to make such an attempt, but it would be useless."

"I hope not, Mrs. Fitzhugh, but, at all events, I may succeed, and there appears to be no other chance of saving their lives. I will try."

"What rational ground can you find to hope for success? It is not probable that you will ever reach Washington. I say nothing of the dangers by the way, for I know you will not be deterred by them, and, my dear child, I cannot say that you ought to be. But if you were in Washington, the authorities will certainly act according to the reports and suggestions of their own officers and adherents in the county. What else can they know of your father?"

"That seems plausible. But I imagine that men in high office must be free from some of the bitter and vulgar animosity which is apt to affect inferior agents. Besides, they are remote from the intrigues of this neighborhood. Surely there is some one in authority who, in spite of political virulence, will feel compassion for the sufferings of so good a man and of his innocent wife."

"Alas, I fear that the military among us are but too faithful representatives of their government. Was not Colonel Tremaine removed to make room for the present commander?"

"These circumstances and many others are discouraging. But I have reflected upon them all. I see discouragement but not impossibility. Since we have thought of no other plan that is even within the range of possibility, I am resolved to try this one. I cannot sit still and see my mother die without an effort to save her. Even the hope which my undertaking will inspire may arrest her decline. I intreat you, if you can, to encourage her and to remove any objection that she may oppose to my attempt."

"If you are resolved, I will not continue to urge arguments which might discourage you without changing your purpose. But how do you intend to travel?"

"On horseback and alone. There is no other way."

"You cannot pass through the Federal lines without a passport."

"I must avoid them. Of course, I cannot obtain a passport from those who have sent my father to Washington."

"I am not thought to be a timid woman, Julia, but the dangers of such a journey through a country overrun with armies, marauding parties and other enemies, appear to me—but I must not frighten you."

"Our Heavenly Father will shield me."

"I pray that He may."

Mrs. Fairfax, when informed of her daughter's purpose, shuddered at the prospect of another separation, and dreaded the perils which Julia must encounter. But the hope of seeing her husband once more, with the appeals made to her by her daughter, and the arguments of Mrs. Fitzhugh, overcame her opposition. After the matter was settled, Julia pleased herself with the fancy that her mother's eyes were lighted with more animation than they had shown since the night of her daughter's return to her.

CHAPTER XXVI.

THE JOURNEY.

BUT little delay was necessary for the preparations which Julia had to make for her long and dangerous journey. Not much could be carried, if she had desired to carry much. The fire which destroyed her father's house consumed her wardrobe, and country ladies had but poor opportunities of shopping in Dixie during the war. She might be ready to travel almost as soon as Arab could be saddled. She had no money, and could obtain none, except a few dollars in specie and a supply of treasury notes, which were almost worthless beyond the Confederate lines, though they were the exclusive currency of the Confederacy. She was to travel alone, as well because nearly all those who might have been her protectors were in the army or driven from the county, as because, in the country through which she had to pass, a male companion might challenge annoyance and could not defend her. It was a country where even an army of Confederates could not hold its ground.

With a brave but sad heart she took leave of her friends. The parting between her and her mother was a severe affliction to both. The hope of her husband's release sustained Mrs. Fairfax, and Julia, impelled by love and duty, would not falter at the first of those trials which she had anticipated. Early in the morning she set out upon her solitary journey, and rode nearly the entire day without pausing to rest.

She felt but little fatigue. She was a delicate woman, and had been nurtured in wealth and refinement but not in luxury. The habits of her life had tended to confirm rather than enervate her strength, both of body and of mind. It was a rare state of society in which nature was thus refined and strengthened at the same time, as iron is changed to steel.

During the first day she traveled through a part of the country that was familiar to her. Without much difficulty she avoided the most frequented highways and places of resort for the Federals, and she neither met any troops nor encountered any impediment. She saw but few people. Not many remained at home, except old men, women and children, and they generally kept close to their houses. Some boys and old men and a few women were at work in the fields. Once or twice Julia saw them plowing, with cows. Horses and mules were not to be seen. Some dwellings were wholly deserted; the doors and windows were broken; the fruit-trees about them were hacked down; the gardens were destroyed; the barns, fences and stacks had been burned. Here and there brick chimneys of wooden houses that had been devoured by the flames, stood as milestones of invasion. A few slaves, old, decrepid or faithful, remained with the white inhabitants, but most of them had straggled off. Now and then Julia passed a negro, lying asleep at the wayside, with his shining face upturned to the sun, or saw stout black fellows strolling about in listless indolence. The lethargy of that race seemed to forebode a relapse into lazy barbarism as soon as the spur and rein of the white man's authority were withdrawn, as the neglected soil was resuming the unfruitful wildness of nature. The desolation which Julia witnessed deepened her sadness. But it is impossible to record all she saw and thought and felt on that journey without overspreading these pages with intolerable gloom. In our reminiscences of those times we must soften the truth if we would obtain a hearing or belief.

Late in the afternoon, Julia arrived at the house of a friend, and there she spent the night. She heard a rumor there, that during the day a party of Federal soldiers had been seen within a few miles of the place. This rumor, however, scarcely added a new fear to the constant apprehension that her journey might be interrupted. The next morning she took the road again, traveling through a district less known to her than that through which she had passed the day before. She was, therefore, obliged to keep on the main highway. When she had pursued her solitary way two or three hours, she looked back, and saw several horsemen about a mile behind her, and apparently moving towards her. Fearing they were Federal soldiers, she put her horse to a quicker pace. They followed, however, still more rapidly than she rode. For a short time they were concealed from her by a hill over which she was passing, when she discovered them. In a few minutes she saw them galloping over the crest of the hill, not more than half a mile from her. Then she imagined that she could distinguish the tall form of Albert Palmer among them.

In fact, he was there. He had not discovered her place of retreat after she disappeared from his father's house. But, being with some cavalry, that were foraging or ravaging near the place at which she spent the first night of her journey, he learned in the morning from the gossip of a negro, that she had set out from there alone.   Immediately he started, with a few followers, in pursuit of her.

As soon as she became convinced that she was pursued and suspected that Palmer was among the pursuers, she put Arab to his utmost speed.   The cavalry behind her used their spurs freely.   Palmer, dashing off before the others, came on at a furious gait.   Julia, a practiced horse-woman, on a fleet and spirited horse, could not easily be overtaken ; but, for three or four miles, the chase pressed Arab to his mettle.   The gallant horse, excited by the race, seemed to share the determination of his rider to distance the pursuers. Gradually he widened the space between him and the foremost of the cavalry.   Relying upon his qualities, Julia rode with steady courage, until, suddenly, she beheld a cloud of dust rising from the road before her.   Suspecting at once that there was a larger body of Federal cavalry in front of her, and that no chance of escape was left, her heart sunk for a moment.   But she looked back, and the sight of Palmer, in eager pursuit, reminded her that, whatever might be before her, she was leaving her most cruel enemy behind. She resolved to go forward.   Onward she flew.   Her rapid flight soon brought her in sight of five or six horsemen who were approaching on the road before her.   Onward still she flew.   She was very near them before she could discern, under the dust which covered them, that their uniforms were of Confederate grey.   Checking her horse, she cried out to them—"I am pursued by Federal cavalry."

"How many?"

"I have seen ten or twelve.   One of them rides far in advance of the rest.   There!   He comes in sight."

"Ride on, madam. You are safe. Colonel Fitz-hugh's regiment is nòt far behind us. We must move forward."

They started at a brisk trot. When Palmer saw them first, he thought they must be Federals. He was almost among them before he discovered his mis-take. Then, wheeling his horse, he was pursued in his turn. Julia saw no more of him. Riding slowly on, and wondering at the chance which brought her so unexpectedly out of danger into the protection of Hugh Fitzhugh, she saw a cloud of dust, which, at a considerable distance, indicated the approach of his regiment.

A spring, near the side of the road, attracted her attention, and she stopped to rest and refresh herself. She sat down on the grass, near the spring, and, after drinking, she bathed her brows with her hands. The spring was shaded by trees and vines. With the in-stinct of a woman, expecting a lover, she arranged her hair and dress, while she waited for the regiment to come up. When the head of the column drew near, she stood upon a grassy knoll near the spring, under a canopy of vines. She held the bridle, while her horse, with distended nostrils, ears erect, and arched neck, gazed at the warlike array. Her veil was thrown back, her fair complexion was rosy with excitement, her hazel eyes were moistened with the mystery of tears that were not weeping, and her graceful form stood a picture of living loveliness in a frame of sylvan beauty.

When Hugh Fitzhugh, turning from the dusty road to the spring, suddenly beheld her, he was amazed, enraptured, alarmed. "My Julia," he exclaimed, as he leaped from his horse, and ran towards her. Hastening to meet him, she threw herself into his arms, and burst into tears.

"Julia, my own Julia, why is this? Why do you weep? Why are you here?"

For some moments she was unable to answer his anxiously repeated questions. But when the paroxysm of emotion was passed, she lifted her head, and looked in his face, while she smiled through her tears.

"Pardon me. It was a woman's weakness. I weep for joy or grief—I know not why. But it is over. I can talk to you now. I must not detain you long, and I have much to say."

Then, glancing at the cavalry, she blushed deeply at the display of emotion which she had made. She drew her veil over her face and whispered, "O, forgive me, Hugh." He pressed her hand, and was leading her to a seat, when they heard a shout. Already her name was passing from mouth to mouth, and as it ran along the ranks, the men began to cheer for Miss Fairfax. Many of them knew and admired her. Others cheered, because they loved their colonel, and knew or suspected that he loved her. Finally, some there were who shouted, simply because cheers are contagious. At all events, the name of Miss Fairfax was echoed with cheers along the whole line. The enthusiasm waxed warmer and warmer, until Julia, turning her face to the regiment, raised her veil, and gracefully acknowledged the boisterous salutation.

While the regiment marched on, Hugh Fitzhugh, seated beside Julia, learned from her the circumstances which led to this meeting. They were soon joined by her uncle, Doctor Dick, who had been with his

company since the opening of the spring campaign.
"What, Colonel Julia, have you come to take command in person?" he exclaimed. Then he shook both
her hands and kissed her over and over. It was not
long, however, before he was seriously engaged in the
discussion to which Julia's communication gave rise.
Both to her uncle and to her lover, her journey appeared too hazardous, and the object of it wholly
impracticable. They urged her to abandon it and return with them. There was a long debate, in which
their solicitude for her safety contended with her
anxiety for the liberty of her father and lives of both
her parents. They found her filial devotion invincible,
and nothing was left for them but to consider how
they might contribute to the ease and safety of her
journey. Colonel Fitzhugh proposed to send a guard
with her, but gave up that proposition when she mentioned her reasons for traveling alone. The doctor
then declared that he would himself escort her. He
insisted that, with his servant, Caleb, he could relieve
her of any troubles and embarrassments to which a
woman traveling alone was liable, and that a little old
man, as he styled himself, and a poor old negro, would
not provoke more hostility than a lady. She doubted
the prudence of the proposition, and would have saved
her uncle from dangers which were useless. But he
combated her objections with some plausibility of
argument, and more pertinacity of purpose. He was
seconded by her lover, and finally prevailed. Colonel
Fitzhugh envied the doctor his office, and would gladly
have taken his place if propriety and duty had permitted. He lingered beside her after this matter was
arranged as long as his conscience allowed, and they
exchanged some of those tender words which are pro-

faned by publication. Besides the natural reluctance
of a lover to leave her, he felt a presentiment that this
parting might be final, for he knew that they were
both going into danger. But the thought of his own
coming danger reminded him of the urgency of his
military duty. Without knowing the design which
he would hasten to fulfil, at the peril of his life, she
knew and appreciated the demands of military service,
and would not detain him. With a sorrowful farewell
they parted.   .   .

Doctor Fairfax summoned the faithful Caleb, who,
with others of his class, was riding at leisure behind
the regiment. He had followed his master whenever
he was with the army, and, in that branch of the art
military which fell within his sphere, he had acquired
the ready skill of an old campaigner. After testifying
his delight at meeting with Miss Julia, by bows and
grins and words of learned length and thundering
sound, he applied himself, under the doctor's direction, to the care of the horses and the arrangement of
the baggage of the expedition in which his master had
just enlisted. With his expert aid everything was
ready for the road in a short time, and Julia, with her
escort, resumed her journey.

During the rest of the day no event occurred to
them of sufficient importance to justify recital. While
they rode along, Julia related to her uncle in detail all
that had recently happened at Roebuck and in its
vicinity. The doctor was often moved to indignation, and the misfortunes of his brother and his brother's wife more than once drew tears to his eyes. As
to her own sufferings, while she was a captive in Mr.
Palmer's house, she maintained a peculiar reserve in
speaking both to her uncle and Hugh Fitzhugh. They

learned from her little more than Marlin and Baxter
had already told them. Even to her mother a sentiment of maidenly modesty prevented her from reveal-
ing all that occurred in her chamber at Mr. Palmer's.
Perhaps, too, a consciousness that her own indignation
was more intense than it had ever been before, and a
scrupulous fear of carrying revenge too far, or of in-
volving others in attempts at extreme violence, restrained her from exposing the whole enormity of
Albert Palmer's guilt. Enough was known, however,
to Colonel Fitzhugh and her uncle to brand Palmer in
their estimation as a monster of iniquity, who had
wronged her whom they regarded as the most innocent and most lovely among women.

At evening the travelers arrived at the house of a
farmer whose name was Bell. He was an acquaintance of Doctor Fairfax, and consented to entertain
them for the night. This was a considerable proof of
hospitality; for, although Mr. Bell had a good farm, he
had nothing to eat for men or horses, except a little
corn and bacon, which he kept concealed lest it should
be taken from him or destroyed. Experience had
taught him this fear and an adroit ingenuity in concealing the remnants of his supplies. Besides, there
was then in his house, awaiting interment, the dead
body of his son. The young man had been a soldier in
Fitzhugh's regiment, and died suddenly within a few
miles of his father's house. As the funeral rites of
"rebels" were sometimes interrupted with insult and
outrage in those parts of the State which were overrun by the invaders, it had been deemed necessary to
bring home the body of the Confederate soldier pri-
vately during the preceding night, and it was to be
buried with equal secrecy the very night of Julia's

18

arrival. Notwithstanding their own destitution and affliction, however, Mr. Bell and his family received the travelers, and did all that was in their power to make them comfortable.

At midnight two or three neighbors had assembled, and, with them, Doctor Fairfax assisted at the interment of the son of his host. They carried the corpse to a remote part of the farm, followed by the father and mother, and lighted only by the stars. Arriving at a spot where a grave was already dug among some old field pines, one of the neighbors lit the candle in a lantern which he had brought. Its scanty light tinged the faces of the mourners with a melancholy tint of yellow, and faintly streaming through the pines, it made the heavy masses of dark shadow more funereal. No word was spoken. The rough coffin was let down by means of ropes into the rude receptacle of mortal dust. The first clods falling with dull rattle on the boards, heard in the dead silence of midnight, and telling that a beloved son was to be covered away from sight forever, so shocked the weeping mother that she shrieked. But the cry af anguish was suppressed, and all was still again. The mournful task was finished in silence.

CHAPTER XXVII.

DOCTOR DICK.

DOCTOR FAIRFAX procured from Mr. Bell a suit of plain clothes, and left his Confederate uniform. He was about to travel through a part of the State exclusively occupied by Federal troops. Not being an enlisted soldier, he felt at liberty to assume or quit the service and its badges for honest and needful purposes at his own discretion. Traveling with his niece for an innocent and pacific object, he thought that an old man, in citizen's dress, might be suffered to pass unmolested where a Confederate soldier would certainly be arrested. He did not explain to Julia that this change of dress might be so interpreted, possibly, as to augment his danger in case of capture. Nor could he bring himself to rely so absolutely on the immunity of age, innocence and a civil suit, that he would leave his revolvers behind. He carried two pistols. Thus he set out on the next day's journey in ambiguous trim, hoping for peace, but prepared for war.

They rode two or three hours of the morning without interruption, and having no occasion for action, Doctor Dick, of course, filled up the time with talk. Julia thought and felt too much for easy conversation. Her uncle was free to indulge himself in soliloquy or in lecture. They came upon a part of the road which passed for a distance of a mile or two through a forest. They were riding at a walk, and Doctor Fairfax had fallen into a disquisition.

"Two rival systems of civilization"—so his discourse was running on—"have been developed on this continent. The Northern has reached its most advanced stage in Massachusetts, the Southern in Virginia. One is founded on trade, the other on agriculture. One flourishes in cities, as in hot-houses, the other ripens in the sunshine of the country. The Northern is of more rapid growth, the Southern more perfect. By some fatality this trial of force between them has been brought on soon enough to give the North all the advantage of its precocious strength, while half the South is not yet rid of the stumps. I fear, as you know, that in this struggle the North will prevail. Then the world and posterity will be taught that the Northern system is the best, every way. The world is sycophantic, and listens to a conqueror. You know my opinions of this Yankee civilization. It makes white slaves, while we use the black slaves made by nature. The leading tendency of our system is to cultivate virtue; of the Yankee system, to sharpen the wits. Our refinements are refinements of virtue. Our fantastic excess is an exaggeration of honor and courage. The selfish principles that we develop as a prop to virtue, is pride—theirs, prudence. We incur among the Yankees the disdain which rustics incur among city fops. The prime products of our social system are noble men and women. The Northern—see—there are specimens now, I verily believe."

The travelers were emerging from the wood, and were in a view of a farm-house that stood at no great distance from them. From the house a lane led to the road on which they were traveling. In the lane, four mounted men, in Federal uniform, leading three horses, had just turned away from the house, and were approaching the road. The doctor suspected that the led horses had just been taken from citizens, and perhaps from the farmer who lived there. The prospect of meeting the soldiers was not pleasant, but there was no way to avoid them, as the doctor concluded, and he resolved to advance without any appearance of distrust. He slipped, however, one of his pistols into the hands of Caleb, with an injunction not to show it, nor to use it, until ordered to do so by his master. Julia begged her uncle to make no resistance, whatever might happen. He assured her that it was his purpose to avoid a collision if possible.

When the Virginians were nearly opposite to the mouth of the lane, the Federal soldiers came out of it and met them on the road. The doctor saluted the strangers courteously, and would have passed on. But a non-commissioned officer, who appeared to be the leader of the party, ordered him to halt. The order was obeyed, of course, and he who had given it, after looking at the horses, and fixing his attention particularly on Arab, said:

"Them's good horses you're riding."

"They are tolerable nags," the doctor admitted.

"We're looking for sich horses, we are."

"We do not wish to sell ours."

"Good; we don't want to buy."

"I believe we are not likely to agree upon an exchange, either."

"You're a comical old cock. Do you take us for horse-traders? Don't you see we're soldiers? We take horses, we do. I've a particular fancy for the woman's horse, but as she's a woman, we'll leave her the old sorrel we got at that house. He'll do for her. Come, Cuffee, take her saddle and put it on the sorrel. We'll just take your horse, and the old man's saddles and all."

While he was speaking, he dismounted, and approached Julia. She said to him in her softest tones :

" I am sure, sir, if you knew how I prize this horse and for what a holy purpose I need him now, you would not take him from me."

" Wouldn't I, though ? Come, get down without any more palaver."

He seized her by the arm and pulled her so roughly downward that she was glad to leap to the ground. He then lifted her veil and said :

" By —— that's a pretty secesh face. I must have a kiss."

He seemed about to suit the action to the word, when the crack of a pistol was heard and he fell dead· Doctor Fairfax had prevented the insult.

Instantly a fight ensued, which was so sudden, rapid and brief, that Julia could distinguish nothing but the firing of revolvers until it was over. She was near being trampled upon by the horses in the affray, but she was below the range of the shots. In a minute the firing ceased. Two of the Federals lay dead on the ground ; the other two were flying and apparently wounded. Caleb was down, bleeding freely. Three barrels of his pistol were empty. Doctor Fairfax sat on his horse, looking at the two retreating soldiers. Presently he said :

" Julia, they have quieted old Dick," and he began to sink upon the horse's neck. She ran to him, and supported him while he slipped to the ground.

" Where are you hurt, Uncle Dick ?" she asked, in great alarm.

"Here, Julia; hurt to death."

"Oh, no, you will not die," she cried, "you will not die."

"Yes, I know—I can live but a few minutes. When the breath is out, you must leave me and save yourself. The villains will send others after us. I'll not keep you long. I finished two of them. I believe another, thanks to Caleb, is not long for this world. Three Yankees the less to destroy our people."

"Your voice is strong, Uncle Dick. Let me examine your wound. I am sure it cannot be fatal. I will go for help."

"You would like to do something for Uncle Dick. But it is useless. Raise my head a little—so—now you have my head in your lap I can breathe a few minutes longer, and I shall die easy. Ah, Julia, what a tragedy of tragedies we have witnessed, with Yankee power for the devil of the scene and Yankee policy for the plot. If I could live a little while longer I would repent of all the sins of the Yankees as they have repented so angrily of our sin of slavery these many years. Poor old Virginia, she was drawn into this war by the action of the States North and South of her, and now she has to fight more and suffer more than any of them. Well, I have done my duty, thank God. Only a few minutes more, my dear girl. I wish he had been a gentleman who shot me—I fear he was a cur. Well, I forgive him; he was a soldier. I am very weak. Here is your purse in my pocket. I was going to leave without giving it to you. I shall not need it where I am going. Ask the people of that house to take care of my body and of Caleb—poor Caleb, I fear he is badly wounded "——

"I's gwine wid you, master," said Caleb, speaking with difficulty, and falling at last from his ambitious phraseology to the negro dialect, "I's gwine wid you, master."

"I hope not, my faithful fellow."

"I bin always wid you; I's gwine wid you now master."

"Farewell, Caleb. God bless you. You have done your duty. Then fly, Julia. Conceal yourself until night in that wood. Save your father. Tell him I die for him and for you and for Virginia—as I would wish to die—for the dearest objects of my love—and I love sister Mary and—— We die, Julia—you are a brave girl—the earth has not another so noble—kiss me, Julia—farewell—we die, but our country lives for- ever—God bless Virginia—light the candle—God bless "——

He spoke no more.

Mr. Hart, the farmer who resided there, now stood beside Julia.

CHAPTER XXVIII.

HUGH FITZHUGH.

WHEN Albert Palmer, abruptly abandoning his pursuit of Miss Fairfax, turned to fly from the five or six Confederates who had met her, he was mounted on a fleeter horse than any of theirs, and not sparing the weary animal, he left them at some distance. He would probably have escaped if his horse had not fallen in descending a hill. By the fall one of the rider's legs was broken, and being unable to move, he was captured. He was carried by his captors into the yard of a house which stood near the road, and there laid on the grass, while the Confederates, giving up the pursuit of his comrades, who had scattered themselves over the country, waited for the regiment to come up.

Colonel Fitzhugh, after leaving Julia with her uncle at the spring, hastened forward. She had told him that some of his men were in pursuit of Palmer, and he had heard enough of that gentleman's recent conduct to fill him with anger. Anticipating the capture of the fugitives as possible, if not probable, he meditated the punishment that was due to such a villain. His fury being the counsellor of his judgment, he was ready to condemn the culprit to extreme torture of any kind that imagination could conceive. In his anger he dashed the spurs into his horse, as if no speed was swift enough for his revenge. Whether his tempestuous thought turned to the perils through

13*

which Julia had passed, or to those which he was about to encounter, or to the sufferings of her father, or to the atrocities recently perpetrated against others, or to the past career of Palmer, he became more and more enraged. In this vindictive mood he dashed on to the head of his regiment.

He was amazed at the scene which he then witnessed, and it recalled his mind to the duties of an officer. That portion of the command which had arrived at the place where Albert Palmer lay, was in the utmost confusion and disorderly excitement. The report which Marlin and Baxter had brought of his conduct had been circulated among the men, and, as usual in such cases, it had gathered additions as it was repeated. It inflamed the minds of the soldiers to the highest pitch of resentment against one whom they regarded as a fiend. The foremost of them, seeing him in the yard, gave way to the impulses of passion. Leaving the ranks and dismounting, they hurried into the yard with threatening cries and gestures. Others followed. Forty or fifty men entered the enclosure. Shoot him —he's a deserter—he's a trator—he's a murderer—he tried to kill Miss Fairfax—he hung her to a bed-post —Mark Marlin had to cut her down—hang him— such were the cries that expressed their purpose or their passion. Some of them who were near the prisoner tried to seize him, but were delayed by two or three officers. A few of the men cried, don't murder him—wait till the colonel comes—let the colonel deal with him. But the increase of the crowd brought an increase of excitement. The uproar of threats silenced the the feeble voice of remonstrance. Every moment it appeared certain that the maddened mob would obtain possession of Palmer and execute instant revenge.

When Colonel Fitzhugh came upon this spectacle of tumult he asked what was the matter. A soldier replied, "they've got Palmer in there."

"What is he doing?"

"Lying on the grass. They say he's wounded."

"What are the men doing?"

"They are going so hang him."

"Murder a prisoner!"

The violence of others struck him in its true light, and restored his reason to the mastery over his passions. He leaped from his horse and into the yard. Pressing forward among the men, he called to them, in a voice of authority that rang above the uproar, not to murder a prisoner, but to return to the ranks. Those who recognized him gave way for him to pass. Others, too intent on mischief to see their colonel or hear his voice, were thrust aside. In a moment he was beside Palmer, and looking round upon the enraged soldiers, sternly commanded them to fall back. They yielded with a sullen murmur to his ascendancy, and slowly retired. He rebuked them for the crime which they had meditated, and ordered them to return to their places. Palmer implored him not to let the men assassinate him, but he made no reply to this supplication until the yard was cleared of soldiers. Then, casting his eyes upon the prisoner, he merely said, "you are safe now." He had Palmer carried into the house, and placed a guard around it, under an officer on whose firmness he could rely, commanding him to remain until the regiment had passed and to follow it, taking care that no men were left behind. He then informed Palmer that he was to be left there at liberty, and required him to give the ordinary parole of a prisoner of war. When this matter had been arranged, the prisoner began to express gratitude, but the colonel abruptly left him and hastened to the regiment, which was again in motion. Some of the men, as he passed by them, muttered, "this was not the way the Yanks treated Colonel Fred." He chose to be deaf to such comments. His own passions, which had been so suddenly quelled, began to rebel again, and he had to ride some distance before he felt perfectly master of himself. He then took occasion to speak to his men in words of grave reproof, and of the dishonor which some of them had almost brought upon the regiment. He assured them that in a little while he would conduct them to a far more honorable revenge, and that the crimes of their enemies should not go unpunished. He informed them that they had a long march before them for that day and coming night, and he relied on their patience, discipline and courage for the success of an important enterprise.

When Colonel Fitzhugh was returning, successful, from his expedition, and had heard of the outrages which had been committed in the county of his residence, he resolved to strike a blow, if possible, which might restrain such inhuman excesses of military violence for the future. The information obtained by Baxter encouraged him to believe that it was practicable, and his interview with Julia did not tend to relax his resolution. He was hastening on with a hope of surprising the Federals at the village. After leaving Palmer he continued the march until a late hour of the night when he was within three or four miles of the village. The regiment was then halted for a brief rest, but, an hour before daybreak, the men were again in their saddles. The colonel then addressed them:

"Soldiers! Virginians! You are about to attack the enemy—not soldiers but malefactors. They have perpetrated their crimes at your own homes. They have desecrated your own altars. They have burned your own dwellings. They have robbed and insulted your own families. They have made war on women and children. They have defiled virgins. As you are men, redress the injuries of women—of your families and friends. Scourge these felons. Here revenge is justice. In such a cause your sabres are sacred. Count no odds against you when Heaven must bless your valor. The enemy is a thousand; you are five hundred; you are enough. Let the word be Eliza Marlin. Follow me."

There was no shout in response to this address. The clenched teeth would not open for cheers. There was an inarticulate murmur. There was a low, continuous clash of iron, as every man felt his sabre or his carbine. Then, in stern silence, the little column moved off.

The force at the village numbered somewhat above a thousand men—a regiment of infantry about seven hundred strong, and about three or four hundred cavalry. License had destroyed the discipline and impaired the vigilance of the entire force.

Availing himself of his local knowledge and of the information which he had recently received, Colonel Fitzhugh led his regiment, undiscovered, to a point near the village, and then dashed into the centre of the Federal encampment before any signal of his approach was given. Officers and soldiers, suddenly aroused from sleep, ran from their tents to be cut down or trampled under foot, or to flee from the merciless sabres. On one side confusion and dismay—on the other shouts, strokes, wrath, triumph. Pistols were fired on every hand—a few muskets or rifles replied. Darkness added to the horror of the scene. But friends and foes knew that the careering horsemen were Confederates and the fugitives on foot were Federals. Here and there a few Federals attempted to stand, but they could stand only to be slaughtered. An enemy who had seen Mark Marlin there that morning would have denounced the heart-broken boy as an unsparing savage. He and his had not been spared. All through that camp the name of his sister was muttered by men who were saved from horrid deeds, perhaps, by the rapid dispersion of the enemy. They were men.

The Federal cavalry, finding that the infantry had been scattered, took to flight without an effort at defence. Some mounted horses without saddles or bridles and galloped away. Others on foot scampered across the adjacent fields. In a few minutes it appeared to the assailants that, of the whole Federal force, none remained near the village but the few who were killed or severely wounded. But it was not so. Colonel Wesel, whatever else he may have been, was a man of courage. Though suddenly awakened by an enemy in the midst of his camp, he did not lose his presence of mind. He soon discovered the real state of affairs, and thought only of retrieving the disaster. Using the opportunities of darkness and confusion, he collected a few men, and with them he threw himself into a house at one end of the village. There he determined to make a stand while he sent some of his officers to rally his flying troops, and a courier to the nearest Federal post for succor. He did not believe that the assailants were numerous or that they would

venture to remain long at the village. He hoped that
a sturdy show of resistance might even cause them to
retire as suddenly as they came.

As soon as Colonel Fitzhugh discovered that the
house was thus occupied, he divined the objects of the
Federal officer, and saw the necessity of dislodging
him at once, and of preventing the fugitives from being
rallied. He knew that it was impossible for him to
hold the village very long under any circumstances,
and that if any part of it could be held by the enemy
until reinforcements or considerations of prudence
should compel him to retire, the effect of his present
success would be neutralized. He sent a considerable
part of the regiment to pursue the fugitives for a time,
and then prepared to assault the house occupied by
Colonel Wesel. When the party organized for the
purpose was ready to make the assault the day was
breaking.

The assailants rushed towards the house, intending
to enter through the windows. When they were
within a few yards of it a well-directed volley brought
several of them to the earth. Mark Marlin, springing
forward, seized the ledge of a window which was
rather above his head, and drawing himself up, broke
in the sash with the hilt of his sword. He climbed
up to the window, and had almost entered, when he
received a shot, and fell heavily back to the ground.
The men behind him, and those directed to other windows, still pressed on. But the defence was so steady
and effective that it was soon found necessary to recall
them, and the assault failed.

Colonel Fitzhugh, still deeming it necessary to dis-
lodge the Federal colonel as soon as possible, made
instant preparation for another attack. He placed

himself at the head of a number of men deemed sufficient for the purpose. Having procured a ladder, he
led them, under cover of buildings, to a spot about
fifty yards from the house occupied by the enemy.
Then, while a false attack was made on another side,
he rushed forward. His foremost men, carrying the
ladder horizontally between them, swung it, as a ram,
against the door until they broke it, but not without
two or three of them being wounded. As soon as an
opening was thus made, wide enough for a man to
pass, Colonel Fitzhugh dashed in, followed by his
men. Within the house there was a fierce fight, hand-
to-hand. It could not last long. Colonel Wesel and
several of his men were killed. The rest surrendered.

The victory was complete, but it was purchased
with some precious blood. Besides other losses, Colonel Fitzhugh was dangerously wounded. He was
carried from the house, bleeding profusely. Calling
the lieutenant-colonel of his regiment to him, he expressed the belief that his wound was mortal, he commended the gallantry of his men, and gave directions
for the burial of the dead, the care of the wounded,
the removal of captured horses and guns, and the
withdrawal of his command from the village. Finally,
he requested that, whatever might be his own condition, he might not be left behind. Although these
directions were given with coolness and clearness,
they were scarcely completed when he became insensible. Afterwards he revived; he was almost lifeless
when, in the afternoon, he was carried from the
village.

The dead body of Mark Marlin was lifted from the
earth and borne with tender respect by his comrades
to the cabin of his father, who sat on his desolate
hearth beside his wife; and she was a maniac.

When Mrs. Fitzhugh heard of the condition of her son she followed the regiment, and taking charge of him, she had him carried, from time to time, by short stages to an interior county. There she took a cottage, and attended only by her faithful Belle, devoted herself to the preservation of his life.

CHAPTER XXIX.

WASHINGTON.

We left Julia Fairfax seated in a highway, holding in her lap the head of her deceased uncle. Near her lay his bleeding servant, and the corpses of two Federal soldiers. Beside her stood Mr. Hart. Notwithstanding the dangers which he and his family might incur if he should afford assistance to those who had provoked the vengeance of soldiery in possession ·of the country, he was prompt to acknowledge the duties of humanity to a woman in affliction, and to the dead and wounded. He addressed her in words of sympathy, and offered her the shelter of his house, and whatever aid he could render. Her delicate frame might have sunk under the load of calamity that had befallen her; but, if she was a woman in the weakness of passion, she could be a woman in the heroism of duty. A sacred duty was still before her. A gush of tears discharged the natural tribute of affection and grief. Then she rapidly reviewed the circumstances by which she was surrounded, and concluded that it was necessary for her to act promptly according to the advice of her dying uncle. She thanked Mr. Hart for his kind offer of assistance. She explained to him briefly that she was obliged to prosecute her journey without delay. She begged him to take charge of her uncle's body, and of the wounded Caleb. That faithful servant assured them that he would not trouble any one long in this world. When Mr. Hart had consented to fulfil all the wishes which she expressed, and she had seen Caleb laid on a bed in the house, she took leave of him with many tears, and, after kissing the lifeless lips of her dear uncle, she bade farewell to Mr. Hart.

She went into the wood to wait for the more secure shelter of night. Concealing herself in a ravine, she tied her horse by.the bridle to a limb, and sat down upon the grass, leaning against the trunk of a tree. There she remained alone several hours. The sun went down, and the retreating shadows at length stole away upon the approach of night, like faithless friends at the coming of misfortune. Darkness made her solitude more dismal. Hooting owls, and wailing whip-poor-wills, broke, with melancholy voices, the solemn silence of the forest and of night. Her clear sense and natural courage usually saved Julia from imaginary terrors. But her heart, already sorrowful and fearful, felt the depressing influence of the scene. She turned her sleepless and tearful eyes to Heaven, and prayed to the friend of the friendless, who sees at midnight as at noonday. It was midnight when she found courage. to venture upon the highway. The night was friendly to her, and, by riding rapidly, she left this dangerous neighborhood far behind her before the dawn.

Afterwards, traveling much at night, she continued her journey through many difficulties and alarms, but without any adventure that ought to detain the reader from more important events, until she arrived within ten miles of Washington City. Then, as she was riding along a public road in the. forenoon, she saw before her a party of Federal cavalry approaching at a brisk trot. To avoid meeting them, she turned her horse and rode back, intending to enter a lane which she had passed, and to wait there until the cavalry should go by. When she was about to enter the lane, she heard from behind her the word "halt." Intending to halt as soon as she turned out of the road, to avoid collision, she went on. She had scarcely turned into the lane, and drawn her rein, when a shot was fired, and the bullet struck her horse. He made one bound and then fell. Quivering with momentary agony, he died. The cavalry rode on. One voice exclaimed—"I guess you'll halt next time," adding some words of profane ribaldry. Julia stood by her horse, not injured by his fall, but overcome with a sense of utter desolation. "Poor Arab," she murmured, "brave, gentle, faithful Arab, will they let nothing live that I love?"

She sat down for a few minutes, weeping. But a thought of her father recalled her to the hard path of duty still before her. She rose, and with a lingering look of regret at the body of her last companion, set out alone and afoot towards the city. She was not much accustomed to walking, and she had not traveled five miles over the hard road when she became very weary, and her feet began to feel sore. Still she walked on, slowly, indeed, and with frequent pauses, but with perseverance. The sun was setting when she found herself within the suburbs of Washington. She stopped to rest, and to consider what was next to be done. She did not know that she had a single friend or acquaintance in the city, except her father. Regarding her soiled garments and wretched plight, she feared that her appearance would excite the suspicion of strangers. She imagined that not only the public offices but the streets were thronged with avowed enemies of Virginia who, she inferred, would be her enemies if she should make herself known. She thought that in her dusty garb, if she entered a respectable hotel, she would be rejected as a guest, and perhaps expelled with insult. Her present perplexities, more than all the perils of her journey, made her plan for obtaining the release of her father appear to herself impracticable. Still, uncertain what to do, she started in the dusk of evening, and walked into the city. She went along Pennsylvania Avenue, that wide and cheerless thoroughfare. Hundreds of persons met her or passed by her. She did not dare to put aside her veil, or to lift her eyes to their faces. She felt that they were all strangers. She imagined that they looked at her with suspicion or enmity. More and more disheartened, more and more uncertain what to do, she still walked on. At length, in passing a corner, she looked into a cross street, thinking that perhaps it might be better for her to turn into it, and so avoid the multitude who thronged the side-walk of the great Avenue. By the light of a lamp she saw a negro man sitting on the curb-stone not far from her. Stepping aside into the cross street, where she could see him more distinctly, she looked at him a moment, and then said, in a low voice—" Dave." He started and looked at her. She raised her veil, and by the lamplight he saw her features. "Miss Julia," he cried, " 'fore God, it's Miss Julia." He seized her hand, which she held out to him. He kissed it. He shed tears upon it. Then, with true African volubility and incoherence, he poured forth a torrent of mixed and incongruous emotions. Julia tried to check demonstrations which began to attract the attention of passengers. She

asked Dainty Dave how he was living in Washington. This was asking a renewal of his sorrows, and
the floodgates of complaint broke loose. It appeared
that from the time he left Roebuck—and he was
among the first to desert—until that moment, his experience had been bitter. "O de fools, de fools us
niggers is"—was his own comment at several stages
of his story. "I's mis'able, Miss Julia, I's starvin', I
ain't got no place to sleep dis night, but dis 'ere pave-
ment."

"Why did you leave us, Dave?" she asked in a
compassionate voice.

"'Case I was a fool, like de other niggers. Master
spiled me, I reckon. He was too good to dis 'ere nigger. I thought I was a gwine to be free when I
done run away. I hadn't got no sense to see I was
free afore, and master was workin' for me as ef he
was my sarvant. My blessed old master! All de
niggers here is mighty bad off, Miss Julia, and dere's
heaps of 'em. Dey is piled in cellars and places, and
kep in dem barracks till dey starves, and gits sick and
dies, and sich dirty niggers. I can't stay wid 'em. I
ain't used to it. But dere dey is, men and women
and children, all wretched, mis'able bein's, and nobody
keers ef dey lives or dies."

"Poor creatures! What can I do to relieve them!
But why do I ask? I do not know where to lay my
own head to-night?"

"What you say, Miss Julia?" Dainty Dave exclaimed, in astonishment, for his attention was now,
for the first time, turned from his own misery to
the condition of his young mistress. "You don't
know whar to go?"

"No, Dave, I am alone, and a stranger in the city.

I have just arrived, and I am not willing to go to a hotel. I am in distress, and I do not know a man or woman in all this great town."

"Why, whar's your cousin Clara, den? She lives here."

"Cousin Clara?"

"Mrs. West, you know."

Julia then remembered that the lady whom he named, a distant relative of her father, had once visited Roebuck. It was when Julia was a child, and she had almost forgotten the lady. She had quite forgotten that she lived in Washington. But Dave, who was older than his young mistress, remembered the visit of Cousin Clara very well. She had importance in his eyes, not because she came to the country from the capital, but because she was "kin to de Fairfaxes." Recently he had been inquiring about her, with some intention of claiming kin to keep himself from starving. Shame had hitherto held him off from her house, but he knew where it stood, and had walked by it more than once with longing eyes. When Julia recollected her distant cousin, and considered that Mrs. West was the only person in the city upon whom she had the slightest claim, she accepted Dave's offer to conduct her to the lady's house. They walked on together, Dave keeping his proper place as a servant, but near enough to her for conversation. He chattered away continually. But little of his chat is worth recording.

"No, Miss Julia, freedom ain't for niggers. Dey can't git de hang of it, and it don't do 'em no good. Free niggers ain't got no friends. De rale friends of de niggers is de good masters and mistresses what takes keer of 'em. It's de ole Virginny blood dat's

de friends of de niggers. Dem's de rale gentlemen
and ladies. Dey knows what to do wid sarrants.
But dey's gwine down. Dey's bin gwine down ever
sence de universal suffrage. I knowed dat would
make mischief to de niggers. And now de ole families is gittin' broke up by de war. Next thing, dey'll
have to marry quarter-masters and other low folks
what's made money by de war. De good ole blood's
a gwine down. What'll become of de poor niggers?"

While his tongue was running on, they arrived at
Mrs. West's house. Julia then divided with Dave
her remnant of cash, and telling him to provide for
himself that night, and come to see her the next day,
she dismissed him. When she entered the house,
and made herself known, she was received by Mrs.
West with affectionate welcome. The kind lady had
a pleasant remembrance of Roebuck, and esteemed
"Cousin Fred." as he deserved. She had a bright,
busy, talkative and cordial manner. With hospitality,
she possessed intelligence and tact. Unlike those
hosts who bid you make yourself at home, and then
leave you to shift for yourself most helplessly in a
strange house, she could make a guest feel at home.
She had heard nothing of Colonel Fairfax's imprisonment, but when Julia told her all her painful story,
she manifested such sympathy and such a warm desire to befriend Cousin Fred., she suggested so many
plausible expedients for obtaining his discharge, and
she offered her assistance with so much apparent hope
of success, that to Julia's eager fancy the prison doors
seemed already to turn on their hinges for her father's
release. Grateful and hopeful, she laid her head upon
her pillow to dream of her father's happy restoration
to his family.

The next morning she was up early, impatient for
the hour when, accompanied by Mrs. West, she was
to start in search of her father. They were to take
the round of many prisons, and, without a clue, to
look for him among an immense number of prisoners
then confined in the city. He had been there so short
a time, and was so completely unknown to all those
who had charge of the prisons, that they could scarcely
expect to find him until they should happen upon the
very room in which he was confined. After breakfast, they sallied forth upon their quest. Although
they traversed the magnificent distances of the city
in a carriage, they had walking enough in visiting the
various places at which they called, with climbing
stairs, and standing, while they awaited the leisure of
those to whom they made application, to fatigue even
the active Mrs. West. Many persons of whom they
inquired, knew nothing of Colonel Fairfax; others
declined to answer any questions. By some they
were treated with politeness, and by others rudely re-
buffed. They were very weary, and Julia was much
disheartened, when, late in the day, they were told
that a prisoner from Virginia, answering to the description which they gave of Colonel Fairfax, was confined in a room before which they were then standing. But it was too late to obtain admittance to the
prisoners that day; the person who had the custody
of Colonel Fairfax was not present; nothing more
could be learned by Julia about her father, not even
about his health. She went away, feeling disappointment and anxiety almost as painful as if she had not
discovered the place of his imprisonment.

The next day the ladies returned. The custodian
of Colonel Fairfax then informed them that they

14

could not be admitted to see him without a special order from higher authority. As to the prisoner's
health, he did not know much, except that "he
seemed to be pretty bad," but he referred them to the
surgeon. Inquiring where the surgeon was to be
found, and receiving a very vague direction, they
started in search of that officer. Besides the anxiety
of Julia to ascertain her father's true condition after
receiving the uncertain but alarming information
which she had just heard, Mrs. West suggested that
a certificate from the surgeon might promote the success of their application to be admitted into the prison.

But it was several hours before they found the surgeon.
He replied to their inquiries with civility, and when
he knew that Julia was the daughter of the prisoner,
he looked at her with compassion, for he was a man
of great benevolence. In tenderness to her he soft-
ened the report which he gave of her father's condition as much as truth permitted, and he soothed her
with general expressions of hope. But, by the use of
a little dexterity, he contrived to inform Mrs. West,
aside, that Colonel Fairfax could not live many days,
if he remained in prison. At her request, he slipped
into her hand a certificate to that effect. This was an
artifice of kindness to save the daughter from distress which, as they feared, might overcome her, but
Mrs. West afterwards discovered that Julia had inferred from the cautious conversation of the surgeon
the actual danger to her father's life. Reserve could
no longer be useful, and the certificate was shown
to her soon after they parted with the surgeon. They
then endeavored to procure the necessary order for
admittance into the prison, but official hours were
over, and another day closed with disappointment.

Such delays would have been painful under any circumstances, but, with the knowledge which they had acquired, Julia spent the following night in anguish.

Wearisome to the ladies, and worse than wearisome to the prisoner's daughter, were the next few days; for so long was it before Julia obtained permission to see her father. Those who have had experience in pressing an application, however trivial and unobjectionable, though official routine, can understand how a whole day may be spent without any progress in such affairs. When the applicants were women, seeking favor for a rebel from the servants of the offended government, it may be imagined that delays and obstacles were multiplied. But Mrs. West was never disheartened. She had been through such trials of patience before. She was one of those women who habitually assuaged the miseries of the war by charities to the unfortunate. To relieve them, she had passed through scenes which were often repulsive, and sometimes revolting to a lady. With officials, her gentle importunity, now pathetic and then laughing, would not be denied. Besides, she had acquired much knowledge of the secret springs of influence at Washington. Finally, with the use of the surgeon's certificate, and of her own energy and adroitness, she succeeded in procuring, not only permission for Julia to visit her father in prison, but an order for his discharge. He was to be set free, however, only upon condition that he would first take an oath of allegiance to the Federal government in a prescribed form.

CHAPTER XXX.

FREDERICK FAIRFAX.

JULIA went to the prison. Her step had lost the
elastic lightness of youth, health and happiness. She
walked with the nervous celerity of painful excitement. The bloom had faded from her cheeks. Above
their pallor, her eyes gleamed with unnatural lustre.
In her fluttering pulse, suffering and heart-sickness
had extinguished the energy of hope and high resolve. But despair was still kept at bay by the expectation of seeing her father, and relieving him by
filial ministrations.

She found him in a small room—a mere cell. It
was gloomy, having only one window, a little grated
opening. He lay on the floor, with no bed, but some
wisps of dirty, broken straw. The close, corrupted
air almost stifled Julia as she entered. The cell contained several prisoners besides her father. They
might have been long there, for their faces had the
dead whiteness and sullen indifference which come of
long imprisonment. They let the spider weave his
web over their narrow window without raising a hand
to brush it away. Colonel Fairfax was looking round
upon them, and, as Julia entered the door, she heard
him faintly utter the words "poor fellows!" When,
by the dusky light, admitted through dirty panes, she
saw him lying on the floor, none but a daughter
would have recognized his form and features. His
wound, his frightful journey to the Federal capital,

imprisonment, suffering, grief had conquered his manly frame. His eyes were sunken; his cheeks were hollow and haggard; his beard was long and white; his grey hair was matted, his form was emaciated and distorted with pain; his garments were soiled by the filth in which he lay. In all this squalid wretchedness nothing could be seen which seemed properly to belong to that noble gentleman but the benignity of his countenance as he looked round upon his fellow-prisoners.

His daughter hastened to his side, and sobbing, "my father, my father," she knelt down and kissed him again and again. Her tears trickled in showers upon his face. Laying her cheek to his, she wept in speechless agony. "Julia, my sweet child," he whispered, "do not give way to despair. God is merciful. We are in his hands." She could answer only with tears. She had come to comfort him, but the first sight of him had dissolved her firmness. She recovered her voice only to cry out, "O God! O God! can such goodness be doomed to such misery? my father, my father!" His eyes filled with tears, and, for a time, he could not speak. At length her paroxysm of uncontrollable grief was past. She recalled to mind the duty which she had come to discharge. She sat upon the floor, and wiped her eyes. But her lip still quivered, and she feared to make an effort to speak, lest her self-control should abandon her again.

"Speak to me, my daughter. Tell me of your mother. My beloved wife!"

"Yes, papa; she is with kind friends. Her great trouble is for you."

"My wife, my wife, my wife!"

"When she knows that you are—are safe, she will be comforted."

"May God comfort her."

"When she sees you again she will be happy. "

"Ah, me!   My unhappy wife!"

"We shall be happy yet, papa."

"Yes—hereafter," he said, looking upward.

"At home, dear papa."

"Yes, in Heaven."

"You must recover your health. We shall go to mother. Then love will make us all happy."

"Do not delude yourself, my daughter. We must now look for happiness beyond this world. My gentle Mary! My wife, my wife, my wife!"

"Listen to me, my dear papa. I have an order for your release from imprisonment."

"Can this be true, Julia?   Then I may live to see my Mary."

He uttered these words with more vigor than he had displayed since his daughter entered the room. His face was suddenly lighted with a flash of joy. He laid his thin hand on Julia's waist, and feebly pressing her to him, he kissed her fondly. The new-born hope of freedom and of household-endearments was very sweet. The calm of resignation, which had before succeeded the extinction of hope, was ruffled. For a few moments he cherished his joy in silence. His imagination flew to her whom he had loved so long, so wisely and so well. The image of his daughter went with him to the side of his wife, and his love revelled in domestic bliss. Julia saw this happiness in his face, and she feared to dash it by an allusion to the condition upon which he was to be released. She was silent until he spoke.

"Why, then, my darling, do we remain here longer?" he whispered at last.

"Are you able to go?" she asked, with compassionate evasion.

"Yes, yes; let me be carried away. I must see my wife. I have not long to live. I must see may wife once more. Why do you look troubled, daughter? I can bear the pain of removal. Let us go."

"O, my dear papa, I must tell you. The order is that you must take the oath of allegiance to the Federal government before you will be released."

He gazed at her a little while, as if he did not fully comprehend the import of her words. Then his eyes closed. His pallid cheeks gradually became livid. His lips moved but uttered no sound. His fingers grasped the straw nervously. Julia trembled with alarm. She feared that the last shock had killed her father. She almost shrieked; but she held her heart to its terrible task. She was still to sustain and comfort her father. Bending over him, she kissed his brow, and whispered, "Papa, speak to me. Speak to your Julia." He opened his eyes and murmured a blessing upon his devoted child. She held his hand and softly pressed it, but again her emotion was swelling so high that she could not trust herself to utter a word. After a long pause, which seemed like death he looked up and said, "I am resigned, Julia. God's will be done." He relapsed into silence, although his lips moved as if he repeated to himself what was passing in his mind.

"I cannot, my daughter," at length he said, "while Virginia remains distinct from the Federal government,—I cannot take that oath. My allegiance is due to my State. I will not abjure her in her dire extremity. I will not betray the cause of my fellow citizens who daily march to death. Let me die with

them. Let me die for Virginia. I can die, Julia,
even thus—my wife—my daughter—even thus I can
bear to die, but I cannot take a false oath. Death has
power over my body only; perfidy would taint my
soul."

"They say, papa, that such oaths, when taken under
compulsion "——

"Tempt me not, my daughter. Tempt not a frail
old man. The struggle has already wrung my heart.
It has nearly put out this flickering life. I might not
be able to resist the persuasion of my beloved, my
unhappy daughter. O, spare your father."

His imploring anguish almost bereft her of all control over her passion. He clasped one of her hands
between both his own on his breast. She laid her
other hand on his forehead. Alternately he lifted his
eyes to Heaven in mute supplication, or fixed them
upon the face of his daughter with an expression of
tender, yearning, unspeakable love.

"Be not too much cast down by our misfortunes,"
he said, when he spoke again, "do not give way to
despair. The Lord gave and the Lord hath taken
away. Blessed be the name of the Lord. May he
protect you and your mother when I am gone." After
a brief pause he continued—"do not let your heart be
corroded with resentment against our enemies. They
are mortals like ourselves, and they are blinded by the
passions of war   Let us forgive as we hope to be
forgiven."

Again he lay, apparently engaged with thoughts
which his waning strength did not enable him to
utter. It was manifest that he was sinking. But he
rallied a little and again addressed his daughter:

"Julia, I loved the Union. I would have given my

life to save it. But it is gone. However this war may end, the Union which I loved is gone forever. The free Union of sovereign States can never be restored, though the South may be subjugated. If our States should be conquered I trust that the spirit of our people will not be debased. The hope of liberty never dies while the manhood of the people survives. Liberty may be destroyed in one form, like this body, and yet live on like the soul. God grant that the freedom of our country may endure forever."

Julia, believing that when her father ceased to speak, his mind was occupied with meditations which she ought not to interrupt, waited in silence for him to speak to her again. But what she next heard was not addressed to her. He was repeating—

"There the wicked cease from troubling, and there the weary be at rest. There the prisoners rest together; they hear not the voice of the oppressor."

When he next addressed her it was to ask if she had lately seen Hugh. She replied that she had, and that he was well.

".Give him my blessing, Julia. He is worthy of you. You will be a good wife. He will be a son to your mother."

These words were uttered with extreme difficulty. Afterwards he was silent, but restless. Sometimes the single word "wife" or "daughter" murmured from his lips.

The changes that came over his face foreboded the near approach of the last change of all. Julia saw that the end was at hand. She sat motionless, gazing upon him and waiting for the dread event. At last a placid calm settled upon his features. His lips moved—"Heavenly Father"—though his lips

14*

continued to move, no more of the last prayer of the good man was heard on earth.

When Julia saw that he was dead she did not shed a tear. She uttered not a word nor a sigh. She placed his head in her lap and kissed his lips, as she might have kissed him in his sleep. She gave no outward sign of sorrow ; her sorrow was unutterable. Thus she sat, when a gruff voice notified her that the time had come for her to retire. She raised her tear-less eyes to the man and said, in a low voice, "my father is dead ; let me stay with him." The man replied, not with particular rudeness, but according to the habit of his place, "it is against orders; you must go." She quietly lifted that venerable head from her lap and laid it on the straw. She kissed the cold lips once more, and then she rose up and walked away without a tear or a sigh. She was benumbed with despair.

It was not until hours afterwards, it was at midnight in the solitude of her chamber, that the icy rigor of despair melted into overflowing grief.

The next morning she was unable to rise from her bed. Mrs. West went out and made application for the body of Colonel Fairfax, in order that he might have the customary rights of sepulchre. Her application was refused. He was buried among strangers. Those who loved him cannot weep over the unknown grave of Frederick Fairfax.

CHAPTER XXXI.

THE END.

In a few days Julia was able to travel. Though feeble in body and bruised in spirit, she would not rest longer from the sad duties that remained for her. She must return to her mother. She must return without her father. She must bear tidings of his death to his heart-broken wife. She must console her widowed mother, or, as appeared more probable, smooth her path to the grave. On such melancholy duties the unhappy but unselfish girl bent her pious thoughts.

At that time the Federal authorities were permitting all women and children to go into the Confederacy, and were sending thither some of them who would have preferred to remain at their homes within the Federal lines. Without difficulty, therefore, Mrs. West procured a passport for Julia to go to Richmond, and took passage for her upon a steamboat, which, under a flag of truce, landed passengers within a few miles of the Confederate capital. Thus was she transported, with her burden of sorrow, to her afflicted but still beloved State.

At Richmond she heard that Hugh Fitzhugh had been dangerously wounded, and that he was lying very low in the county to which he had been taken by his mother. Sorrows thickened about her at every step. That passionate love which, in young hearts, rules with exclusive dominion, would have carried her to the side of her wounded lover. She felt all the ten-

der tyranny of that passion. But her love for her
mother, cherished from her birth, had been through
life associated with a sentiment of duty. It was now
consecrated by domestic affliction. Duty was not
doubtful, and Julia hastened to her mother.

Mrs. Fairfax, during her daughter's absence, continued to decline in health and strength. When Julia
entered her apartment she raised herself with sudden
and unusual energy in her bed. She stretched out
her arms to embrace her daughter. While they
clasped each other she cried, " your father, Julia, have
you seen your father ?"

" Yes, dearest mamma, I have seen him."

" Has he come with you ?"

" O, mamma, mamma, he has not come. He cannot—he will not—O dear, dear mamma, he will never
come."

Mrs. Fairfax silently sunk down upon the bed.
Julia laid her head on the pillow beside her mother's,
endeavoring to comfort her with nestling fondness.
The widow uttered no loud lamentation. A few sobs
and broken sentences expressed her agony. A few
great tears trickled over her temples. She closed her
eyes to shut out the world, which for her had lost its
light. She lay bleeding inwardly. The tenure of her
life was broken.

Thenceforth she faded away. In long hours of
silence, by day and by night, the hope of being united
once more and forever with her husband in a better
world, occupied her mind. Her daughter was always
with her, denying herself almost entirely the repose
which she so much needed. Her sweet, untiring,
patient love soothed the wounds of the heart which no
earthly hand could heal. Sometimes she allured her

mother into conversation, and they talked of by-gone
days, or of those who were most dear to them, or of
whatever subject had interest enough for the widow
to withdraw her attention from fatal griefs. Whether
in conversation or in meditation, religion was always
present to the thoughts of both, for both were sincerely pious, and death, then familiar alike to memory
and to expectation, brought religion constantly before
them as the light of the grave. Mrs. Fairfax was
sometimes visited by the Reverend Mr. Ambler, who
had left the village with Fitzhugh's regiment when
the Federals were driven out, and he was now sojourn-
ing a few miles from the house in which she was a
guest. From him she received those counsels and
consolations which it was his office to bestow, and all
that tender sympathy which the calamities of his dearest friends excited in the bosom of this venerable
man. When they conversed, as sometimes they
must, of the terrible misfortunes which had befallen
their country as well as themselves, and the soul of
Mrs. Fairfax was steeped in sorrow, he presented the
only solace which remained for such misfortunes.
Often she desired her daughter to sing, and her musical voice seemed to alleviate the widow's grief. It was
a severe trial of Julia's fortitude to control her own
agitation and modulate her voice to music, especially
when her mother asked her to sing such hymns as
this:

HYMN.

We cry to thee, O Father of the fatherless,
  Out of the depths, O Friend of the forlorn:
Among their dead the living call in dire distress,
  The orphans wail, the widowed mothers mourn.

The earth is darkened and the heav'ns are as a pall ;
In starless gloom we pray to Thee for light :
Out of the depths, while sorrow overshadows all,
We call to Thee, O Father ; all is night.

To prayer thine ear is ever open as the sky—
To cries of woe or secret sighs of care :
All tears are known to Him who deigned on earth to die ;
Through Him, his tears and blood, O hear our prayer.

Let there be light where crime and fear and anguish fill
With darkness all the circle of our sun :
But if for sin our stricken hearts must suffer still,
Thy name be hallowed and Thy will be done.

When Mrs. Fairfax became certain that she was
about to die she was not only resigned, but was
almost cheerful. Finally she fell into the sleep that
knows no waking, as gently as a babe falls asleep in
a mother's arms.

Julia, after fulfilling her last filial duty, accepted an
invitation from Mrs. Fitzhugh to visit that lady at the
cottage which she then occupied with her son. Before leaving the county, a natural feeling induced
Julia to visit Roebuck, which she had not seen since
she was driven from the house by fire, and snatched
from her parents by violence. She found a scene of
desolation where, according to her fond recollection,
she had known a paradise. The grounds in which
her childhood had played were strewn with fragments
of their former decorations. The garden which she
had left in blooming beauty was covered with a mat
of trampled stems. Here and there scanty patches
of corn were lazily cultivated by the negroes who
remained, but over wide fields the wheat, unhar-

vested, was left to rot, and the corn was overgrown
with weeds. Fences were destroyed, barns were
burnt, fruit-trees were cut down. Blackened, roofless
walls were all that remained of the elegant mansion
in which a happy family had lived so long, in the
unity of love, and in the practice of every domestic,
every social virtue. There, whatever is admirable in
refinement was familiar as a household habit. There,
a generous hospitality, and more generous charity,
were dispensed as duly as the prayer for daily bread
was repeated at morning and evening. When Julia
stood alone, a solitary orphan, on the marble steps
which had been trodden by so many entering and departing guests, she looked through the opening, in
which the hospitable door had stood, and saw nothing
but ashes. The scenes of happiness within those
walls which her memory now recalled, served only to
deepen her sense of desolation. But most sorrowful
of all associations with the scene, were the recent sufferings and death of her father and mother, and of an
uncle whom she had loved almost as dearly as she
loved her parents. As she stood among the ruins of
her home, and wept over the calamities of her family,
vividly remembering the dreadful scenes through
which she had passed, and looking forward to a dark
future, a feeling overcame her, not unlike the despairing sentiment of the Preacher:—"So I returned and
considered all the oppressions that are done under the
sun; and beheld the tears of such as were oppressed,
and they had no comforter; and on the side of their
oppressors there was power; but they had no comforter. Wherefore, I praised the dead which are already dead, more than the living which are yet alive.
Yea, better is he than both they which hath not yet

been, who hath not seen the evil work that is done under the sun."

But the soul of Julia Fairfax could not long dwell in the degradation of despair. She could not long cherish a vindictive feeling. The most unhappy life could not appear worthless to one who valued life for the power of doing good. In misfortune her tender heart yielded the tribute which nature demands, but then, without repining, and without resentment, she turned with firm, though gentle resolution, to the duties which misfortune imposes.

After this visit to Roebuck, she took leave of the kind friends who had given shelter to her mother, and went to the humble cottage of Mrs. Fitzhugh. The old lady received her with motherly affection. Hugh had passed the crisis of danger, and was slowly recovering. Yet it was not deemed certain that his former strength would ever be restored. When he was first brought to the cottage, every one who saw him, except his mother, expected him to die from hour to hour. But the brave and proud woman would not believe that her gallant son was to die. Disdaining to yield to her own infirmity, she nursed him with unremitting care. Others often would have relieved her of this duty, but she regarded herself as a sentinel between life and death for her son, and she would not desert her post. When Julia arrived, he was still feeble, but he was out of danger.

His love was as balm to her heart. Consoling and consoled, she felt the power of mutual love to sweeten sorrow. He desired that their marriage should take place without delay. Whatever objections she urged, he derived arguments so forcible from the circumstances in which they were placed, that, in a short time, with her coy consent, he sent for the Reverend Mr. Ambler, and JULIA FAIRFAX became the bride of HUGH FITZHUGH.

FINIS.

www.ingramcontent.com/pod-product-compliance
Lightning Source LLC
Chambersburg PA
CBHW020946030726
47496CB00005B/1372